CW01498254

IMPOSITION

Detectives hunt a serial killer in this gripping mystery

RAY CLARK

Published by The Book Folks

London, 2020

ISBN 978-1-913516-95-6

www.thebookfolks.com

"Every man has three characters: that which he exhibits, that which he has, and that which he thinks he has."

Alphonse Karr

Prologue

North Yorkshire
Thirty-five years ago

"You nearly done, Eric?"

Elsie rose out of her chair, crossed the room, and placed two pieces of coal on the fire to last them through the news. She then turned up the sound on the TV.

"The hell are you doing in there, love?" she asked, moving a small coffee table between the two chairs.

"You'll be the death of me, woman," he said, closing the door into the kitchen with his left foot while balancing a tray with two cups of cocoa and a saucer of chocolate digestives.

"*They* will," she replied, nodding towards the biscuits. "You eat far too many."

"Only pleasure I get. Anyway, what's the rush? It hasn't started yet."

He stepped back, drawing the curtain between the dining and the living room.

Elsie chuckled. That was her Eric. Tide and time waited for no man but you couldn't rush him into anything.

She was still proud of their small, terraced house. It had been their first and only purchase, bought as a new build. Moved in the day after they were married – back in the sixties. It was clean and tidy but it needed a spruce up. Painter and decorator he might be but he rarely found the time to renovate their own house – too busy doing everybody else's.

Eric parked his carcass. The ten o'clock news had pretty much been a nightly ritual as long as they had been together: a cup of cocoa, a few biscuits, the news and then bed.

"Wonder what's been happening today?" asked Eric.

"Something has. I saw Jean Parkin in the town this afternoon, picking up a piece of brisket for their weekend joint. White as a ghost she was."

"Why?"

"Not sure. She wouldn't say much about it."

"Is she ill or something?"

The newscaster announced the headlines and they immediately noticed a view of the grade II listed swing-bridge over the River Esk before the shot cut to a street of detached houses.

"Don't think so. But if we watch this, I think we're about to find out."

Eric lifted his cup and took a sip.

In the studio the face of the newscaster was solemn. "Detectives have launched a murder enquiry following the discovery of two bodies in a house in the North Yorkshire seaside resort of Whitby earlier today. A member of the public alerted the police when the front door of the house was seen to be open. The names of the deceased have not been released as police continue their investigations and attempt to contact relatives."

"Good God." Eric lowered his cup. "That's a bit close to home, Elsie, love."

The shot changed to an exterior view of the houses from the street with a reporter standing before them.

They must be freezing, thought Elsie; it was mid-November, and she could see his breath. "Neighbours described the deaths as a tragedy in what was considered a very secure area."

"You're not safe in your own home these days," said Eric.

Elsie made no comment. Her eyes were focused on what was happening. Forensics officers wearing light blue protective clothing and white masks flittered in and out of the large tent stationed before one of the houses.

"That looks like the posh area up on the cliff top. Valley Rd, cuts between Mulgrave and Upgang, near to where the pub is."

The camera panned out. The area remained cordoned off with blue and white police tape and uniformed officers standing guard outside. Flowers had already been left outside the property.

"Did the Parkin woman say who it was?"

"No," replied Elsie. "But she reckoned it was a right mess inside."

"What? She found them?"

"No. She doesn't live there, but she's a friend of the woman who lives next door. It was her husband who found them. Blood all over the place."

"Sounds a bit dramatic." Eric took a digestive. "I doubt it was that bad."

"Wouldn't surprise me."

The presenter continued. "No arrests have been made and post-mortems will be carried out."

"Why?" Eric asked, staring at his wife.

"It's Alfie Peterson's place."

"The cockney?"

"The gangster, more like."

"We don't know that."

"I reckon you have a short memory, Eric. I'll not forget what he did to us."

"There was no proof, Elsie, love."

"I don't need proof. I know his type."

"How can you? We've lived here all our lives. Never left the place. How can you know what people like him are like?"

"I know right enough." Tears formed in Elsie's eyes. "Happen our son might come back home if he's watching this."

"Aye," replied Eric, standing up, still staring at the TV. "And happen not."

The news report finished.

"Anyway," she said, rising from her seat. "I've no wish to talk about it." She headed for the kitchen with her cup. "I'm ready for my bed. Are you coming?"

"No. Seeing as it's Friday and I've no work tomorrow I thought I'd pull a late one. Think I'll watch that film Alan Hardacre lent me."

Chapter One

Present day

Desk Sergeant Maurice Cragg heard the steaming kettle coming to the boil in the other room. Peering at the clock above his head he reckoned he had around ten minutes to make his drink before settling down to watch a repeat of *Armchair Theatre*.

Maurice smiled to himself as he stood up. He remembered ITV's flagship drama the first-time round – in the seventies. He and his late wife, Veronica, passed many an hour watching them if he wasn't working the late shift: him with a beer – her with a sherry.

The kettle switched off, breaking Maurice's thoughts. He was in the back room of the police station in Bramfield, which resembled a sitting room, with a table and chairs, a three-piece suite, an open fireplace, a wooden floor covered by an assortment of rugs, and ancient, yellowed wallpaper.

It was all he had, but he liked it.

Carrying his empty mug into the kitchen he rinsed it in the sink, threw in a teabag and poured the boiling water in. Delving into a tin in the cupboard above his head he grabbed a handful of biscuits.

Munching away, his thoughts returned to his late wife again. She'd been gone eight years. Her life had been taken in the middle of Lidgett Hill in Pudsey by a hit and run – a drunk driver. Ran a red light. She'd had no chance – killed instantly. The driver was still in prison. But then, so was Maurice, after a fashion.

He added milk and sugar to the cup before strolling through into the sitting room area, keeping a watchful eye on the front desk. Not that much ever happened in Bramfield during normal hours, never mind after the witching hour.

Following Veronica's death, endless bills from credit card companies, department store cards and catalogues soon mounted. If there was money to be spent, she had no equal. He'd had to sell everything to keep his head above water.

His home, his life and his job were all now based around the small country station in Bramfield. He had friends, although he hadn't seen any of them for a while. That was the late shift for you.

He leaned forward, switching on the TV – the only thing left from the marriage.

Out in the lobby the station door burst open, crashed against the wall, and slammed shut again.

"Christ!" Cragg jumped, knocking into the table. "Where's the fire?" He turned and rushed through, unsure of what to expect. What he saw confused him.

The room was empty.

Chapter Two

The existence of the everyday hard-working burglar had been a whole lot tougher more recently: first a recession, then Brexit. Fucking pandemic wasn't help either: people at home more, keeping a closer eye on their possessions.

The police were tightening up – more sophisticated procedures. But he kept himself in the know. He knew all about DNA 17 technology, the biggest change to DNA profiling in fifteen years.

According to what he'd heard – because he wasn't that hot on reading – DNA 17 was so good that if you farted you left a trace a mile wide.

Manny laughed at that. Sources had informed him that the new DNA 17 profiling had CSIs swabbing glove marks for a full profile. They reckoned that when you put gloves on, you usually touch the outside with your hands, leaving a trace of sweat. The swabs pick it up. There was no way they'd find a trace of him, not with three pairs of underpants and three pairs of gloves, not to mention a hairnet and mask: couldn't take any chances.

Bastards. Why couldn't they leave Manny and his kind alone? Give them a break now and again?

Situated in a part of the town considered well out of the way, Swansea Court had four detached houses. He was pretty sure number two was empty. He'd studied the front of the house for the last half hour, watching the bedroom with the light on, but there had been absolutely no movement: no one coming or going.

Around the back he'd kept watch for a further fifteen minutes. Nothing. Now he'd finally summoned the nerve to stroll down the path it was time to steal and shoot, before someone did come home. Who lived here and where the hell they were was a complete mystery to Manny but he could live with that.

Manny confidently held the window frame, peering around the edge. His eyes opened wide and he whistled through his teeth. The place was a mess. Maybe the gaff had already been turned over. The kitchen was upside down. Drawers had been pulled out of units, cupboard doors left open. The table was piled high with everything: papers, bills, cups, saucers, plates – and the silverware. Stuff was all over the floor.

Manny rubbed his gloves together. The Lord really had given him the green light. If someone else had burgled the place they may have been stupid enough to leave their prints all over the scene, which meant he could go in and take what was left and perhaps be lucky enough to escape hassle free.

The first thing Manny saw was a pair of trainers, and not simply any trainers. These were *Vans* – definitely expensive. He reached down, pulled the right one toward him. With a bit of luck they would fit.

Dropping his swag bag, Manny carefully reached further into the room, to a collection of carrier bags in the corner. He placed one on the floor and removed his shoes. He stepped into the trainers and tied the laces. Perfect. He slipped his own shoes in another carrier and left them on the back doorstep – stroke of genius. Everywhere he walked now, he would be doing so in the trainers of the man who owned the house. And you'd certainly expect to find his footprints everywhere.

He carefully negotiated the room, bag in hand, peering into all the cupboards and drawers. He found very little of interest.

Lousy bastard. Whoever had been here before had no consideration for anyone else.

He checked the fridge before moving on. He found chocolate ring doughnuts in a bag as well as a number of energy drinks. Now you were talking Manny's language. He scoffed two of the doughnuts and downed a can. He threw the empty in his bag. Safety first, thought Manny.

The living room was a little tidier. The TV screen on the wall was probably the biggest he had ever seen, so that was no use to him. It was too well fastened anyway. A number of paintings of horses adorned the rest of the walls. He didn't want those either. The room was also furnished with an incredible amount of equine ornaments: there was even a fucking rug with a horse's face on the floor. Keith Lemon would have a field day. Manny laughed at his own thought.

Turning his attention to the hi-fi unit, Manny froze, almost certain he had heard something from the floor above. Crouching down he waited, listened further. He wasn't sure why burglars crouched down. Stupid really. If anyone came in and switched a light on you'd hardly be perfectly placed to make a move, would you?

He lingered long enough to realise it was probably his nerves playing tricks on him, remembering the first time he'd taken up his new hobby. He was so nervous he actually shit himself. He wasn't too happy but the old hands in his trade had had a good laugh about it. They'd all done it. They hadn't thrown up afterwards, though.

Manny stood back up, using a small pen torch to rifle through the CDs. They were crap, as far as he was concerned. Fetch a few quid in the pubs or on the market stalls but he definitely wouldn't be listening to them. Glam Rock? Who the fuck listens to that stuff?

An entire shelf had been dedicated to Slade CDs, mostly originals, possibly a lot of bootleg stuff. Manny reckoned there was some money's worth here. The owner of the house was very obviously a collector. So was Manny, and *he* was collecting these: proper money here.

Manny bagged the lot and moved on.

In the front hall he came across two things of interest. One was a shitload of music gear: amplifier, speakers, guitar case, leads and extensions. The man of the house was obviously a musician. But if the place had already seen one burglar why would he have left the expensive music gear? The heavy stuff yes, but the guitar…

Manny opened the case carefully. It was a nice bit of kit. Not that he knew much about guitars. It had the Fender logo and he knew they were good. Manny could make a fair bit here. He closed and latched the case and moved that – as well as his swag bag – to the back door.

The second point of interest was an unlocked door. Inside, the cupboard was nothing out of the ordinary. Tall and narrow with a number of shelves containing a selection of boxes.

Manny checked his watch. Well… it wasn't his but he was taking damn good care of it. He really didn't want to waste too much time in case the homeowner returned. A quick peek wouldn't hurt.

It was mostly crap to do with horses: horseshoes, small bits of tackle used for riding. One was even full of hay. Who was Manny robbing tonight?

He forgot the boxes, and shone his torch toward the floor. More stuff connected to music in the shape of vinyl. He checked: more Slade. He figured it was collectible, and he could probably carry it.

The floor of the cupboard was timber. One of the boards squeaked as he stepped on it, indicating it was loose. Manny found a screwdriver, knelt down, forced the board upwards. Inside was a lockable metal box. Very interesting. Peering deeper into the cupboard revealed a key under a carpet. Most people were stupid enough to leave keys nearby. The box was about fifteen inches by twelve, and perhaps a foot deep. He unlocked and removed the top.

Now what do we have here, thought Manny. I think *we'll* have these. Never know what's in them. Silly bastard probably doesn't even know he has them.

Manny closed and locked the top, then put the key in his pocket. What you've never had, you don't miss.

He closed the cupboard door and carried the box to the rest of the stuff he'd piled up near the back door.

Manny was aware that his luck couldn't really last out much longer but he would have to check the upstairs. No burglar worth his salt would leave a possible treasure trove uninvestigated. The room to avoid would be the one with the light on. He doubted anyone was in there but knowing his luck – no matter how good it had so far been – some arsehole outside would be walking his dog, irrespective of the time. That would be curtains for Manny.

But at the top of the stairs, he suddenly froze. Manny had clearly heard a loud click, as if the timer for the central heating had kicked in – but he couldn't be sure.

Chapter Three

Cragg glanced around. It didn't make sense. The door leading outside was perfectly still, as if it hadn't been opened at all. But he knew it had. You couldn't imagine a sound like that. "Hello?"

No reply came.

He moved forward, placing his hands on the counter, his finger on the panic button. To call it a panic button was a bit excessive. What it actually did was send a wi-fi signal to the computer in the patrol car, and the phones of the men in uniform, which basically said, "whatever you're doing, come back to the station".

"Is there anyone there?" he called out again, walking to the end of the counter and lifting the hatch to step into the main room, where he received yet another shock.

To his left, was a man on his knees. Even though he was crouching, Cragg figured he had to be six feet tall at least, with a solid muscular frame. He had wavy black hair, combed back in an Elvis style. His features were chiselled and tanned. He was dressed in a black leather jacket and jeans and wore a check-patterned shirt. His arms were stretched out in front of him with his hands bunched into fists resting on the floor. He was shaking, breathing heavily. "Oh, God," he said quietly.

Cragg moved forward quickly, bending down. A closer inspection revealed the man was sweating. Although the desk sergeant didn't know him his face was familiar. He had seen him around the town on the odd occasion.

"Are you okay, sir?"

The man flinched at Cragg's question. Perhaps he'd been attacked, though the desk sergeant could see no evidence of that. But he knew enough about the way people fought these days to know that they didn't always leave any outward signs.

Cragg put his hands on the man's shoulder. "Come on, sir, let's get you up and into a more comfortable position. Can you tell me your name?"

The man pushed Cragg's arm away – not violently but very gently, considering his size. "I need help."

"Of course you do," replied Cragg. "And that's what I'm here for – to help you. Let's get you to the other side of the counter into a chair and you can tell me what's bothering you."

Once again, he refused Cragg's help but stared at him. "It's not me that needs help, it's her."

"Who?" The situation had suddenly grown more urgent. Cragg needed answers. "Who needs help?"

"My wife." The man suddenly sunk to the ground, placing his head in his hands. "Oh, God, no."

Cragg put his arm on the man's shoulder. "Please, sir, I need to know what's going on. Who are you?"

Cragg was about to ask another question when the man suddenly spoke. "Robbie Carter."

"Good, Robbie. Well done. Now, can you tell me your wife's name?"

Robbie Carter rubbed his hands down his face. Tears formed in the corners of his eyes. "Jane. It's Jane." There was a pause. "I think she might be dead."

"Dead?" Cragg repeated. "You think your wife is dead?"

Robbie Carter lifted his hands and grabbed Maurice Cragg's shoulders. He started talking, fast, as if he was reading out bullet points.

"I'd been out all night. Came home. On the floor, she was on the floor, in the bedroom." His breathing turned to sobs. "Place has been burgled. Mess all over. I think she's dead, sergeant. She needs help."

Cragg stood up quickly. Staring into Robbie's eyes, he said: "Mr Carter, I want you tell me where you live... now! It's very important, please tell me where you live."

"Swansea Court – number two."

"That's out near the leisure centre and the school, isn't it?"

Carter simply nodded.

Cragg moved faster than he had done in years. Around the other side of the counter he picked up the phone and dialled the hospital. When the receptionist answered he barely gave her time to take a breath.

"Louise, it's Maurice Cragg at the station. I need an ambulance and I need it now. Two Swansea Court. There's no time to waste: woman upstairs on the bedroom floor. Her name is Jane. Her husband says she may be dead – he doesn't seem sure. He's very distressed. Quick as you can."

"Right away, Mr Cragg."

Cragg replaced the receiver and came back around the counter. Robbie Carter was still kneeling on the floor. "Mr Carter, I have to ask. Have you seen the offender at all?"

Robbie didn't say anything.

"Mr Carter, I need you to tell me everything you can. It's important."

Robbie stared vacantly ahead, past Cragg.

The desk sergeant couldn't take any chances. He couldn't allow an ambulance crew into a dangerous situation, so he came around the counter and through into the back room. The television had warmed up and the episode of *Armchair Theatre* he'd planned to watch was well under way.

He grabbed the handset on the radio and called the patrol car.

The radio crackled in reply. "What can I do for you, Sarge?"

"I'd like both of you round to number two Swansea Court right now. Ambulance is on its way: woman either dying or possibly dead. Her name is Jane Carter. The husband's here at the station. The house has been burgled. Suspect may still be on the premises and very possibly further life at risk. Proceed with caution and I'll get some more backup out to you."

"On our way."

Out in the lobby the sound of a mobile phone broke through, which was followed by a scream so spine-tingling that Maurice Cragg dropped the handset and raced back to the front desk.

Robbie Carter was still on the floor, staring at his phone with an expression dark enough to curdle milk.

"What's wrong, Mr Carter?"

Robbie Carter's eyes were wide: spittle had formed at the corners of his mouth. He showed Maurice Cragg his phone.

"He's still there," Carter hissed.

Chapter Four

Two squad cars pulled up at the house within seconds of each other, blue lights flashing but no sirens.

The four officers jumped out in unison and Constable Mike Atherton took charge. His partner, Emma Longstaff had only been with the team for three months. She was twenty years old and a direct replacement for the late PC Gary Close.

Atherton recognised the other two officers from Pickering as Dave Reynolds and Steve Smart. He issued orders. "Steve, Dave, can you go round the back? Emma, you come with me."

Swansea Court was a small cul-de-sac with four houses, each one detached: two stood opposite each other on the way in. The other two were located at the bottom behind the small island used as a turning circle. Number two was the only one with a light on in the bedroom. Everyone else was obviously still in bed, unaware of the drama.

Atherton pushed open the gate and raced up the pathway. He had a very uneasy feeling about the whole thing. Cragg had said the woman was either dying or dead, with a possible suspect on the premises. He doubted very much the man would still be there now.

The front door was locked. "Emma, can you wait here? Keep your eyes and ears open and please be careful."

A shout from the back informed Atherton that the officers had found an open window. On both counts, "life at risk", and "suspect on the premises", the scene had to be treated as a co-ordinated fast approach. Fresh in his mind were the five building block principles, of which the first was preservation of life.

Dispensing with formalities he barged straight inside.

The other two were close behind and one of them instantly located a light switch.

His immediate view of the kitchen was a mess. Even pigs wouldn't live in such a sty, which backed up the burglary theory.

Atherton jumped over a variety of items on the floor and pushed his way into the front hall. Switching on another light, he cast a quick glance at the musical gear in front of the main door.

"Check the living room, Steve."

Emma Longstaff followed Mike Atherton as he bolted up the stairs two at a time. Atherton had one hand on his truncheon and the other on the banister, calling out as he did so.

The bedroom with the light on was the obvious choice. Once in, he saw a white female, laid on the floor on her left side, with her right arm outstretched, as if she was trying to reach out for something. She was slim with long black hair, and hazel eyes. She was wearing a fluffy pink dressing gown that had come open at the front, revealing a see-through black negligee underneath and a pair of white panties; no bra.

He immediately knelt down and called out her name. "Jane, can you hear me, love?"

Longstaff had checked the rest of the upstairs rooms, in which all lights were now blazing, before she joined Atherton. "All clear."

Atherton leaned over the woman on the floor. "Jane?"

There was no response. He felt for a pulse, lowered his head to her chest. Nothing. He glanced at Longstaff and shook his head.

"Has she gone?"

"Definitely."

During the initial response it was sometimes difficult to determine if a death was the result of natural causes, an accident, suicide or homicide. Atherton couldn't clearly put it into any of those categories.

First impressions: no blood, and little or no evidence to show what had actually happened. No external marks were evident on her face. He quickly checked the areas he could see for cuts and bruises but found nothing. "What do you think?" he asked his colleague.

Smart and Reynolds had joined them. "All clear downstairs."

"Hard to say," replied Longstaff. "Looks like she was ready for bed. It's still made up. Duvet folded back. Maybe she'd just come up here, used the bathroom and was just turning in."

"Heard a noise downstairs, maybe?" said Smart.

"If she did, she certainly didn't go and check, otherwise why have we found her up here?" Atherton asked.

"In that case, the burglar was obviously pretty quiet and took her by surprise."

"Not sure about that, either," replied Atherton. "Look around the room, I can't see any sign of a struggle, can you?"

"Bathroom's a mess," replied Reynolds. "Maybe it all happened in there."

"Why drag her in here?" asked Smart.

"I'm with Steve on that one," replied Atherton. "Can't see any evidence of that either. If he'd dragged her from the bathroom, surely something would have been left in its wake."

"Not for us to try and determine," said Reynolds. "We'll need the CSIs to work their magic."

Atherton stood up. His bad feeling about the crime scene was still with him. As he glanced around, the five building block principles kicked in again. Preservation of life was out of the window. He'd broken rule two by not preserving the scene so far, but that couldn't have been helped because he was too busy applying rule one.

Although they knew the victim's name, she would still have to be identified officially. As for suspects – there were none, as yet. That only left securing evidence. And there didn't seem to be much of that either: certainly not as far as the death was concerned. He suspected the place would be littered with prints from the theft but as his colleague had said, that was up to the CSIs.

"If the burglar did kill her, how the hell has he done it?"

Longstaff leaned in towards Jane Carter's body. "Can't see anything on the outside, so it must be something on the inside."

"Maybe he's poisoned her," said Reynolds.

"What with?" asked Atherton.

"Could be anything," said Reynolds, eyes darting around the room. "Not that I can see any signs."

"He'll have taken it with him. Can you see any puncture marks on her skin?" asked Longstaff.

"Not on any of the visible areas," replied Atherton.

"It's all a bit strange, isn't it?" said Reynolds.

"How do you mean?" asked Smart.

"There's only four possible options for loss of life." Reynolds held up his fingers to count them off. "Natural causes, which it could always be. Accident, but no evidence to suggest it. Suicide – it doesn't seem very likely to me. Once again, lack of evidence. Or homicide."

The reasoning was left unsaid but Atherton could tell from their expressions that they were all of the same opinion. Something didn't add up.

"In that case, let's get out of here and start treating it like the crime scene it is," said Atherton. "We shouldn't disturb anything else until the big boys get here. Can you two secure front and rear entry? Emma, take one of the cars down the end of the street and block it off. We need a crime scene log. Have you guys got any stepping plates in the car? We need to establish one route in and one out."

"Not enough," said Reynolds.

"I'll call Cragg, ask him to have more sent over. And while he's at it he can call MIT. This one's way beyond us."

Chapter Five

"So... what's happened here, Sean?"

Detective Inspector Gardener was standing over the body of Jane Carter. Having made an initial examination, he was waiting for the Home Office pathologist, Doctor George Fitzgerald, to arrive.

Detective Sergeant Reilly was peering into the top drawer of the bedside cabinet. He pulled out five ten-pound notes. "Not what people will want us to believe, I'm sure."

Gardener had received a call from the desk sergeant about an hour and a half previously. Because Mike Atherton's report was so detailed, Gardener saved time by calling his own team in immediately. Following a meeting with Atherton and a brief inspection of the bedroom, the SIO had issued a number of fast track actions.

Despite time having passed from the initial reporting of the murder, he had decided to apply The Golden Hour principle that the offender may still be in the area. It would only need two of his team to do a house-to-house to talk to possible witnesses, so the rest he sent off around the town.

"What time did Cragg say that Robbie Carter reported the crime?" Gardener asked Atherton, checking his own watch: six o'clock.

"Around two o'clock."

"And the place had already been burgled. He found his wife on the floor, dying or dead. He didn't seem to know which."

"I'm finding that hard to believe," replied Reilly, "but not as hard as the fact that he didn't call an ambulance immediately."

"That's what I was thinking. How long would it take him to get to the police station?"

Reilly shook his head. "Ten minutes if he drove."

"I'm not happy, Sean. He gets home around half-past-one – from wherever – finds the place upside down, his wife either dying or dead. He doesn't call an ambulance. Instead, he goes straight to the police station." Gardener stopped talking, staring at Reilly. "But it appears that he sets the alarm before he goes. Why does he do that?"

"Shock?" offered Reilly. "Grief, maybe: it can make you do funny things."

"I realise everyone reacts differently, but isn't there a basic instinct that kicks in, where for just one second, you don't believe she's dead: where you think that you might just be able to save her no matter what, no matter how much the evidence says otherwise? You would still call that ambulance first. Why didn't he?"

Gardener's thoughts were with his late wife, Sarah, and that fateful night in the centre of Leeds, when she'd taken a bullet. He hadn't been able to save her but he'd made sure an ambulance was called immediately.

"I'm sure we'll get the chance to ask him."

Glancing around the room, Gardener noticed a number of photographs of Jane Carter with a variety of different horses, and only one of her and her husband. At least he figured that was who it was judging by the description Cragg had given them.

He strolled over and picked up one, studying it. "While Robbie Carter was reporting it to Cragg, his phone went off and relayed some pictures of a burglar in the house, from the alarm system."

"Which suggests the burglar had been somewhere on the premises the whole time," said Reilly, stepping out of the bedroom, staring into the corner of the landing, pointing to a motion sensor.

Gardener followed his line of vision but couldn't see any cameras.

"Maybe," said Gardener. "But where *was* the burglar when the motion sensors were set off: up here? There are no signs of a struggle."

"No sign in the bedroom, either."

Gardener walked back into the bedroom, his scene suit rustling as he did so. He pointed to a chair. "That's the only thing that has moved recently. Look closer at the floor, you can see imprints of where it used to stand."

Reilly did so. "Not enough to suggest a fight. And there's money still in the top drawer of that cabinet."

"This alarm business is bugging me. Why did he set the alarm when his wife was in the house – dying?"

"You think he might be in on this?"

"Wouldn't be the first, would he?"

"Insurance scam?"

"Let's see when we talk to him. See if we can figure out his body language."

Gardener turned back onto the landing and walked into the bathroom, to the mess on the floor. Overall, the space was clean and tidy, as was the shower cubicle. On the window ledge he saw toothpaste, brushes, soap in a dish, and a facecloth neatly folded. A bottle of bleach stood at the side of the toilet.

Gardener pulled up the toilet seat to peer inside – clean water.

"That lot on the floor looks like an accident to me, not the result of a tussle."

"If it got out of control in here," said Reilly, "they'd have needed to disable her in some way so they could drag her into the bedroom."

"Which means that some of that stuff down there would have ended up on the landing."

Reilly nodded and turned his head.

"I'm not fully convinced that the burglar is responsible for Jane Carter's death. It almost looks like he hasn't been up here."

As Gardener studied the items on the floor, one in particular stood out.

He bent down and retrieved a small glass bottle of pills. He had absolutely no idea what they were. Couldn't pronounce the name. He unscrewed the cap and shook a few into his right hand. They were small and circular, with a hard shiny polished surface.

"Interesting," said Gardener.

Reilly studied the rest of toiletries on the floor – also inspecting the smashed bathroom cabinet. "Looks like the only bottle."

"Freshly opened as well. The label says there should be one hundred. It won't be far off."

"Prescription?" inquired Reilly.

"Definitely."

"Could be another option here," said Reilly. "Maybe Jane Carter was in the bathroom getting ready for bed when she was startled by a burglar. They have a fight, things get broken. She has a medical problem, takes a turn for the worse and the burglar bails out, leaving her to it."

"Possibly. Either that, or like we said, the burglar didn't make it up here. Maybe Jane Carter was getting ready for bed and suddenly felt unwell: she couldn't reach the tablets in time. She panicked, lost her sense of balance, brought this lot down on herself and ended crawling back into the bedroom when she couldn't find the pills."

"Suggesting she wasn't attacked at all."

A familiar voice from the ground floor broke their conversation.

Reilly smiled. "Is that the sharp, reptilian voice of our beloved Pathosaurus just arriving?"

"Don't you go winding him up," said Gardener.

"As if."

Fitz's tall, lean frame came bounding up the stairs. His wrinkled, grandfatherly complexion greeted them. "Good morning, gentlemen," he said, pushing his half-lens spectacles further up his nose. In his right hand he held a black medical bag.

Reilly held his chest and feigned a fainting.

"What's up with him?" Fitz asked.

"He's probably wondering the same about you," replied Gardener.

"When have we ever called you out to a scene, day or night, and you've greeted us like the human beings that we are?" Reilly asked.

Fitz simply stared on. "You're right. I'm so sorry. Good morning, Stewart."

Both detectives laughed.

Gardener took Fitz into the bedroom, explained what he knew, before informing him that he was going to check on something downstairs while Fitz examined Jane Carter. Before leaving he asked the pathologist about the pills. He couldn't help, so Gardener bagged them and gave them to him to take back to the morgue.

Downstairs in the living room, four CSIs were busy taking the place apart – one in each corner: two on the floor, combing through the carpet, and two others peering into the cupboards.

Gardener made a beeline for the photos on the walnut finished sideboard. As with those upstairs, most of them featured Jane Carter with a number of horses; in three of them she held a trophy. As Gardener glanced around the room, he couldn't locate those trophies: he'd be surprised if a burglar had lifted them, they were too easily traceable.

"Why do you keep looking at the photos?" Reilly asked.

"See if it'll give me a clue to the state of the marriage."

"Looks to me like she was more in love with her horses."

"Precisely." Of all the photos Gardener had seen, only two of them featured Jane and Robbie together: one upstairs, in which they were both smiling, and the one he now held – no smiling.

Gardener made a mental note. "I wonder how he sees the relationship."

"Probably not the way she did, from the look of that pic."

Turning back to the sideboard Gardener leaned further in, noticing circles in the dust on its surface. Yet further evidence that the burglar had been busy on the ground floor of the house.

Steve Fenton, the crime scene manager, entered the room. "We just found this on the stairs."

"What is it?" Gardener asked, staring at an empty evidence bag.

Reilly smirked. "You should have gone to Specsavers."

"You need to look really close," said Fenton. "It's a hair."

Reilly leaned forward, squinting at the bag.

"Looks like I'm not the only one whose eyes don't work," said Gardener.

"Away with you, man. Can't you see I'm trying to concentrate?"

"Thought I could smell burning."

Gardener took the bag from Fenton. The hair was long and black and was almost certainly Jane Carter's. Forensics would confirm.

"We found it at the top, caught in the skirting board," said Fenton. "No doubt we'll get confirmation from those in her hairbrush."

"Could it be the first sign of a confrontation?" asked Gardener.

"If it is, it started downstairs," said Reilly.

Gardener studied the four corners of the room – glancing at the motion sensors – still no cameras. "A heated argument, maybe. Got out of hand?"

"Some argument," said Reilly. "But if that's what happened no burglar would drag her all the way upstairs."

"Surely someone would have heard her screams of protest," suggested Fenton.

"I doubt it," replied Gardener. "There's only four houses on the street and they are a bit of a distance from each other."

"Not to mention the time it was supposed to have happened," said Reilly.

Gardener sighed. That gave them three separate crime scenes now. The body was scene one. Where the body was found was scene two. And scene three was the burglary. The problems were mounting.

"The best we can hope for is plenty of prints," said Reilly.

"Good work, Steve. Keep checking," said Gardener, passing back the evidence bag.

As Fenton made to leave, Gardener called him back. "Have you come across the computer yet?"

Fenton pointed. "In there."

Gardener noticed a desk in an alcove, with a computer tower and monitor on top. Behind, on the wall, were shelves containing books and DVDs, a number of ornaments, and a couple of the trophies he had presumed were in the photos. "Can you pack the whole thing up now and get one of the lads to take it back to the station immediately?"

Fenton nodded.

"It's all a question of timing now. I want to see that system he's got installed. I want to know if the computer recorded the time of the alarm being set, when and where the first motion sensor was tripped, and who was responsible."

Reilly had found a pile of CDs on the floor. "Plenty of these but nothing to play them on. Looking at the marks on the wall I'd say they had a whole lot more than this."

"Burglar obviously has a market for them – and the hi-fi."

"Might be a good place to start asking questions. The market."

Gardener was about to venture into another room when one of the CSIs caught his attention. "What's up?"

"The pathologist would like a word, sir."

The two officers left the living room and headed up to the bedroom. They found Fitz kneeling by the side of the body with a thermometer in his hand.

"You called?" said Reilly.

"Yes. I think you need to see this."

Fitz had positioned Jane Carter onto her back and her negligee was now up around her shoulders. The pathologist pointed to two bruises on her stomach. Both were large, inflamed. The outer edges of both were red, the centre deep blue.

"There's a lot of swelling around the abdomen. It looks unnatural, and in my opinion, this lady will have suffered terribly before she died."

"Any idea what caused them?" Gardener asked.

"Not until I have the chance to examine her thoroughly."

"You don't think it's anything to do with the tablets?" asked Reilly.

Fitz stood up. "No. In my opinion these are contact bruises."

"What, like a truck?"

Fitz continued, "There's no external bleeding, but I suspect she has some damage to the internal organs, which has caused them to swell – pain would have been quite intolerable."

"So she's been attacked with something," said Reilly.

"Very possibly." Fitz pointed to the smaller of the bruises. "That one, I really have no idea."

"And the other?" Gardener sighed.

"It's a different shape, I could hazard a guess."

"Go on," pushed Gardener. "A footprint, maybe."

Chapter Six

It was after twelve when Manny returned to consciousness. He immediately wished he hadn't. Rolling round to squint at the clock on the bedside cabinet, he winced. He had a headache to compete with the world's best. The little men with hammers were working up a sweat. His eyeballs *really* hurt, as if someone had taken a pan scrubber to them. The inside of his mouth felt like he'd chewed a carpet that had been in a skip for six months.

"Oh, fuck me, is that what time it is?" Manny sat up far too quickly. His head fell forward, his eyes nearly vacated the premises, his stomach lurched and his toes curled as a shooting pain passed through his body like a wave of radiation.

"Have a fucking heart, Lord. I know I've misbehaved but the punishment does not fit the crime."

He laid back down, but that only made things worse. As he tried to leave the bed, his foot became caught in a sheet and instead of disentangling he simply dragged the whole thing with him to the bathroom, where he faced the sink and dry-heaved for what felt like forever, leaving his stomach muscles tender, as if they had been put through a mincer.

Manny fell to the floor. "What the fuck did I do?"

Despite the sun shining through the bathroom window he still felt cold and shivery.

He tried to piece things together. He remembered leaving the house with his ill-gotten gains. He hotfooted it through the town, using all the back alleys and ginnels he knew about, and one or two he didn't.

A light suddenly beamed inside Manny's head. He'd passed the off-licence where some kind soul had left a bottle of three-year-old, oak barrel, aged French brandy out in the yard. It had either been forgotten, which he doubted, or the slack bastard that worked there had been intending to steal it. That was when Manny remembered the old saying "the Lord helped those who helped themselves". So he did.

The trouble started in the early hours when he reached his home and deposited everything into the living room. In the kitchen he'd taken another can of Red Bull from the fridge and downed it in one. After eating a sausage roll long past its sell-by date he then opened the brandy and poured a glass, or two – or three. Fucked if he could remember.

Feeling more like moving he stood up – slowly. The sheet fell to the floor revealing everything Manny had, which wasn't much. Prisoners of war from Belsen were in better shape than him. He was about to rinse his mouth but thought better of it. He glanced around the small bathroom: chipped tiles, flaky ceiling, no bath, only a shower with a curtain so old it would have made a better sieve. He continually had to dry the bathroom floor. Sometimes it was easier not to take a shower. Manny made a mental note to acquire another curtain.

It was time to try walking. He lived in a one bedroom flat in the old town in Bramfield, known as Carpenter's Yard – so called because at the bottom of the yard there had been a dry dock where carpenters worked on the keels. It had been very busy down there in the early part of the last century. All that had gone now and in its place were two small flats – his and the woman's next door. Hers had two bedrooms.

Each flat also had a garage. They were huge – even had lofts. Manny's was full of shit – hers wasn't. That was a matter of opinion. Mary had a pale blue VW Beetle. Bastard thing. Especially when she revved the knackers off it early in the morning, going to see her mother in the care home. It was a wonder *she* didn't hear it, and that place was five fucking miles away.

The courtyard had been bricked, with two large gas lamps installed. A patio table and chairs had been dropped dead centre, and a set of gates closed off the secluded area from the world. A number of wooden barrels adorned the courtyard, all of which had been filled with flowers. Mary had bought a truckload of other associated crap like wooden wheelbarrows and gnomes and solar lights to brighten the place up.

Manny glanced into the living room as he passed on his way to the kitchen. Another mess. It was furnished and decorated mostly with stuff he had stolen. He had a small portable TV that he rarely – if ever – watched. No Sky – that costs money.

Strolling through to the kitchen, he opened the fridge, and spotted an energy drink. That's what he needed. A tin of beans with a spoon sticking out the top came into view. He saw the yellow ticket but he wasn't bothered. They'd been there a week anyway.

He took two mouthfuls, chewed and swallowed and washed them down with the drink. After a few seconds, his brain sent a message to every sensor in his body, informing him he shouldn't have attempted that procedure so soon after rising.

Manny closed the fridge and held the edge of the sink, rigid, preparing himself. Seconds of indecision passed before he noticed Mary, his neighbour and current stalker, out in the yard.

"Oh fuck." Manny ducked down. If she saw him, he'd never be able to shift her. He had a soft spot for her. She'd been treated badly by every man she had ever met. They used her because she was too nice, and rather plump. He would never admit to anyone that she was probably the only woman in his life. For reasons unknown to Manny, Mary would do anything for him. She often bought him little things – found any excuse to pop round to his flat.

But he couldn't deal with her now.

Manny needed to inspect his latest haul. He threaded his way carefully around the furniture. He had bare feet.

Any number of hidden dangers could spring a surprise. He never cleaned up; never had the time.

He grabbed the swag bag, noticing the *Vans* trainers. He was pleased with those. He was elated with the Fender. A red Stratocaster; bruised and scratched, it definitely had a tale or two to tell. That would fetch a few quid.

The contents of the bag hit the floor: a collection of Glam Rock CDs, a midi hi-fi, ornaments, jewellery... The watches he could fence, no problem. There was cash, a wad he'd found in the guitar case. That would certainly help his cause.

"This is all good, Manny, my old son."

Running his hands through his hair he quickly reached for the box he'd found in the cupboard. What he'd seen inside in the early hours had been interesting, but he suspected a much closer investigation would be needed.

The clock on the wall read one-fifteen. His windfall had to be moved. To do that he needed a car, and a roll of black insulating tape.

A knock came on his kitchen window. "You ooh, Manfred. Are you up?"

Manny put the box on the floor and stood up.

Fuck it, Mary was here.

Chapter Seven

Reilly brought the pool car to a halt in the car park whilst Gardener quickly reflected on the morning's developments. The undertaker had been and taken Jane Carter's body to the morgue. Fitz had left. The scene had been locked down and the only people in the house now were the CSIs – hopefully collecting concrete evidence.

The police station in Bramfield was large and old-fashioned and resembled a town hall. There were four steps leading to the front door, flanked either side by Grecian pillars, with castellated mock battlements. Above the front door was a wrought-iron canopy with potted plants. The windows were old-fashioned wood and not double-glazed, and the exterior was surrounded by gas mantle lighting.

"Ah, now here's a familiar sight," said Reilly, closing the door and locking the car.

The pair of them climbed the steps to the front door. Once inside, the smell of lavender and furniture polish was ever present. A middle-aged cleaner with blonde hair stood in one corner watering the potted plants. She smiled as Gardener passed.

The lobby was empty as Gardener approached the desk. Maurice Cragg came through from the back with a couple of files in his hand.

"Good to see you gentlemen again."

"It can't be," replied Reilly. "You only ever see us when there's a murder."

Gardener smiled and shook hands with the older man. "Where's Robbie Carter?"

"He's in a holding cell."

"Is he okay?"

"Was the last time I looked – took him a cup of coffee about an hour ago."

"Has he said anything?"

"No. Do you want to see him?"

"Not yet. I'd like to talk to you first. Is there somewhere we can go?"

"Of course, come through the back. Bet you're ready for a cup of tea?"

"I'd like a bit more than that. If I remember correctly, you people have a bakery quite close – a very good one."

Gardener realised how hungry he was. He hadn't eaten anything between the initial phone call and Reilly collecting him – or since.

"Leave it to me." Cragg glanced at the Irishman. "You're a bacon sandwich man if I remember correctly."

"Nothing wrong with your memory, old son. And on this occasion you can make it two."

"And something healthy for you, sir."

Gardener liked Cragg, remembering the last time they had worked together. His features were solid and dependable, which was a good measure of his character. He had close-cropped, iron-grey hair with a hard, rugged complexion, pockmarked. He was stocky but not fat.

Cragg left to sort out the snacks, returning a few minutes later with a tray containing three cups, a jug of milk, sugar, and biscuits to keep them going no doubt. He sat at the table and four chairs, passing out the tea.

"She has died, then?" Cragg asked Gardener.

"I'm afraid so."

"Any thoughts?"

"On the scene?" Gardener inquired. "Only that nothing stacks up."

"I take it you didn't catch the intruder red-handed on the premises?"

"We're a wee bit confused about that," said Reilly.

"Oh, I see. Why?"

Gardener explained. The house had almost certainly had a visitor but he wasn't convinced that the man had made it upstairs.

"So, what do you think happened?" Cragg asked.

"I really don't know, Maurice. What time did Robbie Carter actually come into the station?"

Cragg sipped his tea. "As far as I can recall, it would have been about two o'clock. But hang on a minute, I can tell you better with this." The desk sergeant leaned forward and grabbed a copy of the TV magazine, confirming the time, because it coincided with his program.

"What happened?" asked Gardener.

Cragg explained about the almighty crashing sound and how when he checked the lobby it was empty.

"He wasn't even in here?" asked Reilly.

"Oh, he was in, but on his hands and knees and I never saw him until I went through the hatch." Cragg also confirmed that no one else was with him, either inside or out.

"What did he say to you?"

"Not a lot. He were breathing heavy. I think his only words were 'Oh God.'"

"Did he offer any information about what had happened or did you have to force it out of him?"

"I had to drag it out of him: his name, hers, then he said she was dead, or dying. He didn't seem to know which."

"Do you know him?" Gardener suspected it might be a stupid question because Maurice Cragg knew everyone.

"No. I've seen him around the town a time or two; mostly during the day. I never thought anything of it. His clothes were usually good quality and I wondered if he was on benefits but then one night I left the station and popped in the local down the road for a drink and there he was."

"You sound surprised, Maurice," said Reilly. "Why's that, it's a pub after all."

"I was surprised by what he were doing: singing. There's a small stage in the corner and he was on it. Not karaoke, like, he was the main turn. Got talking to one or two people who knew him a bit better than me and they said that's what he did for a living. Done it all his life as far as they knew. I stayed for a couple more. He was quite good."

That would explain the music gear, thought Gardener. "Any idea how he got here?"

"No, but there's a white van in the car park that I haven't seen before. I reckon that'll be his but I can run a check anyway."

Gardener nodded. "What were the circumstances of him finding her? Did he say?"

"No, not in so many words. He'd been out all night, came home and found her on the floor – the bedroom floor."

"Did he tell you where he'd been?"

"No. Couldn't get much more out of him. I called for an ambulance straight away."

"That's something that didn't stack up with us. *He* didn't call an ambulance."

"Maybe he were in shock."

"Not too shocked to set the alarm before he came here," offered Reilly.

"Alarm?" questioned Cragg.

"Yes," replied Gardener. "The house alarm."

"He set the alarm," repeated Cragg. "I don't understand. Why would you set the alarm before you left the house if your wife was still in the place? A wife who was dying, at that?"

"That's what we'd like to know. But at the moment we're still in the dark as to whether she was dying or dead when he left."

"Either way," said Cragg. "It seems a bit strange to me."

"Could you smell any alcohol, Maurice?"

"No."

"Did he look like he was under the influence of any other substances?"

"Not that I could tell."

"Any marks on him?" asked Reilly. "Scratches, bruises."

"No. Do you think he's responsible?"

"We don't know," replied Gardener. He felt they had three possible options as he explained what they had found at the house, and the mess on the bathroom floor.

"Which could have been the burglar," offered Reilly. "Or it might have been Jane or Robbie Carter."

Gardener continued. "Option one is the burglar surprised and attacked her but may not necessarily have killed her."

"But she could have died afterwards as a result," said Cragg.

"Yes," said Gardener. "But I don't think so. Option two is he came home and something very similar happened. Maybe they had an argument, things got out of hand, the accident in the bathroom happened and he stormed out."

"That doesn't sound likely to me," said Cragg. "If that was the case, why come here and report her as dying or dead?"

"Good point. Unless it was to take the heat off himself," said Gardener.

"Or to cover what really happened," said Reilly.

"What were your first impressions of him, Maurice?"

Cragg sighed and finished his tea. "Well, with all due respect, Mr Gardener, I've been pounding this beat a lot longer than you and I've seen all manner of people – all walks of life. I've come across every criminal known to man and quite a few murderers, I can tell you. He didn't strike me as one."

"You were quite happy that he was in a state of shock and wasn't really aware of what was happening?"

"I'd have to go with my gut instinct on that one and say yes."

"Okay, Maurice, I'll go with that."

"Which leaves us with option three."

"Amongst the mess on the bathroom floor we found a bottle of pills. No idea what they were. My guess is a prescription drug of some sort, not painkillers that you can buy over the counter."

"And you think that she might have been feeling off colour, gone to bed, either taken the tablets or had a fall trying to take them?"

"That's option three," said Reilly.

"But you don't sound convinced by that one, either."

"No," said Gardener, "because it doesn't explain the bruising and doesn't account for the break-in. I don't mind admitting that I'm puzzled. But I need to keep an open mind. So, if it's all the same to you, Maurice, I'd like you to take care of a few things while we speak to Robbie Carter."

"What would you like me to do?"

"The first thing is an incident room."

Before Gardener had a chance to continue, the sandwiches arrived. Judging by the smell and the wait they'd had, they'd been freshly prepared. Gardener's stomach rumbled. Reilly moved so fast that Gardener didn't even see him – all he felt was the breeze as the Irishman passed him.

"Not a problem," continued Cragg, "we can use the same one as last time."

Gardener gave a quick thought to Cragg's comment. The squad lost a very promising young PC in Gary Close who had been killed by an obsessive doctor earlier in the year, hell-bent on seeking revenge for the death of his wife. He'd been in the wrong place at the wrong time.

Gardener quickly continued. "Can you also contact HOLMES, get them here and set them up in the next room?"

"As good as done," said Cragg, standing up and leaving the table.

As Gardener turned, Mike Atherton came through the door.

"Mike," said Gardener, "have you been on duty all this time?"

"No, sir. I've had a few hours at home but I wanted to get back and see if you'd consider using me on this case, to work alongside your team."

"We'd value your help. In fact, I have something specific for you in mind. You must know the area and the people pretty well. We have more than just a murder to investigate, there's a burglary and all the subsequent enquiries that go with it."

"Are you thinking it might be a burglary gone wrong, sir?"

"I have no idea, yet, Mike, but it's looking that way. I'd like you to try to locate it, through handlers or second-hand shops etc. I'd also like you to talk to your Intel cell and ask the CHIS Handlers to press the snouts for info on someone having the gear – or a load of cash."

Gardener felt that Mike Atherton was best placed for that last task. A CHIS is a Covert Human Intelligence Source, in other words, a police informant. Every CHIS had an officer they could trust, called a handler. A CHIS Handler was someone who dealt with police informants. An Intel cell is a group of intelligence officers who work specifically on developing intelligence.

Gardener glanced at his watch. Time was moving on and they needed to speak to Robbie Carter. He also wanted another word with Cragg, whom he found out in the lobby. "Maurice, is Robbie Carter known to us?"

"Not as far as I'm aware."

"What about his wife? Is she known to us for any reason?"

"None that I can think of."

"Okay. Can you check on that and do one last thing for me? I'd like a list of all the known burglars in the area: names and addresses and any whose prints we have on file."

Chapter Eight

Jane Rogers glanced at the clock as the door opened. At shortly after two she was already late for her dinner. Now she had another client. Though not in the mood, she placed her pen on the desk in front of her and smiled. Business had been quiet of late: people don't want to think about moving or buying houses with the festive period approaching.

"Afternoon, can I help you?"

"I hope so. Have you got a brochure on the property in Haygate Lane?"

"Of course," she replied, leaving her desk and heading for the cupboard at the back of the shop. Maybe it wouldn't take too long after all.

The man waited patiently while she found the one he wanted. "It's quite a large place," she said as she returned, "detached, three bedrooms, double-glazed, gas central heating."

"It was my wife who saw it first?"

"Do you have a family?"

"Two children."

"How lovely, sounds like the perfect place. Most of the year the area is very quiet, but it does back onto the showground and the events arena so the summer months can prove quite lively."

"Exactly what my wife was thinking. She has visions that we'll be sitting in the conservatory in the summer, sipping wine and listening to the concerts."

"Sounds perfect. I'm sure your children will be happy with all the space as well."

"They'd be happy anywhere. You know what kids are like. Nothing on the outside interests them these days."

"Tell me about it. Most of them have to be surgically removed from a tablet, and if they are outside all they do is stare at a mobile phone all day. They used to say television killed the art of conversation. Not so sure now."

"I see you have kids then."

"No, just very observant," she replied. Her stomach growled. Breakfast was the last thing she had eaten, following a five-mile run and a shower. She held her stomach, as if she could somehow deaden the sound. "I'm so sorry."

The man smiled. "Don't be. Sounds like someone needs to eat, so I won't keep you any longer."

Well done, stomach, thought Jane, but she held her professionalism to the last. "Nonsense. Do you own your own property at the moment, or are you renting?"

"Renting. We moved up here recently from Suffolk."

"Oh, what made you move?"

"The job."

"What do you do?"

"I'm a police constable at the station in Bramfield." He extended his hand. "Mike Atherton."

"Nice to meet you." Though she never took the offered hand.

"Let me take some details." She turned back to her desk and opened a pad. After writing down his name, address and contact number, she passed him one of her cards. "Please, feel free to contact me anytime. I'm here every day."

He nodded, took the card and left.

Her stomach growled once more. "I'm coming."

Chapter Nine

Known to everyone else as Jane Rogers, Grace Browne stepped outside and locked the door. A number of cars were parked in the high street. Most of the local shops were busy – trade was good. The two pubs advertised a specials board for lunch outside and their car parks had a number of vehicles in. Despite being November, the sun was up and it was unseasonably warm.

She popped across the road to the local mini mart, collecting fresh ingredients for her evening meal ahead.

Having returned, she unlocked the door between the estate agent and the café next door. Three separate locks had to be taken in sequence of bottom, top and then middle. If not obeyed, the tumblers would reset themselves and she would have to start again. The middle one was the awkward one as it had a series of numbers that had to be keyed in.

Once inside, a fresh exotic smell brightened up the hallway. She locked the door, slipped on a pair of latex gloves from the box on the table behind the door, collected her post and took the ten steps leading to her flat. She glanced behind her once more before tapping the electric panel to the left of the door. The oblong shape was made from titanium, five inches by three, with a voice-activated LCD display.

Grace was deeply obsessed with personal security. The alarm system outside the door randomly generated a question from a list of five hundred before allowing entry. The required answer had to be accurate, word for word – otherwise the door would not open.

The voice was clear and concise and picked a question: "Which prime minister was defeated by Margaret Thatcher in the 1979 general election?"

She leaned forward to the small speaker. "James Callaghan."

Nothing more was said: nothing more was needed. A buzzer sounded, followed by a series of sliding tumblers and the door opened.

She stepped into a small hallway with two doors leading to other rooms. One was a large cupboard where she could hide anything she considered clutter, which was very little, as Grace was a minimalist. Everything was a commodity to her, including people. If she had no time for either then she discarded and moved on. She used the space to hang her coats and jackets and leave her shoes.

She took the door into an open-plan living and dining room with wooden floors. She had no TV, only a hi-fi system with low lighting. A number of oil paintings, mainly places of interest like the Yorkshire Coast, adorned the walls.

Passing the wooden table and dining chairs she went into the kitchen and deposited a carrier bag on the countertop. She'd bought chicken breasts, mushrooms, onions, tomatoes, and pasta. She loved pasta and almost anything Italian. Her love of their food came courtesy of two months touring the Italian lakes and mountains. Her kitchen was decorated with a number of oils with scenic views of the Italian coastline. She washed her hands before placing the items in the fridge and cupboards.

Back in the main room she turned her attention to the large wooden crate in the middle of the floor that had been delivered earlier, shipped in from America. Removing a pair of disposable gloves, pliers, a screwdriver and some scissors from a storage unit, Grace pulled out all the staples and systematically set about gaining entry.

Having removed all the items before placing them on the table, she was elated by the quality. The kit contained a number of tactical weapons including a bulletproof vest, as well as a variety of nasty little surprises should anyone wish to try and take advantage of her. It had cost a fortune and, in her opinion, would be worth every penny when the time came. And it would.

She was eager to try it on before returning to work.

Grace skipped back into the kitchen and made herself some fresh Italian coffee before strolling over to the bathroom. After shedding her clothes and using the toilet, she stepped into the shower.

Ten minutes later, wrapped in a bath towel she glanced at the kitchen clock. Half an hour left.

She put her coffee onto a tray, along with two belVita breakfast bars, an apple and a banana and headed for another door. She slipped the tray onto one of the chests of drawers and turned round. There were two walk-in wardrobes in the bedroom, one of which housed her computer and state of the art security system.

Switching on the PC, she retrieved the tray and placed it on the desk, to her right. Grace logged on and sipped coffee while she checked her emails. There was nothing of any importance so she logged out and entered the next site: the important one.

The blue and white homepage of *Findadate.com* flashed into life and she immediately signed in. Her photo stared back at her. She had very stylish, black shoulder-length hair in a fashionable bob, blue eyes, and wide mouth. The outfit she had chosen for the photo had been the very latest fashion. She had maintained a trim figure due to a daily workout. Her make-up had been professionally applied, as always, due to time spent in a beauty salon.

She had perfected the vision that he normally went for.

Having finished the breakfast bars and the fruit, she was almost at the end of the coffee, and the time she had before her return to work was diminishing.

She moved the cursor to the "connections" panel and clicked, glancing at the three candidates she had marked as favourites: two were of no real interest to her but she felt that marking only one would be a little odd.

Homing in on the one she really wanted, Grace noticed that he had taken the bait and picked her out as one of his favourites as well.

She studied his photo for a few minutes, realising it was a complete lie. She had no idea who it was but it certainly wasn't him. The description however, his likes and dislikes, were a different matter. She knew him well enough to have spotted what she needed to know.

She rubbed her palms together, laughing as she did so. Her plan was coming together. And Christ, was she pleased.

It had taken long enough: years, in fact.

She sent him an email.

Chapter Ten

"Perfect timing."

Mary stood in the courtyard with her arms outstretched, holding a casserole in a wrapped towel.

"Well, come on, Manfred, let me in. I can't stand out here all day with this in my hands."

Manny stepped back, allowing her to pass.

Mary faltered, struggling to work out where she was going to put the dish. Places were limited in Manny's kitchen: he'd filled every open space with something.

"Here, let me," he offered, pushing stuff all over to clear a space.

"Be careful, Manfred."

Before he could do any further damage, she stuck it on a cooker ring. "Look at the state of this place. What would your mother say?"

"Doubt she can see it from where she is – she'd need a bloody good pair of glasses."

Mary stood back and crossed her chest. "You shouldn't speak ill of the dead."

"Well she can't hear me, either."

Mary stood with her hands on her hips. "I've no idea what I'm going to do with you. Look at the state of *you*, never mind the flat. Pale and thin. You're not looking after yourself. What were you up to last night, coming back at all hours of the morning?"

"Nothing much."

"Didn't sound like nothing to me. You woke me up with the racket you made."

"Sorry, Mary, never meant to."

"So, what were you doing?"

"Helping a friend."

"To do what at that time?"

"Move house," said Manny.

Mary's face softened. "That's your trouble, Manfred, you're too easy going. People put on you. You were out all day yesterday. I suppose you were helping him all the time, were you?"

"You could say that. But you're no different, Mary. I bet you've been up since the crack of dawn, cleaning, ironing, baking, cooking." Manny pointed to the dish. Mary was a bit of a workaholic, and cared more for others than for herself. She worked at the Forest Pine care home, halfway between Bramfield and Bursley Bridge on the Pickering Road. She had been there for the best part of fifteen years, and her mother had been a patient for five.

"Yes but that's different. That's for you. You need someone to look after you, Manfred."

"I don't do too bad."

"You don't do too well either. You're that busy helping other people you don't get your own work done and you don't eat properly."

Mary left the kitchen and walked through to the living room. "Oh my word, it looks like a bomb's hit it." She turned back to face Manny. "What you need is a wife."

She gave him little time to answer as she started picking items up, carefully rearranging them.

"There's no need to do that, Mary," said Manny. "Really, you must have enough to do without looking after me."

"Nonsense. I like helping you, you know that."

Mary had picked up Manny's box, the one he hadn't yet had time to thoroughly inspect. As she turned it slipped straight into his arms.

"Honestly, Mary, there's no need. Anyway, I can't stay because I have to go back out and help my friend finish off."

"See. What did I tell you? What time are you coming back?"

"Oh, I won't be long. Two hours tops."

"Good. When you come back, make sure you eat that casserole I've prepared. Just needs warming up. I can do that if you want."

"No, Mary," said Manny, ushering her toward the back door. "You've done more than enough already. But if I get back in good time I'll come and see you later, perhaps have a nightcap with you."

Her face brightened. "Would you really?"

"Yes, really."

Mary strutted off with a spring in her step.

Chapter Eleven

"She's dead, isn't she?"

Sitting in an interview room, Robbie Carter was pale and his eyes were bloodshot. Gardener could understand it: he'd had no sleep, had been surviving on only coffee, wondering as to the state of his wife. He was still dressed in jeans and the black leather jacket he had on when he came in.

"I'm sorry, Mr Carter," said Gardener. "I'm afraid she is."

Robbie's arms were folded on the table, next to an empty cup. The walls were bare, no carpet, little in the way of heat or home comforts but that was the way it had to be for now. Gardener and Reilly each pulled out a chair and sat opposite. Gardener had a file in his hand, which he placed on the table in front of him.

Robbie Carter suddenly shot to his feet and slammed the palms of his hands on the metal table, causing the polystyrene cup to fall over.

"I want him caught."

Reilly was on his feet.

"Who?" Gardener asked. It wasn't the reaction he'd been expecting.

"Whoever did this!"

"Sit down, Robbie," said Reilly.

"Are you listening to me, copper? I said, I want whoever did this to my wife caught."

"So do we," said Gardener.

"And I said sit down," Reilly repeated.

For a few seconds, the stand-off remained. Gardener did not want a showdown, he simply wanted to interview the man, to try to arrive at the truth. Gardener realised that grief affected everyone differently, but Robbie Carter's seemed contrary to what they'd heard of him so far. Eventually the man did as asked and sat back on the chair. "It was the burglar, wasn't it?"

"That's what we're here to find out."

Reilly returned to his chair but Gardener could tell his partner was more than ready should Robbie Carter repeat his performance.

"What do you mean?" asked Robbie.

"I appreciate this is a shock for you, but we need to ask you some questions."

Robbie Carter placed his head in his hands and sighed. "I come home to find my house turned over and my wife dead and you're questioning me."

"Dead?" Reilly asked.

Robbie Carter glanced upwards.

Gardener pulled the sheets of paper from the file.

"When you came into the station to report the offence you weren't sure whether she was dead or dying."

"Now you are," said Reilly.

"Dead, dying, the outcome was the same."

Robbie Carter's answer and blasé attitude shocked Gardener. He realised they were going to have a lot of trouble with him and it was very unlikely that he would be able to continue questioning without detaining the man further. He would need a Superintendent for a twelve-hour extension, and then, if necessary, a magistrate for another twelve to take it to forty-eight.

"Let's start at the beginning, shall we, Mr Carter? If you cooperate, we'll all be out of here a lot quicker. You have to understand it from our point of view. If you want us to catch whoever did this to your wife, remaining calm will help you remember as many details as possible. Do you understand me?"

Robbie Carter merely nodded. "Can I have another coffee?" He pushed his empty cup forward.

Gardener nodded and Reilly left his seat and banged on the door. The PC on the other side answered and the order was placed. Reilly returned to the table.

"Just for the record, can I have your name, address and phone number?" Gardener asked.

"Carter. Robbie Carter. Number two Swansea Court." Robbie followed up with his mobile number.

"Your statement to the desk sergeant basically states that you found your wife when you came home. Where were you until then?"

"Working, at a club in Leeds. I'm a musician."

"Which one?" Reilly asked.

"Seacroft Working Men's."

"Go on," prompted Reilly.

"I finished the gig about half eleven. Packed up the gear. Had a quick drink then I came straight home. And before you ask I was not over the limit. Got into the house about one-thirty."

"You're not likely to be if you only had one," replied Gardener.

"What was the drink?" Reilly asked.

"Pardon?"

"The drink," repeated Reilly. "What did you have?"

"Half a lager. I never drink when I'm on stage, apart from still orange maybe. When I've finished, I always have a half."

"So you're a musician, Mr Carter. How long have you been doing that?"

"All my life."

"How old are you?"

"Fifty-five."

"You should be pretty good, then," said Reilly. "What do you play?"

"Look, is all this necessary?" Robbie Carter asked. "I thought we were here to talk about my wife being murdered."

A knock on the door meant the coffee had arrived. Reilly took the tray and brought it back to the table.

Gardener noticed two coffees and something herbal. Good old Maurice.

"It is necessary," said Gardener. "I want to establish your movements and the build-up to what you found."

"You mean you suspect me."

"I didn't say that."

"You didn't have to."

"Would you just answer my partner's question, please?"

Robbie Carter glanced at Reilly. "Guitar and vocals. Glam Rock: T-Rex, Slade, Sweet, The Glitterband, all the big names."

"How did you get the booking?" Reilly asked.

"My agent. Steve Crossman. Has an office in Leeds."

"How long have you worked for him?"

"About four years."

Reilly made a note of the answers. "Do you have his contact details?"

Robbie Carter rattled them off.

Gardener was eager to press on and immediately brought the subject back to the evening itself. "So, you had a half and then what?"

"Left the club."

"What time?"

"About quarter to one, a little later maybe."

"Who were you having a drink with in the club?"

"The manager, the compère, and one or two regulars."

Gardener passed Robbie Carter a sheet of paper and asked him to write down the names. "Did you drive straight home?"

"Yes."

"When you got home, can you tell me exactly what happened: how you found your wife, and when?"

"I've already said, I got home about one-thirty."

"Did you find her straight away?"

"No. I put the gear in the house first. Called out her name a few times. She often goes to bed before I get in. I went upstairs and she was on the floor."

"Where on the floor?" Reilly asked.

"What do you mean, where?"

"Was she near the door, near the window?"

"Near the bed – she must have fallen out."

"Go on," said Gardener.

"Well, I panicked. I'm not used to coming home and finding my wife on the floor. I knelt down, called out her name. She didn't answer. I couldn't feel a pulse, hear her breathing."

"So you assumed at that point she was dead?"

"Wouldn't you?"

"Why didn't you call an ambulance?"

"Pardon?"

"We asked why you didn't call an ambulance," repeated Reilly. "You'd been out, came home early hours of the morning, went upstairs to find your wife on the floor, either dead or dying. The first thing I would have done is call an ambulance, but you didn't."

"Why?" Gardener asked.

The longer it took Robbie Carter to answer, the less Gardener liked it. He seemed to be stalling. Was he thinking of a suitable answer? At the same time, what possible reason could you give in such a situation?

"Come on, Robbie, old son. Surely it's not that hard to answer. Are you a doctor as well as a musician?"

"Oh, I see, so this is the game," said Robbie.

"Game?" repeated Gardener.

Robbie stood up. "I see what you're up to. Good cop, bad cop routine. What comes next, the thumbscrews?"

"Sit down, Robbie, we've told you once."

"You gonna make me?"

Reilly rose to the challenge. "You know something, Robbie. If it was my wife who'd been killed, I'd be in bits, so I would. I'd be a bit of a mess, working out how the hell I was gonna live the rest of my life without the woman I love. Can't say I've seen anything resembling that emotion so far."

"I was in shock, okay," shouted Robbie Carter. "I didn't expect to come home and find my wife dead, did I? I didn't fucking know what to do. She was dead on the floor. I panicked. I wasn't thinking straight. I didn't know what to do for best. We're not all fucking policemen, you know."

At that, Robbie fell back into his chair, tears finally beginning to show.

It was the first time Gardener had seen anything close to how he should have been reacting.

"Okay, Mr Carter. We'll accept your explanation of being in shock. You had any first aid training?"

"I'm a musician, not a medic."

"So the answer to that would be no?"

"No, I have not had any first aid training."

"When you arrived home did you park at the back of the house, or the front?"

"The front door. That's where the gear is, isn't it – in front of the front door?"

"It was when we last saw it," said Reilly.

"Did you notice any lights on in neighbouring houses while you were unloading?"

"I don't think so. Most of my neighbours either work for the railway or on local farms, so they're up pretty early."

Gardener made a note and continued. "Does your wife normally go to gigs with you?"

"Sometimes. She's seen and heard it all before. Same songs, same order, different clubs, it's how we work."

"We?"

"Musicians. We can't learn new numbers for every gig."

"Okay," pressed Gardener. "After having shouted out her name, there's no answer, so you go upstairs and find her dead, or dying. You panic. You're frightened: you've never been in this situation before. What next?"

"What do you mean, what next?"

"What did you do next?"

"I'm not sure." Robbie Carter put his head in his hands again.

"You're not sure?" repeated Reilly. "You must know what you did. You know what you didn't do, and that's call an ambulance."

"Okay, okay," said Robbie Carter, testily. "I'm trying to think. I guess I must have gone downstairs."

"Did you use the bathroom?"

"The bathroom?"

"Yes. Did you use the bathroom? Did you feel queasy, want to throw up? Did you need the toilet?"

"No. As far as I can remember, I just went downstairs."

"Did you see the bathroom as you went past?"

"What the hell are you two getting at?"

"Simple question," said Reilly. "You didn't use the bathroom but could you see inside? It's not that far from the bedroom and you have to pass it on your way down the stairs."

"I didn't take any notice, for God's sake. My wife was dead, the bathroom was low on my list of priorities."

"The wife you didn't call an ambulance for," said Reilly. "Yes, we remember. Were you in a rush?"

"Probably. I was panicking – still didn't know what to do."

"You didn't rush into the bathroom, or knock into anything on your way past?" Gardener asked.

"No. For fuck's sake, how many times? What's so special about the bathroom?"

"Someone had left it in a mess. All the shelves had come down. A cabinet that should have been on the wall was on the floor, along with smashed glass, toiletries... you name it."

Robbie Carter's eyes widened. "What happened?"

"That's what we're trying to establish," said Gardener. "What happened next, after you'd gone downstairs?"

"Well, that's when I found out the place had been turned over."

"So you hadn't actually been anywhere after you'd loaded the gear into the house and before you went upstairs?"

"No," replied Robbie. "The two rooms at the front of the house were in darkness."

"Do you keep your musical gear in front of the front door?"

"No. Once it's all inside I move it to another room."

Gardener resumed his questioning from earlier. "You came downstairs. Which room did you go into first?"

"Er..." Robbie Carter was scratching his head. "The kitchen. Place was a mess. Drawers pulled out. Cupboard doors open, stuff all over the table. I wondered what the fuck had happened, so then I went into the living room – same thing there."

"You didn't see anyone at the scene?"

"No. Maybe my wife woke up and startled him – whoever he was. If you reckon there's a mess in the bathroom, that's probably where he attacked her. Maybe that's where he was hiding from me. I wouldn't know, would I? I never went in there."

Gardener thought differently. Working out what had happened in the bathroom and who had been there was going to be the case-breaker.

"He must have been somewhere, because your phone indicated that. It went off while you were in the station and you saw him at your house."

"Exactly," shouted Robbie.

"Your explanation of what happened doesn't add up, does it?"

"What do you mean?"

"You think your wife must have startled him and he attacked her in the bathroom, maybe dragged her to the bedroom..."

"Yes."

"But then you'd have seen the mess in the bathroom, Robbie," said Reilly. "At the very least you might have seen a trail across the landing."

"Only you claim there *was* no mess," said Gardener. "We're very confused here about the timing of things, Mr

Carter. So you see how important it is to us that you understand the difference between dead and dying?"

Robbie Carter hung his head again. "Oh Christ, what a mess."

"So which one was it? Was your wife dying when you got home, or dead?"

Robbie started to bite the nails on his right hand. "Dead."

"Are you sure?"

"She must have been; I couldn't feel a pulse."

Gardener paused to take notes before continuing.

"You came down the stairs, found the place had been burgled. What then?"

"That's when I came straight round to see you lot. I really couldn't take any more. My wife was dead, the house ransacked. I needed help."

"You left straight away."

"Yes."

"Back door, or front?"

"Back door. I couldn't get out the front door, could I? My gear was in the way."

"Did you lock it behind you?"

"Lock it?"

"Yes. Did you lock the place up?"

"I... I can't remember. It wasn't a priority. I was a mess by that time. I can't even remember getting to the police station."

Gardener scribbled more notes.

"You left immediately – didn't do anything else?" Reilly asked.

Robbie Carter diverted his gaze to the Irishman. "What do you think I did, make a coffee and have a game of backgammon?"

"No, and this is why we're confused as to the timing of things," replied Gardener. "We think – at that point – that you set the alarm."

"The alarm?"

"Yes, the alarm. You left the house, went to the police station and while you were there your phone pinged and you said to the desk sergeant, 'he's still there.'"

"I set the alarm?" questioned Robbie Carter, as if he couldn't quite believe he had done it himself. "Why did I set the alarm?"

"That's what we'd like to know. Your wife was in the house, and as far as you are aware, the only person in the place. She's dead. Your house had been burgled and you're all over the place, yet you set the alarm before you leave. Why would you do that?"

Robbie Carter shook his head a few times, opened his mouth but nothing came out.

"Let's be honest, Mr Carter, your wife wouldn't have set it before she went to bed, would she, knowing you were still out?"

"Is there anything you want to tell us, Robbie?" Reilly asked.

"Such as?"

"I've no idea. You say your wife was already dead and your house had already been burgled before you got home. But nothing you say seems to confirm what we've seen. So we're starting to wonder about something."

"Starting to wonder what?" Robbie Carter's expression was grave, as if he had suddenly worked out what Gardener and Reilly had been thinking all along.

"That maybe you know more than you're letting on."

Reilly had ignited Robbie Carter's short fuse again. "What the hell are you saying – that *I* set all this up?"

Gardener and Reilly remained tight-lipped.

Robbie Carter stared directly at Gardener. "You're out of your mind. I had nothing to do with this... nothing at all."

Both detectives sat silently – arms folded.

"If I'd done it, why would I set the alarm? I mean, what, you think I killed her and then arranged for a burglar to come in and turn the place over, take the heat off me?"

"Did you?"

Robbie Carter was on his feet. "How dare you?"

"Maybe you had a change of heart, old son," said Reilly, "thought you were out of your league, or that something would go wrong and you didn't want to go down so you'd get rid of both of them."

"You take that back, you Irish bastard," shouted Robbie.

Gardener had to admit that his partner had a way of provoking a reaction. Robbie Carter had risen to the bait, but Reilly remained calm and collected.

Gardener stood up, pushed his chair back and collected his folder.

"I think we'll take a break, Mr Carter."

"We're done, are we? It's what he'll be if you stay much longer," said Robbie Carter, pointing to Reilly.

"Sorry if you think we've been a bit tough on you, in view of everything that's happened, but we have a job to do. Not very nice at times, I grant you."

Robbie Carter nodded. "It's okay." He stood up and placed his chair under the table. "So, I can go now?"

"Go?" asked Gardener.

"Yes, go, go home."

"I'm afraid not, Mr Carter. We haven't finished yet."

Chapter Twelve

The windows on the car had steamed up, on account of the fact that it had no heater, and the temperature outside was dropping fast.

Manny was freezing. He put his hands to his face and blew into them. The end of his nose felt like a Cornetto – it was too cold to even run.

Trust him to pinch the only car in Bursley Bridge that was fucked. The owner was probably laughing all the way to the bank: doubt he would even report it missing. If he did, it would be ages before the authorities found it. He had his mate, Stitch, to thank for that one. He'd taught Manny how invaluable a roll of black PVC tape could be on number plates. Soon change an F to an E. Mind you, the silly bastard put paid to that trick when he'd forgotten which letter he'd changed on the front: altered a different one on the back and was nicked in no time.

Manny was in the car park of The Black Bull in the middle of Rawston. There were some rough areas in Leeds but very few worse than here. He avoided Rawston because there was fuck all worth nicking. Even the seagulls flew upside down because there was nothing worth shitting on.

Manny raised his right arm and squinted at his watch. Ten minutes after seven. A rap on the window frightened the life out of him. He came close to soiling himself, which would have been really bad news because he'd had a shower after Mary had left – his first in ages. He'd then spent another half hour mopping and drying the bathroom floor. He'd eaten half the casserole she'd made and then disappeared before she saw him leave.

He rolled the window down. "Yes?"

"Manny?" asked the silhouette.

Manny was parked under a street lamp and all he could see was a long dark trench coat and a pair of black pointed shoes.

"Who wants to know?"

"Don't fuck me about," the man shouted. "Guitar?"

Manny waved his arms. "Keep your voice down, mate. I don't want everyone knowing what's going down."

"Everyone? Fucking place is deserted."

"Walls have ears," said Manny.

"Which is more than you'll have if we're here much longer."

Manny rolled up the window and opened the door. Not that it had any effect on the bloke standing next to the car because he didn't move, made Manny squeeze through the gap – inconsiderate bastard.

"Where is it, then?" asked trench coat.

"Well it isn't in me pocket, is it?"

"I don't know, do I? I can't see it."

"I'm hardly gonna walk around Rawston after dark with a fucking Fender Stratocaster, am I?"

Manny trotted round to the tailgate and unlocked it, lifting it so that the street lamp illuminated the guitar case.

"You sure it's a Strat?"

"That's what it says on one end."

"The neck?"

"How do I know what a neck is?" said Manny, opening the box. "I'm not Eric Clapton."

Trench coat whistled through his teeth, giving the game away. Manny soon realised there was a few quid to be had: add that to the two hundred he'd found inside the case and today was a real winner.

The man picked it up, inspected it from every angle.

"What do you think?" Manny asked.

Trench coat stared at him. "You in a rush or something?"

"No, I just love hanging round pub car parks putting my life at risk."

Trench coat went back to his inspection. He put one leg on the back of the car and rested the guitar on one knee, running his hands up and down the strings.

"Feels okay, but I need to test it properly."

"What do you mean?"

"Need to hear it."

"Put it through an amp, you mean?"

Trench coat nodded.

"Oh, good," said Manny. "For a minute there I thought you were serious." He glanced around. "Only I don't see any fence posts with sockets on, do you?"

"No problem. Follow me."

Manny was doubtful. Straight in and straight out was all he wanted. Now trench coat was walking to a big van. There could be anything in the back of there. Like Manny's carcass when a dozen blokes had finished with him.

Trench coat opened the back doors. "See, I got everything we need." He pointed to an amp. "Cordless. Amazing what you can get these days." The man connected the guitar to the amp, switched it on, struck a chord and nearly blew the windows out of the van.

"Fucking hell," shouted Manny, ducking. "Look, are you gonna buy this thing or what? I don't want to be here all night, and I don't want to advertise to the world what we're doing."

"Good enough for me. How much?"

"Four hundred," said Manny.

"For this battered piece of shit?"

"Battered?"

"Look at the state of it." Trench coat pointed to all the scratches.

A group of seven men wandered into the pub car park. They were big, probably rugby players. Luckily they paid no attention to Manny and his companion, heading straight for the main door instead.

"Two hundred," said trench coat.

"Behave yourself," said Manny. "That's a quality machine. You can tell by the sound." Not that Manny knew one end of a guitar from the other but he was going to have to put some pressure on. He had too many other things to do.

"Three hundred or I'm leaving... with the guitar."

* * *

Ten minutes later, Manny was on his way home with his pocket bulging. What a day: five hundred quid richer from the day's takings.

Within an hour he'd offloaded all the CDs, the hi-fi, and the car, which would no doubt be used later in a smash and grab. It wouldn't matter to Manny. As always, he'd worn three pairs of gloves.

Manny glanced at an ancient timepiece in his kitchen. It was nine o'clock. Enough time to shovel down the last of the casserole and pay Mary a quick visit. He felt like he ought to apologise for earlier, ushering her away so quickly.

He strolled into the living room, fully satisfied with the food and drink. He thought about another glass or two of brandy but decided against it.

Dropping into a chair, Manny picked up the box at his feet. He unlocked and opened it. The thing was full of cameras. Manny unloaded them one by one and although he knew very little about cameras, he recognised some of the names, Kodak being one. He saw a pocket camera in a leather case. As Manny rifled his way through, he figured there was very little of interest, or anything that would fetch money. He wondered if any of them had film inside.

Manny sat back in his chair. Why would someone go to the trouble of hiding a box of old cameras?

Returning to his find, the last one in the box really caught his interest. He pulled the case out, rubbing it between thumb and forefinger. Manny was no expert, but if felt very much to him like snakeskin, or crocodile.

Carefully removing it from the case, he could see that it was gold plated and had a 50mm Elmar lens – which meant fuck all to him. The name informed him it was a Leica Luxus II.

Manny placed the whole lot – apart from the Leica – back in the box, taking care to lock it, and sat back. They may not make him any money but he liked the Leica, a lot.

He had plans for that one. And for that reason, he was keeping it.

He figured there was no safer place than Mary's garage. He could gain entry through the connecting door in the firewall; he wouldn't even need her key.

Chapter Thirteen

"You can't do this to me!"

Robbie Carter was back in the interview room, still dressed in jeans but with a different T-shirt. He was on his feet, banging his fists on the table. "I know my rights."

Gardener closed the door. Reilly was behind him with a tray containing three hot drinks. "So do we, Mr Carter. We know *your* rights, *our* rights, and we know the law, and we're acting within it."

"You can't hold me for more than twenty-four hours."

"As a matter of fact, we can, especially when we're not satisfied with the answers to our questions."

"Satisfied!" he repeated. "It's *my* fucking wife who's dead – not yours."

That sentence struck a raw nerve with Gardener but he had to let it pass.

"I'm being victimised here. I'll have your badge for this."

"You've been watching too much television, Robbie, old son. Now sit down and drink your coffee."

"I can detain you for a lot longer than twenty-four hours if I really want to, so don't bother complaining about rights. Your wife had them as well: we're also doing our best for her."

Robbie Carter took his time but eventually sat down, taking a sip of his coffee.

Gardener opened his file, placing sheets of paper on the table. "Let's start with where we left off last night: your alarm system."

"What about it?"

"Come on, Robbie," said Reilly. "Don't make this any harder. Tell us about your alarm system."

"It's nothing special. The CCTV system is linked via the wi-fi. It's cheap and fairly common and streams straight to a website. Sends me a text if motion is detected."

"Is it connected to your computer?"

"No, only the wi-fi, and seeing as I have a smartphone that's all I need."

"So you don't have any cameras around the house?"

"No. It's a simple system for the musical gear. That stuff costs a fortune and so does the insurance for it. If you want proper musician's insurance, you pay through the nose for it."

"Be worth it, wouldn't it?" Reilly asked.

"Probably. I had a mate who insured his drums properly. He reckoned he could leave them in the middle of the garden and they'd be insured. Cost him about four thousand pounds a year and that was ten years ago."

Gardener would need to check, so he passed over a sheet of paper and asked Robbie to write down the details of the website that the alarm was linked to and where he'd bought it. "What time did you get home?"

"Are you for real? How many times did you ask me that last night?"

"I'm asking again."

Robbie Carter sighed heavily. "One-thirty. This is getting boring now. Haven't you two found anything fresh to ask me overnight?"

"We're finding it anything but boring," said Gardener. "We simply can't get our heads around the timing of everything. You get home and find your wife dead. You don't ring for an ambulance, you decide to go and get help."

"That's because I'm a law-abiding citizen."

"Come again," said Reilly.

"It's true. You lot say I shouldn't tackle a burglar on my premises. It would be against the law if I was to smash his face in."

"You're allowed to use reasonable force."

"We both know that doesn't work. He isn't going stand and wait for you lot to turn up. Chances are he's going to attack me and I would have to defend myself. Anything bad happens to him and he'll sue me, and he'll get away with it. Oh, no, mate, I'm not falling for that one."

"But I still can't understand why you set the alarm before you came to see us."

"I've told you," shouted Robbie, slamming his fists on the table. He stood up quickly and kicked the chair back. "I've told you I can't bloody well remember setting the alarm."

Even though Reilly was up, the policeman outside the room opened the door and rushed in.

Reilly held his hand up. "It's okay, son, there's no threat."

The young constable's expression said he didn't believe Reilly but he left anyway.

The Irishman walked around the table, picked up the chair, told Robbie to sit. "Quite a temper you have, old son. Maybe it was a good job you didn't find that burglar. We might have two murders to investigate."

"I'd say I was provoked enough."

"Is that what happened last night, Mr Carter?" asked Gardener. "You were provoked by something: you came home and you and your wife had a row. She provoked you, you hit her, things got out of hand – all went a bit too far..."

"Maybe it's you two who have been watching too much TV. I've told you a dozen times I came home and found her like that. I panicked. I cannot remember setting the alarm before leaving the house, or whether or not I locked the back door. But I'd say it was a bit bloody pointless as the place had already been turned over."

"At least you're sticking to your story," said Reilly.

"Must be true, then."

"Let's move on," said Gardener. "Perhaps you'd like to tell me about your wife."

Robbie Carter finished his coffee and Gardener noticed him stiffen a little at the mention of his other half. "What do you want to know?"

"How long have you known each other?"

"About three years."

"Where did you meet?"

"I met her at a pub in Thirsk. Strange, really, I was actually there to meet someone else, and so was she, but neither of our dates turned up. She was ready to leave, so was I. We bumped into each other on the way out. I made a joke about being stood up. She laughed, said the same had happened to her. As neither of us had eaten I offered to buy her a meal and we stayed till they chucked us out."

"Did she live in Thirsk?"

"No, Sowerby."

"And you married, when?"

"About a year after we met."

"Is that when you started living together, after you were married?"

"Yes."

"Did she sell her house?"

Robbie Carter shook his head. "It was rented."

"How would you describe the marriage?"

"How would you describe any marriage?" countered Robbie. "It wasn't perfect. We had our ups and downs but we worked at it. It was a second marriage for both of us so we'd had a bit of experience. It sometimes helps."

"Any financial problems?" asked Reilly.

"No more than anyone else. We didn't really have any debt. Both of us worked hard – paid our way."

"What did your wife do?" asked Gardener, remembering the photos and the trophies.

"She worked for Matthew Atkinson. He owns stables in Thirsk. That's who she rented the house off as well."

"Did you go out much around the town?"

"Of course we did, like most other couples. We shopped in the town, went out for meals. So in case you're wondering, plenty of people saw us together."

"Any family?"

"No. Neither of us had children in any of the marriages. Her parents died years ago."

"Any close friends?"

"Not that close. We never went out with the neighbours. Jane sometimes had girly nights out – mostly her mates from the stables."

Gardener passed over the sheet of paper again, asked Robbie Carter to write the names and addresses.

When finished, Gardener asked: "How old was she?"

"Fifty."

"When was the last time you saw her, Mr Carter?"

"That would have been before I left for the gig."

"Which was what time?"

"Six o'clock. I always leave early for gigs: never like to arrive late. I like plenty of time to set the gear up – sound check."

"How did she seem?"

"Tired. She'd had a full day at the stables. Like I said, no idea what she'd been doing. She only got back home about fifteen minutes before I was leaving."

"Apart from tired."

"What do you mean by that?"

"What we say?" said Reilly. "People can be tired but sociable. They're not usually sociable if something's bothering them. So how was your wife? Was she tired but pleased to see you – gave you a kiss? Appreciated the fact that you'd made her a drink, or perhaps had a glass of wine ready for her?"

"Jane was Jane. She was an Aquarian, not the most talkative of people anyway. They're a bit cold – to the point. But her heart was in the right place. She was fine. I made her a coffee before I left but not before she got home because I never know what time she's getting home."

"She didn't text you, then?"

"No. Like I said – Aquarian. They don't waste much time on small talk."

"Did she mention that she would be doing anything special during the night: having a friend over, maybe?"

"No. She was tired. It's my guess she would have had a nice long, relaxing bath, something to eat and maybe a glass of wine."

"Did she drink much?"

"No. She liked a drink – doesn't everyone? But she knew when she'd had enough, which wasn't usually very much."

"How would you describe her health?"

"Pretty good. Then again, it would be, wouldn't it? Eating all that stuff: fruit and berries and seeds and shit – live forever, you will." Robbie Carter glanced up, as if his final words hit home with him. "Look, I know what you're thinking but I had nothing to do with this. It was probably the best relationship I'd ever had."

"Have you had many?" Reilly asked.

Robbie Carter smirked, one of those irritating lopsided grins that made up for a thousand words.

"Okay," said Gardener, not wanting to give Robbie Carter an excuse to rattle on about his conquests, "she drank moderately; ate well. She worked outside in the fresh air. She was healthy. Was she taking any medication that you know of?"

Robbie Carter finished his coffee. "You mean the little yellow pills she kept in the bathroom cupboard?"

Gardener nodded, surprised.

Robbie Carter folded his arms and sighed. "I knew about them, but I'm not sure what they're for."

"You've known her for three years but you don't know if she had any health problems?" Reilly asked.

"Whatever it was she didn't want to talk about it. The first time I saw them and asked, she said there was nothing to worry about. She could handle the problem, and had been for years."

"But you have no idea what the problem was?"

"No."

"You ever question it again?"

"Once or twice but I always got a similar answer. She seemed..." Robbie Carter paused, "embarrassed is the only word I could think of."

"You think it was personal?"

"It was to her. Nothing sexual, she assured me that much. But, as I said, it was her problem and she said she was dealing with it. And she obviously had been. I never saw her really ill during the time we were together. Colds, maybe, but nothing bad."

Another dead-end for Gardener, which meant he would have to push Fitz. He figured they were important. He felt he was running out of things to ask on which to incriminate him. He requested Jane Carter's doctor's name and address.

"Were you aware of any disagreements that your wife had recently?"

"What, like neighbours from hell – that sort of stuff?"

"Not specifically. The impression you gave earlier is that you didn't socialise with the neighbours," said Gardener. "I'm talking everyday life – could have been a few words with someone over a parking space at the local shops; a run-in with a client at the stables. Had she come home anytime during the last few weeks and mentioned anything of the sort?"

Robbie Carter ran his hands through his hair, scratched his head. "Nothing I can think of. She wasn't the type. She didn't like confrontation."

"Did you argue much?" asked Reilly.

"No more than any other couple. But if we did, she didn't like it – had this annoying habit of turning the other cheek and walking off."

"That bother you?"

"Did at first. I sometimes think a good row clears the air. When you first get together you're always a bit bothered about the first argument in case it all falls apart. She never really rowed with people. As I said, she would rather walk away."

"How was she after a row?"

"She could sulk for England. It was usually me that had to make the first move."

"Any enemies?" Reilly asked.

"Enemies?" Robbie Carter's expression was one of disbelief.

"Yes, enemies. Look at it from our point of view. We've listened to everything you have to say and she seems a model citizen. But your house was turned over and your wife is dead as a result. Now, it's either a burglary gone wrong, or it was someone who had it in for you and used the burglary to hide things."

Robbie Carter hung his head in his hands. "I really don't know. I'm not aware of any enemies, or disagreements that were so bad that my wife would end up being killed. I've told you everything I know. I've also told you I didn't do it, so why the hell are you keeping me here?"

"We need to be sure, Mr Carter. You might think our job is easy, but it isn't. Someone out there has burgled your house and killed your wife. We need to know everything about your relationship and what happened that night.

Build up her movements, so that we can get a much clearer picture of the person who did this."

"Like I've said, I've told you everything."

"Have you?" Reilly asked.

"Can you shut him up?" Robbie Carter asked Gardener.

"He's talking about the bruises."

Robbie Carter's eyes were intense. "Bruises? What bruises?"

"Your wife had some very serious bruising to her abdomen. It's possible that it may have a major significance on how she died."

"I don't know anything about the bruises. Where were they exactly? How big?"

"You didn't notice any bruising anywhere?" Reilly asked.

"No, but I only checked for a pulse and put my ear to her lips to see if I could hear any breathing. I didn't check anywhere else."

Gardener nodded, made a note. Once he'd finished, he placed the file in the folder and stood up.

Robbie Carter thought for a moment. "Bruises? They could have come from the accident a couple of weeks ago. She was out with a group of friends. They went for a hack. They were one side of a hedge with a main road on the other. She said something about a car backfiring, the horse reared and she fell off."

"Did she go to hospital?"

"No. It was only a fall – she's had a few. She knew how to land."

"There were no after-effects during the last two weeks?"

"Not really. She was bit stiff for a couple of days."

"She fell off the horse two weeks ago," said Reilly. "Plenty of time for the bruises to come out but you still hadn't noticed them?"

"Why would I?"

"You did have a physical relationship with your wife, I take it? I'm sure you would have noticed."

"Our physical relationship is our business," replied Robbie Carter. "But like I said, she'd fallen off the horse, she was a bit stiff for a few days and probably because of that we hadn't been very physical of late."

"And not for any other reason?" quizzed Reilly.

"What other reason could there be?"

"You tell us, son."

Robbie said nothing.

"Okay, I think we have enough to go on for now," said Gardener, collecting his files.

"Can I go this time? I've been here for thirty-six hours."

"We know that. There are a number of things I want to check on and we'll come back and see you later."

Gardener and Reilly left to a torrent of abuse.

Once outside, Reilly turned to Gardener. "Are we charging him, or letting him go?"

"I think we'll have to let him go, Sean. I simply don't have enough to hold him on much longer. Even if we do extend it to forty-eight hours, I still don't think I can question him on anything else. It's time we started digging elsewhere."

Chapter Fourteen

Gardener studied the incident room that Maurice Cragg had arranged. The whiteboards had been positioned ready for action, with a number of photos: one of Jane Carter on her own, one of Robbie Carter, and two with the couple together. Positioned alongside those were the photos of Jane Carter in death, all taken from a variety of angles. Despite the pain she must have suffered, the expression on her face was calm. The bruises told a different story.

Gardener's team comprised of Colin Sharp, who was chewing the fat with Dave Rawson and Paul Benson. Bob Anderson was sitting in a corner sipping coffee with Patrick Edwards. Gardener also had the experience of the Bramfield police station resident, Maurice Cragg, and two of his team, Mike Atherton and Emma Longstaff, both of whom had been taken off the nightshift.

"If I can have your attention, please," said Gardener.

The noise didn't stop immediately but everyone did as he asked. Before he delved into the meeting, Gardener formally introduced DC Sarah Gates. They all knew Sarah from a previous case when she worked under DI Goodman. He explained that Sarah had transferred from Bradford and was now a part of the team. For the time being she would be replacing Frank Thornton who was on compassionate leave. Sarah was mid-forties with a tanned complexion and red hair cut fashionably in a bob. She wore a two-piece navy trouser suit, with a crème blouse and a blue leather jacket.

"You all know that Sean and I were called out at two-thirty yesterday morning to a house in Swansea Court in Bramfield to investigate a murder." Gardener pointed to a photo. "Fifty-year-old Jane Carter was discovered dead on the bedroom floor by the time we arrived."

He pointed to another photo. "Her husband, Robbie Carter, had reported the incident at two o'clock here in the station, but he wasn't sure whether she was dead or dying at the time he found her." He detailed Carter's actions upon arriving home and finding her body before adding, "It's what happened afterwards that gives us a real problem. Carter claims when he came down the stairs, that's when he noticed the place had been turned over."

"So he says the place was burgled?" questioned Anderson, a solid officer who could always be relied upon in a crisis.

"Yes."

"But you think otherwise?" asked Sharp.

"From what we saw at the scene, yes." Gardener went on to describe what he and Reilly had found in the bathroom and why, in their opinion, they were questioning whether or not the burglar had even made it upstairs.

"Is it definitely homicide?" asked Rawson.

"We think so," said Gardener, pointing to the photos taken from the scene. "If you take a close look at these you will see Jane Carter's body bears two large bruises that, according to Fitz, were very recent. One, he felt, would need further investigation; the other, in his opinion, could be a footprint."

"Do you have any ideas, sir?" asked Patrick Edwards, the youngest member of the team – a fresh-faced constable at twenty-one years of age, with one earring and curly blonde hair.

"Not at the moment. Robbie Carter has an alibi. He is a musician and was working at Seacroft Working Men's club for the night so he should have no shortage of witnesses when we check that one out. To be honest, Patrick, you may as well do that – being a budding musician and all that. Establish and clarify Robbie Carter's movements. Talk to his agent – Sean has the details. Speak to staff at the club, and the manager. Get a list of everyone in the place on that night and speak to those as well. Find out what time he left the club and how long it takes for him to drive home."

Patrick Edwards had trouble keeping up with Gardener as he wrote his instructions down.

"This is a tough one, guys, with a lot of ground to cover. As usual, the discovery of an unexplained death presents us with a series of questions that we need to structure our investigation around. Firstly, is it a homicide?" Gardener nodded at Rawson who had already asked the question. "Yes, we think it is. Secondly, who killed the victim? That we don't know, but I will elaborate on that later with Maurice's help. So, let's stick to the basic murder investigation formula: what, why, when, where, how, and who?"

Gardener took a pen and drew three large, interlinking circles on the whiteboard. In the middle section he wrote, Homicide. On the outer edges he wrote the words, Location, Victim and Offenders, knowing that within a day or two the board would hardly be recognisable.

"Usual points to consider here." He pointed to *Location*. "Selection, transportation and escape. Has the offender chosen the location deliberately? How did he travel there and how and when did he escape? Planning: is there any evidence? Was the incident spontaneous, or planned? If it was planned, what level of planning was required? What did the offender do to avoid detection?"

Gardener then pointed to *Victim*. "There's a whole wealth of information to be chased up here – lifestyle being one of them. We need to establish Jane Carter's movements for the whole day, and the night in question. Sean and I are going to talk to her employer, Matthew Atkinson, he runs stables out at Thirsk."

Dave Rawson was quick off the mark to connect the stables and the bruises. "Is it possible something happened at the stables to cause those bruises?"

"That's one of the things we want to ask about," said Gardener. "According to her husband she had a riding accident a couple of weeks back."

"But you said those bruises on her body were fresh."

"They were," said Reilly. "We don't *think* they were caused by a riding accident."

"So why did the husband mention it?"

"He claims he knew nothing about the bruises we found on her, and the accident a couple of weeks back was the only thing he could think of."

Bob Anderson threw his hand in the air and Gardener nodded.

"I'm thinking out loud here – about the burglary and everything that you've said. Was it a burglary gone wrong, or was it made to look like that? Was Jane Carter entertaining someone? Things not right in the marriage – her husband's out of the picture – she decides on a quiet night in with someone else."

"Good point," said Gardener. "But it wouldn't explain the mess that's consistent with the burglary."

"You said yourself," Anderson pointed out. "You didn't think the burglar had made it upstairs. Yes, there was stuff on the bathroom floor but that could have been her. Maybe she was drunk, fell over, brought everything down."

"We'll have to wait for Fitz to confirm toxicity levels but I'm not so sure about the drunk bit," said Gardener. "According to her husband she didn't drink that much, and we found a bottle of tablets in the bathroom cupboard, which suggested to me a medical condition that meant she had to be careful with her diet."

"What were they for?" asked Rawson.

"The husband doesn't know."

"He doesn't know?"

"He knew she was taking them, but not why?"

"More evidence that the relationship wasn't all it was cracked up to be," said Gates.

"Does Fitz know what they are?" asked Sharp.

"Not on first glance. We need to find out who her GP is, talk to him and check her medical records."

Gardener once again pointed to *Victim*. "So, lots of things to consider here: routine, vulnerability, lifestyle, associates, links to the scene, physical appearance, and relationship."

Patrick Edwards raised his hand. "We need to check her social media status: Facebook, Twitter, Instagram, LinkedIn, and any others."

"Good thinking, Patrick. We have the computer. We'll go through that with a fine toothcomb. I also want someone checking all the phones – landline and both mobiles. The other thing that worries us is the alarm system. When Robbie Carter came to the station to report the incident, his mobile phone pinged, alerting him that a motion sensor had been triggered and an intruder was on the premises. We will ask technical to lift the evidence from the phone and run it through our computers so we can see it more clearly."

"Hold on a minute," said Rawson. "His wife's dead at home, he doesn't call an ambulance but sets the alarm and comes to the police station to report it: what's all that about?"

"He can't *remember* setting the alarm," said Reilly.

"Cobblers," said Anderson.

"You mean he doesn't want to," offered Rawson.

"This whole thing isn't adding up," said Gates.

"There's a lot that doesn't add up, Sarah, but we've grilled him for two days and at the moment we can't pin anything on him. He has a perfect alibi."

"Where is he now?" asked Anderson.

"Still here but we can't hold him much longer. We'll let him go, but we'll make life awkward for him. He can surrender his passport and make daily calls into the station while we continue our investigation."

"What's your take on Robbie Carter?" asked Paul Benson.

"Sean," said Gardener, nodding to his partner.

"He's a bit of a character," said Reilly. "Because he's a musician he thinks he's God's gift to the ladies: he wanted us to know there was no shortage of them. He has a bit of a temper: it flared up a couple of times with us. He's a big lad and I don't reckon he'd think twice about throwing his weight around. But is he a killer? I'm not sure."

Gardener pointed to *Offenders*. "We only have two options at the moment. The burglar, or the husband. We'll have our work cut out and from what I can see, both of them fall into most of the categories: motive; was it for some financial gain? If it was the husband we need to check out her financial status – get a copy of her will, if she made one. If it was the burglar then it's certainly a financial gain to some degree. There are other motives: jealousy, revenge, sex, thrill, hate. Was it planned for any of those reasons? Could have been, so scene disguise is a big one here: what degree of scene arrangement or rearrangement has taken place? Sadly for us, quite a lot."

"It's me again," said Bob Anderson. "What if she was entertaining and he came home and caught them in the act? Would that account for the mess – a fight as opposed to a burglary?"

"Or maybe she wasn't entertaining," said Rawson. "Maybe he came home and they had a massive row about something – judging by how she was dressed, maybe he was feeling horny and she wasn't. He gave her a slap, or two, and then turned the place over to make it look like that."

"They're all good theories and we wouldn't be doing our job properly if we didn't consider them. Once again that's where we have to keep walking and talking. Patrick can determine his movements from the people at the club. We can have another go at the neighbours. I know the initial results yielded nothing but there are more houses in the area. Widen the net, speak to people in other streets, maybe one of them has seen something to shed some light. Robbie Carter claims he came home at one-thirty, but did he?"

The team continued jotting notes.

Gardener glanced at Mike Atherton. "Any news from the CHIS Handlers or the Intel Cell?"

"No, sir. I think it's a bit too early yet but I will have another go this afternoon. Trouble is, it's quite a big area, there are lots of places a burglar could unload his stuff."

"Okay," said Gardener. "Keep at it."

He addressed them as a team again. "So far we have concentrated on the husband as the prime suspect. What if he's telling the truth? Maybe he did come home to find the place turned over and his wife dead. If that's the case, then we need to study the local burglars and here's where Maurice comes in."

Gardener stepped aside, allowing Maurice Cragg to take control.

"Thank you," said Cragg. "I went through the files in the station earlier today of all known burglars. There are five and we have their prints."

Maurice pinned five photos on the board and wrote a name under each one. "The first one here" – he pointed– "Jimmy Pinner, we can discount. He's already doing a five-year stretch for armed robbery with violence."

Maurice moved on to number two, a man with short grey spiky hair, glasses, and three teeth missing from his lopsided smile. "Alan Bond, lives in Pickering. Low-life scum, would sell his parents if they were still alive. He's mixed up in drugs, prostitution... you name it. He'd steal anything that's not glued down to pay for his addiction. But I'm not sure about the violence. He has no record for that – but there's always a first time.

"Number three, Derek Rutter. He's very distinguishable because he's only got one eye. Blew it out with a shotgun one night when he was cleaning it. Nearly took the side of his head off, which is why he's only got one eye and a head like a Brazil nut."

Gardener's team was in uproar.

"He lives out near Thirsk and he's definitely a possibility. He has used violence before but he tends to go more for establishments – post offices and the like."

Maurice Cragg moved on to number four. "Manny Walters. He's made a career out of this lark. He's not the sharpest tool in the box but he's got his hands into everything – if there's a con on the go somewhere in town, you know Manny's got a piece of the action: everything from hooky Sky TV cards so you can view movies for free, right through to fake Viagra tablets."

"Fake Viagra tablets?" said Rawson. "What's that all about?"

Maurice Cragg was on the verge of laughter. "You'll love it. We picked him up for a straight theft. Student officer didn't search him properly and he dragged a packet of twenty tablets out of his arse and swallowed the lot."

Shouts of disgust followed by peals of laughter.

"Fucking hell," said Rawson. "He must have had a boner for weeks."

"Oh, no," said Cragg. "They weren't Viagra, they were sedatives. Nearly killed himself. If brains were a disease, Manny Walters would be in the best of health."

Not one single officer had kept a straight face, including Gardener and Reilly.

When it had calmed sufficiently, Cragg continued. "But he's not violent. He lives right here in Bramfield and he's definitely worth talking to.

"And number five, Chrissie Ward." Maurice pointed to the only woman in the line-up. "She is a very nasty piece of work; a bit like Jimmy Pinner. She'll stab you as look at you. She lives out near Leeds. Rawston, if any of you know it."

"Do we," said Gardener.

"Anyway, we've got prints and details of the lot so we should have no trouble following them up."

As Cragg had finished, Gardener thanked him and took centre stage again. "I think we've just about covered everything. Does anyone have any questions?"

Steve Fenton, the CSI manager raised his hand.

"Not a question, sir, but something you might want to think about seeing as you are considering burglars."

"Go on," said Gardener.

"There were absolutely no signs of forced entry."

Chapter Fifteen

Shortly after nine o'clock on Monday morning, Gardener and Reilly entered Robbie Carter's cell to a tirade of abuse. He jumped to his feet before he started shouting. "You two have abused my rights and my privileges. It's high time I had a lawyer and I'm damn well gonna use that phone call to make sure I get one. I'll tie you two up so fucking tight you'll think you're in an iron straightjacket."

Gardener turned to Reilly. "Maybe we should go."

"I think you're right. Sounds like he needs to calm down."

"Are you listening to me?" hollered Robbie Carter. "I've just told you you're out of order."

"Don't have much choice *but* to listen," replied Reilly, "level of noise you're making."

"Too right I'm making a noise. What you've done is illegal."

Gardener sympathised with Robbie. They had held him a little longer than necessary but he'd been waiting to hear from the website where Robbie's alarm streamed to, to confirm the timing of everything; ensure that it was live and not somehow pre-programmed. They did confirm Robbie's story of a motion sensor being tripped whilst he was in the police station reporting to Maurice Cragg, and that the alarm had also been activated around one-forty-five from his mobile.

To add to that, Gardener's time to detain him had expired at around four in the morning. He didn't think Robbie would appreciate being woken at that time.

Gardener lifted the file he was carrying. "If you'd like to close your mouth for one minute, Mr Carter, you might hear something to your advantage."

"That'll be a first."

"Follow me, please."

Gardener gave him no time to complain as he left the room immediately. Robbie Carter went after him with Reilly following behind.

"Where are we going?"

Gardener didn't reply but led Robbie Carter to the front desk. There was little or no activity and the only person in the room was once again the cleaner.

Maurice Cragg appeared with another file of paperwork, passing it to Gardener, who made a point of showing it to Robbie.

"What's this?" he asked.

Gardener opened the file. "In here is an inventory of everything we found in your house."

He separated the papers into three piles. "Over here we have a list of everything we have taken. In the middle is everything that we left in your house. The last set is your conditional release paper."

Robbie Carter smirked, something that irritated the life out of Gardener, resulting in him biting his tongue.

"Knew you couldn't keep me."

"Please read through them and sign."

"You know, for someone whose wife has died very recently, I have not seen one ounce of remorse from you," said Reilly.

"Remorse," repeated Robbie Carter. "You think I aren't gutted about all of this? I find my wife dead, my house burgled, and I'm kept at the police station for two days and questioned because you lot think I did it. Of course I'm gutted, but I'm not prepared to let you lot see what you've done to me. And if you think this is over then you can think again."

"We're shaking in out boots, so we are," said Reilly.

"Mr Carter, the quicker you read through the paperwork and sign, the quicker you will be out of here but I must warn you there are conditions."

"What conditions?"

"I want your passport..."

"What the hell for? You think I'll have time to leave the country with everything I have to sort out?"

"Let's hope not, because I'd like you to come down to the police station every day and sign your name for us."

"I know how to sign my name, don't need to come here to do it."

"You do if you don't want to come back for a much longer stay, especially if we have to come and find you."

"Are you joking?"

The pair remained silent.

"Here you go again," shouted Robbie Carter, throwing his pen down on the desk. "You're treating me like *I'm* the criminal. You're fucking priceless, you lot."

"There will also be an evening curfew. A house arrest if you like."

"Brilliant. And how am I supposed to do my job?"

"We'll be speaking to your agent, Mr Carter."

"I have bookings for Christ's sake, clubs relying on me. You can't cancel gigs at this late date."

"Are you the only artist on his books, then?" asked Reilly.

Robbie Carter sighed loudly. "What do you think?"

"Then I'm sure he can rearrange your bookings."

"I might never get any again when you lot have finished." Robbie Carter clenched and unclenched his fists, as if ready to strike. "I do have rights, you know."

"So you keep telling us, sunshine," said Reilly. "Your wife had some as well. Remember her, do you? She's the lady who died. I reckon she'd prefer a few rules imposed on her and sleep the night in her own bed... instead of the mortuary."

"Mr Carter," said Gardener. "Maybe you should try looking at this a different way."

"What's that then, the fact that I'm lucky to be alive?"

"You said it," replied Reilly.

"We're only trying to do our job," said Gardener. "We want your wife's killer behind bars as quickly as possible.

Now, while you think we are persecuting you, you might want to try thinking that what we're actually doing is protecting you. Has it crossed your mind that your wife may have been first? The killer might not have finished with you by a long stretch. You might be next. You may have been lucky when you came home in so far as you either disturbed the killer and he fled, leaving you for another time, or he may have left of his own accord when he couldn't find you. By putting all these things in place, we can keep an eye on you."

"You lot must think I was born yesterday. This has got nothing to do with protection. You still think I'm guilty." Robbie Carter only stopped talking because he was pointing at one of the lists. "What's this?"

"What?" Gardener asked.

"You said this is a list of everything that's in the house. Where's my guitar?"

"Not in the house, obviously," said Reilly.

"It was before you lot invaded the place."

"You're certain of that?" said Gardener. "Where exactly was it?"

"With the rest of the gear, at the front door. And apart from the guitar there was my wages for the night inside a little compartment in the case. Two hundred quid!"

"I can promise you, Mr Carter, that we have not taken your guitar or your money. We have inventories of everything in the house. If the guitar is not on the list, then it isn't in the house."

"That guitar is an heirloom. I've had it over thirty years, from new. It's been everywhere with me."

Gardener frowned. If what Robbie Carter had claimed was true then there really had been a burglary. Either that, or he was one hell of an actor. "Have you checked the list for the rest of the gear? Is there anything else missing?"

Robbie Carter went through it. "It looks to be all there apart from the guitar. But I can't say for certain; I'll need to see the place."

"One of my officers will escort you home. You can go through the list with him. Once you know what's missing, come back here and let's have it on file."

"I don't need anyone to run me home. I've got the van outside."

"You can collect your van when the officer brings you back to the station."

"Why can't I have my van?"

"We've just told you," replied Reilly.

"This is all bullshit. Persecution is what this is. I'll be speaking to *my* lawyer and *your* superior about this." Robbie Carter turned as if to leave but then faced both detectives. "I want that guitar found. Maybe now you'll both believe me."

Once Gardener had seen Robbie Carter and PC Benson off the premises he returned to the lobby.

"Why are we keeping his van?" asked Maurice Cragg.

"So we can put a tracking device on it, Maurice. I genuinely want to keep an eye on him."

Chapter Sixteen

Gardener and Reilly parked outside a barn at Matthew Atkinson's stables, and both jumped out. The air wasn't quite as fresh as Gardener had anticipated, though he suspected the smell would be much worse in the middle of summer. It was overcast with a fierce, biting wind cutting into everything it touched.

Glancing around, Gardener figured business must be good. There were four large stables. Staring into the nearest he saw three horses tied to a round pole supporting the roof, eating hay from baskets.

Outside, a young blonde-haired woman was giving a lesson in a paddock. Agricultural vehicles littered the yard – everything from combines to quad bikes. In the distance, Gardener admired the large three-storey farmhouse. A plume of smoke from the chimney created an inviting scene.

He stopped one of the riders and asked where he could find Matthew Atkinson.

The young lady pointed to another stable. "Just over there. He'll be in the tack room."

Gardener thanked her and both detectives set off.

The tack room felt homely and inviting. Along the back wall was a medium sized multi-fuel stove with a basket full of logs. The red glow from the glass said it all. As he studied the room, he noticed hooks on the wall with saddles hanging down; a range of boots lined up on the concrete floor along the perimeter. Hats, jackets and horseshoes shared space with saddles, whips and crops along the walls.

A small TV and tea-making facilities stood on an open wooden dresser off to one side. Tucked into each of the shelves were a number of wicker baskets. On the wall next to the dresser was a telephone. In the middle of the room stood a table and six chairs, where someone sat cleaning a saddle. Gardener saw a couple of dustbins containing what he imagined to be horse feed stationed near the far corner.

The odour was sweet, like candy floss, mixed with the smell of old leather and something else he couldn't distinguish – possibly oil, used for cleaning or maintaining the leather. The most surprising aspect was the peace and tranquillity. Despite what was happening outside in the yard, you could barely hear anything in here. It was dead silent.

"Can I help you?" asked the man at the table.

"Matthew Atkinson?"

"Who wants to know?" Then, laughing, he added, "If it's the police I left half an hour ago."

Gardener appreciated the joke but flashed his warrant card anyway.

Atkinson straightened his face. "Sorry, I was only joking."

"Not to worry."

Gardener took a seat, as did Reilly.

Atkinson was middle-aged, wearing a Barbour jacket and a flat cap. What Gardener could see of his hair it was brown. His eyes and his ruddy complexion bore the wrinkles of years outside in the sun, though his teeth were white. He had a slim build and Gardener figured that he probably worked all day long with the horses, which had allowed him to keep it that way.

Atkinson stopped cleaning the saddle. "What can I do for you?"

"We'd like to talk to you about Jane Carter."

"She's okay, isn't she? Only, I haven't seen her today – since Friday for that matter. I was expecting to see her before now because she has a lesson at four o'clock."

"I'm sorry to have to tell you this, Mr Atkinson, but Jane won't be in again. I'm afraid she died sometime over the weekend."

Atkinson removed his cap and stared at Gardener and Reilly as if he wanted them to retract that last statement. He put the saddle and the cap on the table and placed his hands on his legs, rubbing his thighs slowly, staring at the saddle.

"Are you serious?" he asked. "You must be, mustn't you? I mean you wouldn't come all the way here to tell me that if it weren't true."

"I'm so sorry. From your reaction you must have been close."

"Aye." He replaced his cap and nodded. "Please, call me Matthew. I thought she was a fantastic lass. Do owt for anyone and ask nowt in return. I really thought a lot about her, especially the kind of life she'd had."

Atkinson glanced around the room, as if he was lost. "Look, do you mind if I make a cup of tea? I'm gagging for one. Not had a drink all morning. I'm sure you could do with one."

Both detectives nodded, allowing him his moment of respect, a chance to reflect. No one spoke until he'd made the tea and returned to the table.

"Thank you," said Atkinson. "I still can't believe it. Jane, dead? How did it happen?"

"We're not entirely sure, Matthew," said Gardener, taking a sip of the tea. "We were called out to the house at two-thirty on Saturday morning. Her husband had reported it at two o'clock."

"Robbie?"

"Yes. It's all a bit of a mystery. He came home around one-thirty, to find his house had been burgled, and his wife, Jane in an upstairs room."

"She was dead when he found her? And you don't know what happened?"

"Not yet. But we would like to ask you some questions about her. If you can give us some general information and perhaps tell us what Friday was like, the last day you saw her, I assume."

"I'll do my best," Atkinson replied.

"You mentioned something about the kind of life she'd had," said Reilly. "Are you aware of any problems?"

"Aye, mostly personal. She'd not been too lucky where men were concerned. Though I don't know why, some men never know when they're well off."

"How long had she worked here?"

"About ten years, though work's a strong word for it." He took a sip of tea and then put his hand up. "I'm sorry, I didn't mean it like that. She were a damn good worker but she didn't need to work."

"Why's that?" Reilly asked.

"She was born and bred in Staithes but she moved out to Dallas when she were about seventeen, working for a racing stable. They taught her everything. She were one of the most experienced riders I'd ever seen. A terrible accident finished that career."

"What happened?" asked Gardener.

Atkinson rose from the table and tottered over to the multi-fuel stove. When he opened the door the difference in temperature was immediate. He threw a few logs on, closed the door and returned to the table.

"I don't know everything. It all happened years ago, the Kentucky Derby I think. She got caught up in a terrible explosion: ended up with a broken arm, three broken ribs, one of which pushed upwards and restricted the flow of blood to and from her heart, damaging a valve in the process. The biggest blow was a damaged liver. She never went into details about that."

"That might explain the tablets," said Gardener to Reilly.

"Oh, you found them, did you?"

"Yes, but we couldn't work out what they were for."

"She had good and bad days and I only found out because it was a bad one. She never talked much about it. I'm not sure what they were for but I didn't get the impression they were painkillers."

Gardener found it interesting that Matthew Atkinson knew more about Jane Carter's health than her husband, Robbie. He also realised that Fitz would need to clarify what Atkinson had told him.

"Anyway, about five years after that, her husband died. That's when she came back home to England. I needed someone to help out and a woman called Carrie Fletcher stabled her horse here and she introduced us.

"Jane had been with me a couple of years when she met her second husband, Peter Strange. He ran the local Land Rover dealership and I wanted one. After spending the afternoon together, I bought the car, and Peter asked Jane out. They started dating and married shortly after."

"That obviously didn't work out, either," said Reilly.

Atkinson shook his head. "No, she reckoned there was no love in the relationship and all Peter had wanted was a housekeeper and cook. She never told *me*, mind, she told Carrie all of this. Peter wasn't bad to her. She had a new vehicle and all the housekeeping money she wanted but it weren't enough. All he ever thought about were his cars. He rarely took her out unless it were a business meeting. He'd quite happily ply both himself and the customer with drink in the hope of netting a contract and then ask Jane to drive them all home. He even tried to stop her working here. She refused, the marriage fell apart. There were no children."

Reilly was busy making notes but stopped to ask, "Does Carrie Fletcher still stable her horse here?"

"Oh, aye, but she lives in Thirsk." Atkinson gave them her address.

"You reckon she didn't need to work," Reilly said. "What did you mean by that?"

"She had a nice little nest egg in compensation from the accident, and her first husband left her well provided for when he died."

Gardener's curiosity was piqued. He wondered whether or not Robbie Carter knew anything about her financial status – he certainly didn't appear to know much about her health.

Atkinson continued, "I don't want to speak ill of her but she was a bit too old for the heavy tasks like mucking out. She'd spent her life around horses, just couldn't keep away. She was always made welcome here. She knows horses inside out. Can spot a mile away when they're off colour. She could diagnose problems as well as any vet and she knew all the treatment required..."

Atkinson had stopped talking, his eyes welling up. Gardener felt for him.

"Are you okay, Matthew?"

"Christ, I'm going to miss her." He shook his head. "Don't worry about me. Whoever did this to her wants catching, and I want to see him caught as much as you."

He sipped more tea. "She'd even do all this stuff." He pointed to the equipment on the walls. "Clean all the tack. She could turn her hand to anything and she did it because she loved being here."

"Did you see much of her on Friday?"

"Only in the morning, we had a cuppa together."

"How did she seem – anything bothering her?"

"Just the opposite, I'd say. She seemed full of life. Had a couple of lessons booked, were looking forward to them. I had to go to a meeting, down in Northampton. I took the wife, made a bit of a day of it and we stayed over."

That had answered an awkward question for Gardener. Not that he had suspected Matthew Atkinson but there would have come a point when he'd need to ask. "Where did you stay?"

"Only a Travelodge, Junction 16 off the M1 as you're going in. You'll no doubt want to check, and don't worry, you're only doing your job. I watch all the murder mysteries on the telly."

"I shouldn't believe much of what you see on there," said Reilly.

"Is it possible you can get me a list of all her clients' names and addresses?" asked Gardener.

"Of course," said Atkinson, rising from his chair. "Though I doubt any of them will know owt."

"You'd be surprised," said Reilly.

"They probably won't, Matthew, but one of them might know something you don't."

"Aye, I'm with you."

Atkinson walked over to the phone, lifted the receiver and jabbed three buttons. "Lizzie, love, it's me. Can you get me a list of all Jane's clients, names and addresses?"

Atkinson listened to his wife before saying: "I'll tell you when you bring 'em over. We're in the tack room."

When Atkinson returned to the table, Gardener asked if Jane Carter had her own horse.

"No, there were plenty to choose from here. Most of the people who stable the horses can't make it every day so apart from cleaning out their stables, the staff here exercise 'em as well."

"Did she have any particular favourite?"

"No," replied Atkinson. "She loved them all. Could ride them all equally, even the difficult ones."

"Was there many of those?" asked Reilly.

"One or two, but Jane knew how to handle them."

"Can you tell us about the accident she had a couple of weeks back?" Reilly asked.

"Accident?" questioned Atkinson.

"Yes. Apparently she was out with a group of friends," said Gardener. "A hack, or something?"

"Aye, a hack, just a gentle stroll. No racing involved, it's all nice and easy. Accident, you say?"

"Yes. They were near the edge of a field and a car backfired at the other side of the hedge. Upset the horses and they took off, only Jane Carter fell off."

"Who told you this?"

"Her husband, Robbie," said Reilly.

"Well no one's told me."

"Do they usually?"

"Oh, aye, it'd be a real talking point when they got back to the yard. Especially if it were serious. If owt like that happens I always make them go to the hospital, get checked out. You can't be too careful."

"Maybe it wasn't anything serious," said Reilly. "They just forgot to tell you."

"No," said Atkinson, shaking his head. He stood up and reached into one of the dresser drawers, removing a large red book, before sitting back down.

"Accident book, Mr Gardener. For insurance purposes, everything gets recorded in here." He leafed his way through it. "Last accident was two months ago."

"So you know nothing about any accident Jane Carter was supposed to have had?" pressed Gardener.

"No. Like I said, a very accomplished rider. I'm not saying she couldn't have had an accident but when a horse gets spooked you have to know how to handle them and she certainly did. I'd back her against any jockey I've ever come across."

Reilly made a note.

Gardener was unhappy. There were holes appearing in Robbie's story.

A woman entered the tack room. She had long black hair, blue eyes and a rugged complexion like Atkinson. She was dressed in jeans, riding boots and a Barbour jacket.

"What's all the rush, Matthew?"

"Lizzie, love," he said, standing up. "These gentlemen are the police."

"Has something happened?"

"It's Jane. She's died, love."

Lizzie Atkinson put her hands to her mouth. "Oh, dear God, no. How did it happen?"

"I'll tell you later."

"Did you see her on Friday, Mrs Atkinson?" asked Gardener.

"Only through the car windscreen." She glanced at her husband and then at Gardener. "We were going away and as we drove out of the yard I waved. The poor love." Lizzie Atkinson sat down. "Ooh, I've gone all cold."

"Before you go, you might want to speak to some of the people in the yard," said Atkinson. "Most of the staff were here on Friday and they'll have been with her all day. I'm sure they can tell you more than we can."

"Thank you, Matthew, we'll do that. You can't think of any recent disagreements with anyone? Clients, staff?"

"Jane?" said Lizzie. "I don't think I've ever heard her argue with anyone, or have a bad name for anyone."

"Or them for her, for that matter," added Atkinson.

"How well do you know her husband, Robbie?" asked Reilly.

"We don't," replied Atkinson. "He came to the yard a couple of times to pick her up but he never spoke to anyone. I got the impression he didn't like the place."

"Not everyone does," said Lizzie. "It's a bit raw. There's no in between. You like, or you don't."

"Aye, horses are not a job. They're a dedication."

"Take a lot of looking after," added Lizzie. "But you were asking about her husband. The impression I got is they were a bit like chalk and cheese, but then they do say opposites attract."

"What gave you that impression?" Reilly asked.

"Most of the staff here said so. They were all her friends. They had nights out together. Women talk, just like men."

"Any examples?" Reilly asked.

"Nothing I can think of."

"Maybe we shouldn't speculate, Lizzie, love," said Atkinson. "After all, we didn't know him, and we're only going on what other people said."

Lizzie nodded. "I know, and I'm not going to tittle-tattle. You should speak to the staff, they'll know more than us."

Gardener figured the meeting was at an end. He didn't think the Atkinsons could tell him much more so he collected the names and addresses of Jane's clients from Lizzie.

On his way out, Gardener turned. "I believe she rented one of your houses in Sowerby for some time."

"Aye, she did," said Atkinson. "Big rambling old farmhouse. It's not actually in Sowerby. If you leave this place and take the A168 it's a couple of miles before you get into the town itself. Can't miss it... big white farmhouse... part of a windmill. It was my grandmother's. She left it to us."

"Sounds like a big house for one person," said Reilly.

"She pretty much had it for nowt, part of the job. Never thought anybody would rent out a house that big but we couldn't just let it go to rack and ruin."

"That house'll not go to rack and ruin," said Lizzie. "Too well built."

They were about to leave when Atkinson piped up again. "Mind you, had no trouble re-letting it when Jane had left, did we, Lizzie, love?"

"Managed to find a family, did you?" Reilly asked.

"No. Funny thing that – another one on his own. Ronald Critchley. Rang us pretty much after Jane moved out."

"Yes," said Lizzie. "Only two or three days later."

"He said he were up here on business, looking to move into the area from down south."

"He gave us references," added Lizzie.

"Everything checked out."

"Good tenant?" asked Gardener.

"Very good," said Lizzie. "Pays on time every month, never misses. Keeps the place clean and tidy by all accounts."

"When he's there," said Atkinson. "Which isn't often."

"Probably why we've never met him," said Lizzie.

"You never met him?" asked Reilly.

"No," said Atkinson. "Not once. On the odd occasions I've been over to do a couple of small jobs there's never been owt out of place."

Gardener tipped his hat. "Well, thank you for your time. If we need anything else, we'll be back."

Out in the yard, people were still busy despite the cold. Gardener watched the women standing outside one of the stables busy talking to each other and their horses, feeding them all manner of fruits and vegetables.

"What do you think, Sean?"

"I'm not happy about the phantom accident."

"Do you think Robbie was making it up?"

"Not sure," replied Reilly. "Maybe she told him she had an accident to cover something else up."

"In which case he'd be telling the truth, as far as he knew. But why lie to him?" Gardener asked. "She didn't sound the type if you listen to what the Atkinsons say."

"They weren't married to her."

"Fair point. I'm concerned about her finances. We need to jump on to that one as quickly as we can."

"I wonder how much Robbie knows about them."

"How much she was really worth?"

"Money's always a big motive."

"Okay, Sean," said Gardener. "Something to concentrate on in the incident room. Meanwhile, let's have a talk with some of the staff."

Chapter Seventeen

Ronald Critchley made himself a coffee before going back to the living room table. He sat down and opened his laptop. He needed to catch up on what had been happening in the outside world.

While the machine booted up, he glanced around. The place was old, big, a pig to heat, but he wasn't there very often. At least it was clean and tidy.

Once the machine was up and running, he let the virus protector and the anti-malware do their stuff before setting to work, logging in to the dating site. It didn't take him very long to catch up on the activity regarding his profile. He'd had fifteen views over the weekend, resulting in four winks, three of them adding him to their favourites. And one email he couldn't wait to open.

"Oh yes," said Critchley, rubbing his hands together. "You little beauty."

He'd been after her for a while, and she'd finally taken the bait. Better than that, she'd actually sent him an email to see if he was interested in meeting up with her.

Was he?

Critchley thought she was stunning. She had uploaded more than one photo, so he checked them all out again. That had always made him laugh. There were women on here that actually expected to attract a man by leaving only one photo – some of them never even left that. How the hell did they think they were going to meet someone? Why would you join a dating website to go on a blind date?

But J was something else. No name, only an initial. He liked that. Added mystery to the game. She had the lot. Black shoulder-length hair, stylishly cut, beautiful blue eyes, wide mouth, white teeth. She had a figure to die for, dressed in the tightest black jeans he had ever seen, with a pale green low-cut top. Not too much make-up. Quite young. She was exactly the kind of girl that he went for.

Her profile said she was a professional in the fashion and beauty industry, earning north of fifty grand a year. He could certainly tell. She liked going out for meals in intimate surroundings; loved music and cinema. She exercised regularly. She had no animals or children. Smoking was a no-no. The tag line said she was "searching for that special man to spend the rest of her life with". Could she be any better?

Every single photo was perfection. What he wouldn't give for a taste of her. He'd played it cool from the beginning, nothing more than glancing at her photos twice a week, to start with. She had eventually taken notice of him, winked at him. He'd returned the gesture. She had logged in again, clicked the *I'm interested* tag.

Now he had an email. It would be rude not to reply. Critchley sniggered and cracked his knuckles.

"Well, well, well, J, welcome to the pleasure dome."

Chapter Eighteen

Grace opened her front door and entered the small hallway. Removing her coat and shoes she placed them in the small cupboard on her right. Her next destination was the living room. Switching on a couple of small wall lights she padded through and entered the kitchen. The first thing she did was reach into a cupboard for an antiseptic wipe and clean the worktop before washing her hands thoroughly. She then prepared and switched on the coffee machine.

Back in the living area she threw a copy of *The Bramfield Echo* on the table. She'd had a pig of a day – business should have been slowing down for the time of the year, but you never had two days alike. Yesterday was quiet; today, the complete opposite.

After pouring her coffee she picked up the newspaper. Her vision closed in as she read the headline, as if she was reading it through the long sight of a telescope. She felt weak, and tried to control her breathing as she pulled out a chair and sat down.

Grace placed the paper on the table and finished her coffee. She needed to stay focused.

* * *

Aged seventeen, Grace Browne was working in a beauty salon when her mother met and married a man called Raymond Culver. The couple met through an internet dating site. The pair of them appeared to hit it off through a variety of emails before finally meeting. Grace's mother – Jane – had short black hair and blue eyes. She loved music, life, and being a free spirit.

They were contented at first and took great pleasure in telling everyone how much they loved each other. She was happy, pretty – confident. Her outgoing personality remained, enjoying a good circle of friends.

The change was gradual. After a couple of years Grace noticed her mother's appearance had altered radically. She began to suspect her mother was being subjected to beatings. Black eyes and other injuries were blamed on domestic accidents such as falling from ladders, or walking into doors. One time her mother had front teeth missing but blamed it on a dental problem.

Grace's world, however, completely fell apart when her mother told her that she and Raymond were going away for the weekend, hiking on the moors.

It was a trip from which she never returned.

Grace finished her coffee, shuddered at the thought of what had happened next.

She had pieced together that on the day they were due to return home, her mother woke up well before Raymond. She left a note saying she was going for a walk.

The official story was that she never came back.

Grace couldn't accept all that Raymond told her about the weekend and called the police immediately. They exhaustively interviewed him for three days solid and could find nothing on which to hold him. He told them where they pitched their tent, listed the places they visited, the pubs they frequented – everything that could be corroborated.

They searched for three more days but neither the woman nor a body matching her description was found. They also confirmed that the husband, Raymond, was beside himself and they did not consider him guilty. The local police in Billingham were informed about the incident but for all their investigations, they couldn't reach a satisfactory conclusion. Grace was not happy. She knew her mother: she suspected foul play.

She travelled up to see Raymond. He acted withdrawn, saying her mother had left him and he couldn't go on.

She harangued the police constantly but they said there was nothing they could do and, at one point, Raymond even blamed her for making up stories.

Within a week of returning home, however, Raymond disappeared. Grace never heard from him again.

* * *

She put the empty coffee cup down on the kitchen counter and headed for her bedroom, having forgotten all about food.

In the bedroom she removed the bath towel, slipped into her dressing gown and opened the walk-in wardrobe that hid her state-of-the-art security system.

She reached down to the titanium trunk on the floor and eased it forward. She smiled as she checked her arsenal. It had everything. Some would consider it overkill. Grace figured you could never be too careful, especially when dealing with the man she was after.

In the next wardrobe her computer pinged. She opened the doors and switched on the monitor, leafing through her emails, one of which had come from *Findadate.com*.

She logged on. Sure enough, he had taken the bait.

Grace had him exactly where she wanted him. The time had come for him to pay for everything he'd done.

She rubbed her hands together and smiled. Time to set another trap. She typed out the message and hit "Send".

"Welcome to the arena, Mr Critchley, or whatever your real name is."

Chapter Nineteen

At a little after eight in the evening, Maurice Cragg had organised everything for the final incident room meeting of the day. Two trays full of hot and cold drinks were waiting on a desk; he'd also spoken to the local bakery and asked if a tray of snacks could be sent over. He knew a bunch of tired, overworked coppers who would put them to good use – one in particular.

As they filed in, their expressions of fatigue immediately altered at the sight of the spread. Gardener had spent a few minutes gathering the information he and Reilly had found out at the stables. He updated the whiteboards whilst everyone helped themselves to the refreshments.

The SIO finally turned and addressed them. "Thanks for coming in guys. I know we're less than twenty-four hours in and you've only had eight hours in the field but hopefully we've picked up something useful."

"I have now," said Reilly, his hands around a steak slice.

"Bet you didn't see this, Irishman," said Dave Rawson, parting his jaws for a jam and cream filled Devonshire split.

"I did, but it's bad for me."

There was instant uproar around the room. "Since when did that stop you?" shouted Bob Anderson.

"When you're getting older you need to look after yourself better."

"You mean Laura thinks you should," said Gardener.

Reilly shot him a glance. "You're my commanding officer, so you are."

"Meaning what?"

"You should be backing me up, guiding me, looking after me."

"Fucking hell," shouted Rawson, giggling. "A pet Stegosaurus would be easier to look after."

"And train," added Gardener.

"Don't think there's much difference, myself," said Anderson.

Reilly put his steak slice down. "You can go off people, you know."

"What makes you think we haven't?"

"Okay," said Gardener. "Now we've amused ourselves at Sean's expense, let's see if we've found out anything useful."

He tapped the whiteboard and pointed to the heading, *Neighbours*.

"Anyone have any news?"

Sarah Gates spoke up. "Me and Bob have covered these. As you know, there's only four houses in Swansea Court so there were only three neighbours to talk to. None of those were up so late that night so they couldn't offer anything."

"They didn't hear anything?"

Gates shook her head. "No."

"Have any of them noticed anything different about the comings and goings at the house? Any guests they don't recognise?"

"Not really. The Carters pretty much kept to themselves," said Gates. "Of the two, they felt they knew her better than him, despite the fact that it was his house originally."

"Why was that?" Reilly asked.

"She was more willing to talk. If they saw her out in the garden, she was more approachable than him. She would stop and speak."

"All they got out of him was a nod and the odd word. They didn't find him unsociable, just quieter," added Anderson.

"Interesting," replied Gardener. "According to him she was a typical Aquarian: only spoke when she had to and didn't bother wasting words on people. No sense of humour."

"Maybe he was mixed up, talking about himself," said Rawson.

"Not sure about that," said Reilly. "He had plenty to say to us."

"What's your next step?" asked Gardener.

"We've started planning," said Gates. "Basically, there are houses all around them, lots of fields in between so you wouldn't exactly class them as neighbours but we made a map and figured out a plan of attack."

"We've spoken to some," said Anderson. "A few of them worked nights so we'll have to call back, but so far, nothing. No one was out and about at that time."

"So, what he's telling us can't be proved or disproved," said Cragg.

Gardener made a note before turning to the youngest officer. "Patrick, what do we have from Seacroft?"

"According to the manager of the club, Robbie did the gig, had a good night. Apparently, he's been there a couple of times before and they like him."

"At least someone does," said Reilly.

"Anyway, he finished the gig and he had a half a lager like he said, but he left the club at twelve-fifteen. By my reckoning, at that time of night the drive home only takes about half an hour, so he would have been home by twelve-forty-five at the latest."

"Not one-thirty like he claimed," said Reilly.

"Did you get the names and addresses of everyone in there that night?" Gardener asked.

"Yes, got them all. Took me nearly all day."

"Well done. Spoken to any of them?"

"The ones I've seen haven't confirmed anything. They all went straight home or round to the nearest chip shop."

"So, what was he doing?" Reilly asked.

"Maybe he hung around in the club car park for a while; he might have spoken to someone," offered Gates.

"Maybe he went to the nearby chip shop."

"Did you get the name of it, Patrick?" asked Gardener. "We'll need to speak to them."

"I'll check them out, sir. I think there's two."

"Did he go somewhere else before going home?" Rawson asked.

"It's possible. If you listen to him talking there was no shortage of women after him," said Reilly. "Maybe he got lucky and serviced one of them first."

"Didn't leave him much time," offered Sharp.

"Which brings us back to square one," said Gardener. "How much of what *he's* telling us is true? Maybe he did leave at twelve-fifteen, spoke to no one, arrived home thirty minutes later. We've already considered that he and his wife argued. So, did it get much worse than that – to the point of violence? All of which might take us to one-thirty but we're still short of witnesses. We need a neighbour to confirm something. Sarah and Bob, you stick with that, please. Patrick, you continue interrogating the people in the club that night. We need to get beyond the conjecture."

Chapter Twenty

Gardener spent time updating the whiteboards before asking if anyone had checked the computer taken from the house.

Emma Longstaff attracted Gardener's attention and he nodded to her to take the floor.

"Had a good poke around this, sir, and it's all her."

"What do you mean?"

"Everything on there has been put there by her. She has files for her clients at the stable, so I made copies of those for tonight – thought we could put them to good use."

"Well done, Emma."

"Thank you. There were a lot of photographs on the PC, mostly of horses and the stables and her work. There were quite a few photos that I suspected were of her and friends on nights out."

"Any of her and Robbie together?" Reilly asked.

"Only a couple, and I'd say they weren't recent."

"Another contradiction to the quality of their relationship," said Gardener. "Sean and I heard a similar story at the stables today. Emma, is there *anything* on the computer connecting him to the house?"

"The only thing I noticed was a gig guide: a list of all his bookings, where he was on which date, how much he was paid, what commission he paid out – not to mention tax, and what he was left with."

"So it was a ledger," said Gardener. "Could have been done by him."

"I'm not sure," said Longstaff. "I could only find one password. Surely there'd be two if two people used the machine?"

"They could have used the same one, instead of switching users," said Sharp.

"Not likely, though, is it," said Cragg. "It's not the impression I get of Robbie Carter. I reckon secrecy is his middle name."

"Maybe he had his own machine," offered Gardener. "Most people these days have more than one." He made a note on the whiteboard. "If he has, I want it."

"What about her social media status?" Patrick Edwards asked.

"She had accounts on them all," replied Emma. "Facebook, Twitter, Instagram. It's going to take me ages to trawl through that lot."

"Just keep going, Emma," said Gardener, "but get help. Ask the HOLMES lads, they're pretty good with that sort of thing."

Gardener was about to move on when Patrick Edwards drew his attention. He nodded.

Edwards turned to Longstaff. "Did you notice if she was friends with Robbie or any of them?"

She raised her finger to gesture a good point had been made. "I never checked."

Gardener sorted through the printed documents on the table in front of him, locating the one that covered the alarm. It didn't really tell him anything new, apart from the fact that it was set at one-forty-five and the first detection of movement was after two o'clock.

He mentioned it to the team. "If the burglar had been hiding somewhere, would he have waited for half an hour after Robbie had left the house before making an appearance?"

"No," said Sharp.

"You'd want out first chance you got," said Reilly.

"Unless he hadn't turned the place over properly," offered Rawson. "Maybe he hadn't been at it long when Robbie came home. He hid while the coast was clear and then carried on."

"Too risky," said Gates. "Most burglars would bolt at the first sign of trouble, especially if he'd witnessed anything untoward happening between the Carters."

"So where did he hide?" asked Gardener. "We've seen the house, it's not that big."

"Okay," said Anderson. "Let's assume it was exactly as the boss had said: Robbie gets home early, they argue about something, it turns violent and the burglar witnesses everything from his hidey hole."

"Which would be another good reason to find him," said Gardener.

"But if he was downstairs, he won't have witnessed anything," said Rawson. "Especially as we think the violence was upstairs."

"Maybe the place wasn't burgled, then," offered Gates. "Maybe the argument between him and his wife got heated, turned to violence, he came down and trashed the place and then disappeared."

"All good points," said Cragg. "But it doesn't allow for the fact that someone was hiding downstairs. Robbie Carter would surely have found him."

"You'd have thought so," said Anderson. "Because we know that someone was moving around in the house while Robbie was in here talking to you."

Gardener keyed in on that. "What about the footage on his phone – anyone checked that?"

One of the HOLMES team said he'd run it through the computers but it was too dark to see anything. The more they tried to enhance it, the worse it became.

"*Could* it have been his wife?" asked Reilly.

"Maybe," said Paul Benson. "But I took him home and his guitar was missing, along with the money he'd earned that night – amongst other things. She couldn't have done that."

"No, but *he* could have done all of that before he came here," said Rawson.

"I'll go along with that, Paul," said Gardener. "I think it's ironic that someone was in the house after he'd set the alarm and claimed it was burgled. That leaves us with one big question: *was* he in the place before Robbie came home? Until we find that person we won't know. Which reminds me, what did the phone history show?"

Benson answered again. "I checked most of the landline calls. I managed to identify the stables a number of times. If I can cross reference the list that Emma has, I can probably identify most of her clients and friends. Same with the wife's mobile, a lot of the numbers appear on both."

Gardener nodded.

"What about his?" Reilly asked.

"Still checking," said Benson. "Her number is on it quite a lot, and the landline. He also called his agent on a regular basis."

"Did he call his wife on the night in question?" asked Gardener.

"No. He didn't call anybody that night."

Gardener asked Mike Atherton about the CHIS Handler's and the Intel Cell, both of which had proved negative. As yet, no one had tried to fence any of the missing stuff locally.

Gardener shook his head. Nothing was making sense. He glanced at the clock. It was approaching eight-forty-five, so he told the team what he and Reilly had discovered at the stables, and what Matthew Atkinson and his wife had said about her. The stint in America, the time she'd worked for them, how excellent she was with horses, finishing with the Atkinsons' reaction to the accident that Robbie had claimed she'd had.

"The Atkinsons knew nothing about the accident?" asked Benson.

"No," replied Gardener. "They have an accident book, but nothing was recorded."

"From what you've said about them they've been in business long enough and don't look the type to have slack practices," said Paul Benson.

He was talking from experience. Gardener knew that his wife had horses and he'd spent a lot of time on the family farm as a youngster.

"I can vouch for that," said Cragg. "I've known the Atkinsons a lot of years. They're good people."

"Did Robbie know who she was with when she had the accident?" asked Sarah Gates.

"He never said. He didn't show any interest in her professional life at all," answered Reilly.

"If you ask me, he didn't show any interest full stop," said Anderson.

"Okay," said Gardener. "We have a few more actions from that lot. All her contacts – friends and clients alike – need to be checked out. Build up more about her and her personal life. According to Lizzie Atkinson, Robbie and his wife were like chalk and cheese, but Matthew wasn't prepared to comment further because he didn't feel he knew them well enough as a couple."

"I want to know about the accident," he continued. "*If* it happened, who knew about it and why wasn't it recorded in the book? If it didn't, Robbie is lying and I want him back in here. I want someone over to Peter Strange, the owner of the Land Rover dealership. I know they're divorced but they may have stayed friends; they may have talked recently."

"I'd like someone at Thirsk to talk to Carrie Fletcher. She introduced Jane Carter to the Atkinsons and they indicated that she was a close enough friend for Jane to have confided in if things were wrong, and the impression I got was that things *had* gone wrong before in the relationship, if not now. I want someone at the house in Sowerby that she used to rent from the Atkinsons. There are neighbours, few and far between but they might know something."

Gardener passed sheets around the room containing the address and the name of the current tenant.

"The fact that she had money and was comfortable means we need to find out who her solicitor is, if she's made a will, and who stands to benefit," Gardener added.

"Do you want *me* on that one, sir?" asked Colin Sharp.

"No," said Gardener. "I have something else for you."

Rawson grabbed Gardener's attention. "Don't suppose the Atkinsons knew anything about those tablets you found, did they?"

"A little," said Gardener, briefing them on what had been said. "So I need someone to find out the name and address of her GP. When you do, Sean and I will pay them a visit. I want the name of her solicitor so we can speak to them as well."

"Has Fitz come back to you?" Cragg asked.

"No," said Gardener, making a note on the chart. He was sure if Fitz had found anything important they would have known by now. Nevertheless, it had to be followed up.

"Maurice?" said Gardener. "While I'm thinking about it, what movement have we had from the tracker on his van?"

"Nothing," replied Cragg. "He came and collected it about four o'clock, signed in then went straight home."

"And he's been there ever since?"

"Yes."

"Is he still there?" Reilly asked.

Cragg nodded. "Hasn't moved."

"So, what was it you wanted me to do?" Sharp asked.

"You can concentrate on the man himself – Robbie Carter. I want everything you can find on him: how long he's been here, where he was before that. Is he telling the truth about the way he earns his living? I want his bank details, his national insurance number, everything. Run him through the computer; does he have form? If he has so much as a parking ticket I want to know when and where."

More notes went on to the whiteboard before Gardener turned. He glanced at Cragg. "Maurice, you gave us a list of names to investigate for the burglary. Has anyone spoken to any of them?"

"We did, sir," said Sharp, pointing to Paul Benson. "Three of them anyway. We started with Alan Bond in Pickering – a real piece of shit."

"Yes." Benson nodded. "He was interrogating a woman when we turned up at his place: looked like he'd been at it for a while."

"How do you mean?" Reilly asked.

"She was black and blue," said Sharp. "Anyway, to cut a long story short, it wasn't him that robbed the Carters. She vouched for his movements."

"We had a good look round the place. Plenty of drugs and shit but nothing matching the description of the stolen goods."

"Didn't really think he'd be involved," said Cragg.

"I don't think Rutter was either."

"What was his alibi?"

"A&E," said Benson. "Seems someone had caught up with him from a previous job."

"He won't be very active for a while," said Sharp. "Two broken arms and a few fractured ribs."

"His face was a mess," Benson added.

"How could you tell?" asked Cragg.

"The colour."

"What about Chrissie Ward?" Cragg asked.

"You were right about her. She spoke to us from the other side of the door and she was holding a knife."

"She wouldn't let you in?"

"No. Said she didn't believe us, despite the badge. Said she hadn't done anything wrong and she wasn't out that night. She wouldn't let us in and we couldn't push it without a warrant."

"You'll have one in the morning," said Gardener. "Get yourselves round there mob-handed at five o'clock and flatten the place if you have to. Turn it upside down and don't leave until you're satisfied that she had nothing to do with it. And if you're not sure, arrest her and bring her in. She can have half an hour with Sean. She'll be singing a different tune when he's finished."

"She'll be lucky if she can sing at all," said Rawson.

"Too right," added Reilly.

Gardener addressed Maurice Cragg. "Who else was on the list?"

"Manny Walters – right here in Bramfield."

"Any luck?" asked Gardener.

"We haven't found him yet, sir," said Benson.

"Find him tomorrow, Paul," said Gardener. "It's vital that we eliminate all of these from our inquiries for one reason or another."

Gardener stared at the boards and the clock on the wall. It was nine-thirty.

"I think that about wraps it up. Don't be too disappointed. We haven't yielded many results but we are further on."

A knock on the door interrupted his final briefing. Steve Fenton came in and closed the door.

Gardener nodded. "Steve."

"Found something important."

"Go on," said Gardener.

"Results are back. There is no DNA evidence to show that the burglar was ever in the bedroom or the bathroom. If he did kill her, it wasn't upstairs."

Gardener wasn't too disappointed. He'd suspected as much. "How many sets of prints did we find in the bedroom?"

"Only two. Hers and Robbie's."

Interesting, thought Gardener. That could rule out any illicit relationships.

Fenton still stood his ground. Gardener knew there had to be more so he nodded.

"There is no trace of any prints of any known burglar in the area in that house."

Chapter Twenty-one

Grace screamed loudly as she threw herself out of bed, hitting the floor with a bump. She was bathed in sweat, panting heavily and shaking like a leaf. She had managed to knock over the lamp and the clock from her dressing table, as well as bringing the pillow from the bed with her.

"Oh, God." She sighed.

Everything had been so real. She could see, hear, and smell her mother. She had been able to talk to her.

She shouldn't be surprised. It had been no different from any other nightmare she had had over the last twenty years.

She always came so very close to saving her mother but then the whole scene ended abruptly and she was snatched away once again.

In a fit of temper, she threw the pillow at the wall. "Please, God, why?" She stared at the ceiling, as if that's where God lived. "Why have you done this to me?"

There was no answer. There never was. "Why am I supposed to believe in you when you've hurt me so much?"

Following a few calming seconds, she forced herself to her knees and then to her feet, grabbing her dressing gown from the bed.

* * *

Later, in the kitchen she washed and dried her hands – twice. She put fresh coffee in the machine and switched it on.

She noticed it was nine-fifteen. As her colleague had returned to work yesterday, Grace had been allowed to take her day off today.

She padded through to the living room. Sitting at the table, the sorrow of losing her mother returned all too quickly. She had never had closure; had never been allowed to grieve. For all she knew her mother could still be out there. Though she doubted that very much. She couldn't imagine any possible scenario in which her mother could still be alive and not make contact for twenty years.

She would *not* have walked out on her daughter, no matter what the circumstances. A mother's love wouldn't allow it.

No, that could not have happened. Her mother had suffered at the hands of that fucking lunatic. Raymond Culver had also disappeared very abruptly in 1999, after the disappearance of her mother, never to be seen again. When the time came and the circumstances were right, Grace would have her moment, and all the answers she required – before payback.

She thought back to the period when her life had nose-dived: when she thought it was over for good.

Two years passed before it was clear to Grace that her mother was never going to return. Decisions had to be made, and she had to toughen up if she was going to survive in such a callous world.

Grace had put their house up for sale. Once the proceeds were in her bank account, she changed her lifestyle completely. Grace remained convinced that Raymond had had something to do with her mother's disappearance and if it took her the rest of her life to prove it, or find him, then so be it.

She moved away from the North East, settling in Kingston upon Hull. She enrolled at the college of further education and took a secretarial course. She found herself a small but tidy one bedroom flat in the old town, within walking distance of The Marina. Once she had fulfilled her course requirements she signed up with an agency, working on temporary contracts. Whilst she was doing that, she enrolled at the college again and studied IT and computer literacy. The five-year course gave her a degree and taught her numerous skills in a number of areas.

Over the years she invested a lot of money and moved again, to Harrogate, working in the legal profession. She changed her lifestyle again, became a health freak, eating only the very best food, supplementing her diet with multivitamins. She signed on at a local gymnasium, working out four times a week. She studied self-defence. Grace passed her time reading law books and collecting items of personal security should the time come when she might need them – and she knew she would, one day.

Eventually, she realised she could take things easier due to the serious amount of money she had accumulated. She could choose to work when she wanted. She stayed in Harrogate, devoting the rest of her time to finding the man she believed was responsible for her mother's disappearance.

Her starting point was her hometown of Billingham. She wanted to know if anyone else remembered him. Had they seen him recently? Some of the locals had, but no one had seen him since that unfortunate business.

Her quest led her to Flamborough, and her questions raised local interest due to the photographs of her stepfather she was showing the locals. A visit to the post office unearthed the name Jane Thornton, but they didn't know his name. The couple running the post office believed she originated from Scarborough. They remembered Jane Thornton leaving town under a storm cloud. No one had seen her since.

It took her some time to follow the trail in Scarborough but she eventually tracked down Jane Thornton's best friend, Cynthia Morrell, from a school register, who couldn't tell her much. She vaguely remembered a man called Richard Clayton. He was older than Jane Thornton.

Cynthia thought Richard had treated her friend well enough at the start of the relationship. Inevitably, things went wrong. Jane Thornton's parents died in a car crash. She struggled to recover from their loss. The relationship fell apart. Cynthia figured it was more than the death of her parents. She reckoned Richard was a bit of a dark horse, that he wasn't treating her well. The relationship deteriorated further.

The last Cynthia heard, Jane Thornton skipped town, was residing in Malta, and refusing point blank to return to Scarborough while that man was still breathing.

Cynthia never saw Richard Clayton again. He'd somehow vanished off the face of the Earth around 1991.

She may have discovered the whereabouts of Jane Thornton, but Richard Clayton's whereabouts were a complete mystery.

The trail had ended very abruptly.

Grace finished her coffee and poured another. She believed that Richard Clayton, Raymond Culver and the man she now knew to be Ronald Critchley were one and the same.

Chapter Twenty-two

Terry Jones heard the shop door open, and then close. The Lord only knew how, with the two Herberts that were in the back room testing guitars and amplifiers. They'd been there the best part of an hour – since he'd opened at nine – and the row they were making was enough to make anyone's ears bleed.

Neither of them could play a note, but they certainly assumed they could, like karaoke kings. That was the problem nowadays. *The X-Factor* and *Britain's Got No Talent* and other shit like it was responsible for people thinking they could become rock musicians overnight and earn a fortune, then retire after a year or two and live a life of luxury.

Still, should he complain? He'd been running the music shop in Bursley Bridge for a couple of years. He was making money off them. The reason he didn't like it was because he was a seasoned professional; he knew what he was doing, and had for many years.

Terry glanced up and saw the young man standing in front of the counter with his guitar case.

"I'll be with you in a minute, son."

The young man nodded.

Terry put down the soldering iron, switched it off and shuffled his way to the door leading through to the back.

The room was full of amplifiers and smelled of leather and lavender polish. A number of guitars were in glass cases. All the expensive stuff was in the showroom in the shop front; under lock and key, the stuff that could easily be walked away with: effects pedals, leads and radio microphones. The back was mainly a testing station for people who wanted to know what something sounded like. The real musicians would spend hours trying every combination of equipment but they also spent money.

"Okay, lads." He clapped his hands.

The music stopped and they stared at him. Both were six feet, as thin as sticks and covered in spots. One had hair that resembled an explosion in a mattress factory – all over his head. The other one was starting to lose his. One wore glasses, the other didn't. Their clothes were either held together with safety pins or had bloody great cuts in them. He thought they were dirty but apparently that was the style.

"What do you think, then? We have a guitar to suit you?"

"They're all good, man," said the hairy cornflake.

"You gonna buy them all, then? That should be a good day for me."

Both of them laughed and pointed at him and then glanced at each other.

No-hair reached into his pocket and drew out some cash. "Can we leave a deposit on these two guitars?"

He pointed to the ones they were holding – bass and rhythm.

"Of course you can," said Terry, pleased he'd made a sale when he didn't think he would.

"We'll come back next week and pay for 'em when *we* get paid. That all right?"

"No problem, son. What about an amp?"

"When we pay you next week we'll talk about that, if you don't mind."

"Not at all. Always pleased to help."

He led them to the front of the shop, completed the paperwork, took their money and bade them a good day.

"Sorry about that," he said to the man who had waited patiently. "How can I help you?"

"I've just bought this. I wondered if you could re-string it for me and give it the once over."

Terry took the case, moved to the end of the counter and laid it on top. He opened the lid and whistled through his teeth. "Nice machine. Seen a bit of action."

The red Fender Stratocaster was definitely a model from the late seventies. Not a copy, the genuine article. He lifted it out and the plate on the back confirmed it was built in the USA.

He ran his hands up and down the body. The scratches and dents were real and original. None of them had been touched up. In some respects the battle scars added to the value. The guitar had seen a lot of action but Strats were built to last. He checked the case. That was original as well. He noticed a small round hole on the outside that had been repaired. He suspected a music stand had gone through it at some point. It had happened to him many times over the years; one of the hazards of being on the road. With every sale he now tried to persuade people into buying a flight case, they were much stronger.

"You say you've only just bought it?"

The man nodded. "Yesterday."

Terry sized him up and down. He was probably in his late teens, well dressed: good quality shoes, hair neatly trimmed and combed. He was clean-shaven, smelled spicy. For all that, Terry had the impression he didn't know the first thing about a guitar. He was probably working off what someone else had told him.

"How much did you pay for it, if you don't mind me asking?"

"Five hundred pounds. I've been saving for one of these for years. My Dad reckons they're the best, especially if you want to play *Shadows* music. He helped me with the last hundred. Was it a good buy?"

"What's your name?"

"Stephen Whiteley."

"We'll soon find out, Stephen," said Terry, immediately feeling sorry for the young man. "Where did you buy it?"

The answer to that question wasn't so forthcoming. "Everything's okay, isn't it, Stephen?"

Stephen sighed. "Truth is, I bought it through a friend of a friend, so I don't exactly know where it's come from. But he said it was all above board. Just... didn't tell my dad."

Terry nodded and smiled. "I'm sure it was."

But he didn't think so. Terry hated to see people being ripped off – whoever they were, never mind decent people like Stephen appeared to be. Even the two Herberts who had been in the back of the shop for an hour. He wouldn't have liked either of those being ripped off. People who bought from him always ended up with a fair deal. That's why they came back.

"Let's go through the back and have a listen, shall we, Stephen?"

Stephen smiled and followed him.

"Sit yourself down there, son." Terry pointed to a chair.

He put the guitar strap over his neck, plugged it into a Marshall amp and switched it on.

Terry played a few chords in different positions. The guitar was going out of tune and he detected fret buzz. He placed the Strat in a wooden jig and made a few adjustments. Sure enough, the neck was warped. He turned to Stephen and pointed it out to him.

"Can you repair it?"

"I don't know, son, depends how badly damaged it is. Even if I can, you might have to shell out a bit more money."

"What's caused it?"

Terry raised his hands.

"Could be anything, son."

Chapter Twenty-three

Robbie Carter was on surveillance duty. He'd spent two hours yesterday camped outside the music shop in Bursley Bridge, watching and waiting, in case the parasite who had emptied his house decided to try and sell the goods.

Nothing. It was eleven o'clock.

Robbie decided it was time to go in, put the feelers out.

He opened the door and stepped inside. The place was empty – the atmosphere suited his mood.

The man behind the counter glanced up. He was probably mid-fifties with silver hair, a chubby face, stocky body; he wore a brown apron, white shirt and brown tie. A radio on a shelf above him was playing seventies music, which suited Robbie. The man was sitting on a stool reading the paper, with a cup of tea in front of him.

He placed the paper on the counter. "Morning. Can I help you?"

"I'm not sure," replied Robbie. "What have you got?"

"We have everything here. If we don't have it, we can get you it."

"Sounds good to me. Do you have much second-hand stuff, or is it all new?"

"Depends how good the used stuff is, and where it comes from."

"Can I?" Robbie gestured with his arm that he would like to go through to the back.

"Of course. Help yourself. All the amps and speakers are in the back, some of the guitars. The smaller, more expensive stuff is where I can see it, in here."

"Can't blame you, mate. The bastards will steal anything not nailed down."

"Sounds like you've had a few problems yourself."

"I'll say." Robbie nodded.

"Terry," he said, sipping his tea. "Terry Jones."

"Robbie Carter."

Robbie noticed Jones flinch a little.

"Robbie Carter. Where have I heard that name?"

"Probably from that paper you're reading."

Jones opened his eyes wider, started turning pages. When he found the relevant article he quickly scanned it and lowered the paper back to the counter.

"Oh, God. I'm sorry to hear about your wife."

"So was I," said Robbie, "but she wasn't all I lost."

"I hope they catch the bastard who did it."

"So do I," said Robbie, before adding. "At least before I do."

"Know what you mean." Jones folded the newspaper up. "What brings you in here, Mr Carter?"

Robbie wondered why he'd asked that question. Either the article he was reading hadn't concentrated on the stolen guitar, or he genuinely didn't know about it. Or he did and he was being coy. Robbie would find out which.

"I'm looking for a guitar."

"You've come to the right place," he said. "Go and have a look in the back. If you want to try anything just give me a shout. I'll not bother you; I'll just carry on reading my paper. Maybe you need a bit of time to yourself."

"I'm okay but you've misunderstood me. I'm not looking to buy a guitar, I'm looking for the one that was stolen from me."

"Stolen? When?"

"The night my wife was murdered."

Terry Jones picked up the paper again but put it down quickly, as if he had no idea what to say, or do.

Robbie could tell by the expression in his eyes that he desperately wanted to read the entire article.

He moved in for the kill, walking as close to the counter as he could, so that the pair of them were less than three feet apart.

"Yes, Mr Jones, stolen. You see the bastard that broke into my house to steal my personal possessions not only took the money I'd earned from the gig that night, he made the mistake of taking my most personal possession..."

Robbie left the sentence unfinished, seeing which way the music man would go.

"The guitar?" Terry asked, screwing his face up.

"Nearly," replied Robbie. "But I meant the wife... this time."

Terry Jones could do nothing other than nod his head. Robbie knew he had the upper hand from the body language. It was something he had learned over the years: how to read body language and how to take charge of the situation.

"Now," continued Robbie, leaning closer still, placing both hands on the flat of the counter. "I can't get my wife back, so I'm going to have to make do with something she bought me."

More silence from Robbie forced Jones into talking.

"The guitar?" he said, for the second time.

"You're learning."

Jones blinked. Always a good sign.

"What was it?"

Robbie glanced around the shop, studying all that was on offer. He left the counter and strolled slowly into the back before returning and placing both hands flat on the counter again.

"A Strat."

"A Fender Strat? What colour?"

"Red."

A very thin sheen of perspiration had built up on Jones' forehead. Robbie sensed he knew something.

"You seen it?" asked Robbie.

"No," replied Jones.

More silence. The screws were tightening.

"Are you sure?"

"I think I'd know."

Robbie leaned back and placed his hands inside his jacket pocket.

"Good." His mood lightened, even though he figured he was being lied to. "You'll know when you do. It's an early eighties model, bruised and battered. The case has a small repair where a music stand made a mess of it."

Robbie pulled out his wallet and extracted fifty pounds. He put the wallet back inside his jacket. "When you do see it, I'd like to know."

He held the fifty pounds aloft.

Jones kept his eyes on it.

"And I'd like to be the *first* to know," said Robbie, placing the money in Terry's hand, squeezing it shut, but not too tightly. He didn't want to frighten the music man. "Before the police do, if you get my drift?"

Jones nodded.

Robbie Carter let go of his hand, leaned back, smiled, collected his wallet and made for the door.

He turned before opening it. "I'll be seeing you."

Chapter Twenty-four

Grace waltzed through to the bedroom and switched on her PC. Sitting down she immediately logged in to *Findadate.com*.

She had seven emails, four winks, and had been favourited by three more men. Out of interest she gave them the once over. Two of them were far too old. She cringed. She couldn't even if they paid her.

The third was quite interesting: very appealing with his dark brown curly hair and straight white teeth. She glanced quickly at all the icons covering the screen. He'd had 1,331 views. Ten had made him their favourite; twenty had winked at him.

But then came the catch: an icon further down the screen said he was not available, yet the information at the top said he had logged on within the last twenty-four hours.

Grace laughed. What the hell was all that about? Why did they do that? If they're not available why keep logging on? Why make someone else their favourite? What was it with these people? Dating websites were simply a home for parasites.

Talking of which, Grace opened her emails, immediately locating the one she was after.

Critchley had replied. He was upping the ante, suggesting that they meet. He thought she was very nice, a class above anything else he had seen on the site, and he would really love to meet her for a drink.

Grace laughed out loud. "I bet you do."

She leaned back in her chair, a smug expression on her face. Grace had worked so hard for so long to trap the bastard. She was so close to achieving her goal but rushing into something would not pay dividends.

She stared hard at the screen, realising that she had him exactly where she wanted him. He thought he was in control.

How wrong he was.

She needed to be patient.

Hunting him down had been one hell of a journey.

Following the revelations in Flamborough and Scarborough, it had taken her another two years to put a system in place for capturing him. It was pointless going to a private investigator. Everything they could do, she could do – they strung people along to con as much money out of them as possible.

The hardest bit about tracing someone who changed their ID constantly was trying to work out who they were in the present, which is why she had to think very carefully.

She had to start somewhere; the first point being, how does he pick his ID? That much she didn't know and it would be a massive undertaking. He could use a completely random system like walking round a graveyard, or checking the newspapers for deaths, or, worse still, simply pick a name out of a hat. Or make one up.

The next question to work out was what made him drop off the radar every few years? Did he go inside? Unlikely. If he went inside they would never let him out, fucking lunatic.

Living in Harrogate and working as a legal secretary had been perfect, so she had run with the names she had – which had yielded nothing: neither Raymond Culver nor Richard Clayton had ever done time.

She also knew that past performance is the best predictor of future behaviour.

Did he travel abroad? If he did, once back home, does he change his image?

If she could work out how he arrived at his identity, then she might be able to figure out what was coming next. She knew her target was a predictable creature of habit, so she made a list of patterns to help her identify him: his taste in food, music, TV, and films, amongst other things.

Eventually, she made her first breakthrough. She remembered her mother claimed to have met Raymond on a dating website, but couldn't remember which one. If he was using social media websites, the chances were he would let himself down.

She googled something called *The Way Back Machine*, a site that scanned and recorded the content of all indexed webpages online. It would prove useful if she knew one of the last identities he'd used, and roughly when it was used. It was next to impossible these days for someone not to leave a digital footprint.

She'd made name checks on eBay and Amazon, and followed up by running the sellers' usernames through *The Way Back Machine* to check it against other sites to see where else it turned up. Her biggest single hit had been the dating website *Findadate.com*.

The shock, however, had been that the site had led her to two different places, with two more victims lying in wait.

Grace picked up her empty cup and skipped through into the kitchen where she made fresh tea.

She ran back into the living room, picking up the newspaper from the previous evening, remembering something she had seen on the entertainment page.

Flicking through she found the advert. A new nightclub at the back of the Corn Exchange in Leeds, called

Silhouettes, was having a singles' night with a seventies theme.

Perfect, thought Grace.

Skipping back into the bedroom she put the cup on the desk next to the mouse and took a very deep breath, closing her eyes, trying to concentrate on how best to proceed with the trap.

She opened her eyes and read through his latest email. He'd even had the audacity to use the word "pleasuredome" in it.

How crass. "You sad, sad man."

She constructed her reply carefully, arranging a blind date for the following evening in Leeds, hitting the send button.

"It *would* be a pleasure, Mr Critchley. But not for you," she said under her breath.

Chapter Twenty-five

Malton was a market town located on the Derwent. A famous connection to the town was the author Charles Dickens, who it is believed wrote *A Christmas Carol* whilst visiting. Malton was known locally as Yorkshire's food capital.

At a little after two o'clock, Robbie was taking a late lunch on the outskirts of the town in a pub called The Royal Inn, a traditional establishment with wooden tables and chairs, a jukebox, a dartboard, and a pool table. Though clean, Robbie placed it only slightly higher up the ladder from a spit and sawdust saloon.

It was under new management and they were keen to impress, so the first thing they had done to attract custom was hire a damn good chef and create a winning menu. Robbie had ordered the rump steak and chips with all the trimmings, asking them to lose the salad.

He'd taken a glass of red wine to a table outside in the courtyard and was enjoying what had to have been the hottest day in winter he had ever known. The sky was blue and cloudless with no breeze to diminish the heat. Inside, someone had cranked up the jukebox and he could quite clearly hear The Rubettes singing *Sugar Baby Love*. Great song but well out of Robbie's vocal range.

He had the area to himself but hopefully that wouldn't be for long. Robbie checked his phone – there were no text messages or missed phone calls.

The barmaid appeared with cutlery and napkins. She asked if he would like another glass of wine when his food came. He nodded.

Two minutes later she brought both and told him to enjoy. The mound on the plate was so large that he didn't know whether to eat it or climb it. The steak was done to a turn and bigger than the advertised weight, accompanied by chips, peas, mushrooms and onion rings. The barmaid dropped a basket of condiments on the table and Robbie applied salt, pepper, and French mustard.

He ate a couple of chips to start his appetite, and was about to cut a piece of the steak when the light above him darkened slightly. Robbie still cut the steak and sampled it before glancing upwards.

"You Robbie Carter?"

"Who wants to know?"

The figure leaned in a little closer. He was bald with a wizened face and a pockmarked complexion. His eyes, nose, mouth and two bucked teeth were so close together that Robbie had trouble working out where one started and the other finished. He was wearing a T-shirt and shorts that hadn't seen the inside of a washing machine since he'd bought them. His arms and legs were covered in tattoos of all descriptions but you couldn't miss the pentagram on his head.

"Didn't your mother ever tell you it was rude to answer a question with another one?"

"Yes," said Robbie, smiling. "Just before I killed her."

The man laughed and took a seat without being offered.

"You must be Wilson," said Robbie.

The man sitting opposite didn't answer Robbie's question but stared at his plate of food. "I'll ask the questions, if you don't mind."

Robbie was dying to laugh at the man who obviously thought of himself as hard. Word around town, however, was that if you wanted to know anything, Wilson was your man. He knew everything that went down and, according to rumour, everything meant everything: who'd been turned over; who'd been beaten up; who'd been killed, even.

"I hear you're looking for someone," said Wilson, leaning over and pinching one of Robbie's chips.

"That's right," replied Robbie, rather put out. That would have been the next chip for his fork.

"What's he taken from you?"

Robbie put down his cutlery and wiped his mouth with his napkin, taking a sip of wine.

Wilson obviously saw it as a sign because he grabbed another chip.

"My wife."

Wilson laughed. "What, and you want her back?"

Robbie smirked. "Are you kidding?"

A bigger laugh from Wilson brought about more mirth from Robbie until he silenced the man with his next comment.

"I can't. She's dead."

Wilson stopped laughing. "What do you mean, dead?"

"What do you think I mean?" asked Robbie, picking up his cutlery, resuming his eating. "Someone killed her."

Wilson took an onion ring next.

Robbie really couldn't remember inviting him to do that. Nor did he expect Wilson would pay for half the meal, which was what he would end up eating soon.

"The burglar killed your wife?"

"Word has obviously travelled because I don't remember telling you I was burgled."

Wilson ignored the comment. "Why don't you let the police deal with it?"

"I have. They think it was me."

Wilson grinned. "Was it?"

"They tell me you know everything, Wilson. That much is obvious from the comment about the burglar. So, I want to know who turned my house over, killed my wife, and pinched my heirloom of a guitar?"

Wilson leaned over the table slightly. "What's in it for me?"

"You get to live," said Robbie, glancing at the sky, sipping more of his wine.

Wilson's expression darkened. "Are you threatening me?"

Robbie returned the man's glare. "I don't make idle threats, Wilson."

Wilson reached out for another chip, which was a big mistake. Before his hand made it to the plate, Robbie brought the razor-sharp steak knife down through the middle of it – dead centre between two arteries and bones – pinning it to the table.

A small trail of blood oozed up through the skin, around the knife, before meandering its way onto the table.

Wilson tried to scream but for some reason his vocal cords had stopped working. All that came out of his mouth was a strangulated noise that sounded like a cross between a wheeze and a fart.

Robbie stared him in the eyes. "Like I said, I don't make idle threats."

Wilson's chair legs grated across the ground as he tried to move it away from the table to stand up.

Robbie brought both his shoes down hard on Wilson's toes, quickly pushing his fork upwards into Wilson's neck. The skin delved inwards but it didn't pierce, allowing Robbie to use the fork as a hook, pulling Wilson toward him, ensuring he was going absolutely nowhere until Robbie said so. "Are you sitting comfortably, Wilson?"

"Yes," Wilson wheezed, eventually.

The barmaid popped her head around the corner of the courtyard. "Everything okay, gents?"

Wilson had his back to her so she couldn't see anything.

Robbie smiled and nodded. "We're fine, thanks."

"Does your friend want a drink?"

"No, he's okay. He's not stopping."

She disappeared back inside the pub.

"Now," said Robbie turning his attention to Wilson, who had paled significantly. "I want to know who robbed my house, killed my wife, and stole my guitar. Do you understand?"

Wilson nodded, but judging by the expression on his face he wished he hadn't. Another strangulated cry escaped his lips.

"Do you know who it was?"

"Y… y… yes," struggled Wilson.

"When you give me the name, I'll let you go."

Wilson's breathing was pretty erratic and Robbie hoped he wouldn't pass out. "So, what is it… his name?"

"M… M… M…"

Robbie sighed. "Come on, Wilson, I don't have all day."

Wilson obviously made a supreme effort. "Manny Walters."

"Manny Walters?"

"Yes," whispered Wilson.

Robbie removed the fork from under his chin, and his feet from Wilson's – but not the knife from his hand.

Wilson stared at his hand as if it was in danger of becoming extinct within the next few seconds.

"Wasn't so bad, was it?" Robbie passed him a napkin.

Wilson made a show of wiping his face and his brow whilst still breathing heavily. "You've still got me fucking hand."

"I know I have," said Robbie. "Do you think I'm stupid?"

"Why?"

"Why what?"

"Why have you still got me fucking hand?"

"Because I want to know where he lives."

"Carpenter's Yard, Bramfield."

"Thank you," said Robbie. Standing up he pressed hard on Wilson's arm and slid the knife out very quickly.

"Oh Jesus," screamed Wilson.

"Enjoy the rest of my lunch. You've earned it."

Chapter Twenty-six

Gardener and Reilly were coping with heavy traffic in the centre of Leeds. They were on their way to see Fitz for a post-mortem report on Jane Carter.

Gardener's thoughts were consumed with the information they had collected during the morning, and another early morning meeting in the incident room with his team. Once actions had been given, they decided to pay Robbie Carter a visit. His van was parked on the drive.

When they knocked on the front door, he came from around the back to see who it was.

Robbie had not cleaned the place – as far as Gardener could see he hadn't actually lifted a finger; everything was still as he'd left it on the previous Friday night. The man was in no better shape. His hair was a mess: he was unshaven, dressed in jeans and a T-shirt that had not seen the inside of a washing machine for some time. His feet were bare.

Both detectives declined a cup of tea.

Once Robbie was seated Gardener had asked for the names and addresses of his late wife's doctor and solicitor. He obliged, but when questioned about her will, he claimed he had not seen a copy. He figured there were more important things on his mind. The grief was starting to hit home. He wasn't sure what to do next. Gardener had offered the services of a family liaison officer; Robbie declined. Before Gardener left he asked Robbie – rather casually – if he had any other computers apart from the one they had found in the house. Robbie said he hadn't but they were more than welcome to do another search if they didn't believe him.

Having left the house, they drove into Bursley Bridge to the doctor's surgery, who had a full book of appointments. Gardener left a card and asked if the doctor would make contact.

From there it was over to an address in Thirsk. Solicitor Gerry Rowland had an office in the market square above one of the bigger shops. He'd been very sorry to hear about the death of Jane Carter, and had found her a lovely woman to deal with on all occasions – her last appointment having been approximately six months ago. Gerry Rowland confirmed that Jane Carter had decided to change her last will and testament.

Gardener and Reilly were all over that like a rash. The previous document had included a sum of money to be left to her husband, Robbie, who had yet to make contact with the solicitor. The new one excluded him completely. She had given no reason. Rowland was completely satisfied that she was of sound mind, fit and healthy. He did not question the matter further. She was his client – not the other way around.

The new will saw the largest portion of the money left to Atkinson's riding stables, in the hope that he would set up a riding school specifically for new riders wishing to follow their dreams in horse riding, show jumping and racing as a profession. A further amount was to be left to fund an on-site vet, which Jane Carter felt they badly needed. The rest was to be divided and paid to a small number of close personal friends.

Rowland confirmed it had been witnessed and signed by her good friend, Carrie Fletcher.

On leaving the solicitor, Gardener phoned Dave Rawson and gave him the heads up on the news before asking him to visit Carrie Fletcher. After that, they had a quick bite to eat in one of the local cafés.

Gardener was suddenly aware that the car had stopped and they were outside the morgue.

"You okay, boss?" Reilly asked. "You were miles away."

"I was just thinking about Robbie Carter."

"And the will?"

"What else? Do you think he knew?"

"Not sure," said Reilly. "But the new will suggests he had nothing to gain by killing her."

"You'd like to think so."

"And everything else he's told us all fits perfectly. He has an alibi for the night of the murder, with witnesses to say where he was and what he was doing, but he could have got there in time."

"Trouble is, no matter how much you listen to his story something about it doesn't ring true." Gardener sighed and left the car.

Fitz was sitting behind a clinically clean desk in a spotless office, listening to an opera that Gardener could neither name nor understand. He glanced up, reached over, turned down the volume. "Coffee?"

Gardener nodded. It was the only coffee machine in the world that he would drink from, knowing it had cost Fitz at least a month's wages nearly two years ago and he always had the most mouth-watering flavours on the go.

The pathologist poured three cups and took his position behind the desk again.

"What have we got this time?" Reilly asked.

Fitz took a sip. "Pecan Nut Pie flavour."

"Where the hell did you find that?"

"Over in Ulverston. Wife and I had a day out, visiting relatives, and The Laurel & Hardy museum. Bloody thing was closed but at least we managed to buy some excellent coffee."

Gardener nodded. "You look tired, Fitz. Everything okay?"

"A bit understaffed. Richard, my assistant, is on holiday, and I had a bit of an emergency on Sunday morning when Ruth was taken into hospital."

"Anything serious?"

"She's been struggling for two weeks with vertigo. At least that's what the doctors thought but it was taking longer to shift than it should have done. Anyway, they had her inside, ran tests and scans and we're just waiting for the results."

"I'll keep my fingers crossed."

"Do *you* think it's serious, Fitz?" asked Reilly.

"It's not my area of expertise." The pathologist shifted uncomfortably, glanced at his desk, sifting through reports. He changed the subject. "Anyway, let's move on to something that is. Jane Carter, I have some very interesting things to tell you about her."

Gardener didn't like the sound of that.

"There was nothing natural about the way Jane Carter died. But then we suspected that from what we found. There was a lot of internal damage and I'm recording the cause of death as shock and haemorrhage, owing to bleeding into the abdomen from the ruptured renal vein."

"That doesn't sound good," said Reilly.

"It sounds painful," added Gardener.

"From the bruising we saw developing on Friday night, it was obvious that her abdomen had come into contact with some serious external force."

Fitz leaned forward and bridged his hands underneath his chin. That action alone worried Gardener because he knew they were in for a lecture.

"The abdomen lies under your diaphragm, which is approximately the bit beneath your rib cage. Inside your abdomen lies your liver, pancreas, gall bladder, stomach, small intestines and large intestines, bladder, and kidneys, and your sexual organs, if you're a woman."

Reilly glanced at Gardener. "Why does he do this?"

"Do what?"

"We visit him to talk about a case and he rattles on about anything but."

"It's his age," said Gardener.

"If you two have quite finished I'm trying to educate you!"

Both detectives nodded, like chastised schoolchildren.

"If you crush the abdomen, it usually results in a massive internal haemorrhage, or bleeding, to the layman, which reduces the amount of blood in your circulation so that the brain cannot be perfused with oxygenated blood. End result, you die. This is called circulatory shock.

"If you are lucky, the bleed may be smaller, which delays death long enough for an emergency operation to prevent shock. If this is possible, it depends on the nature of the damage. Occasionally there may be no noticeable bleeding, but damage to the internal organs may cause them to swell, which results in extreme pain. With all of those organs in your abdomen, there is no room for swelling or even bleeding without pain.

"If the internal bleeding is massive enough and the intestines or stomach are damaged, there may be bleeding from the mouth but it doesn't often happen despite what you see in war films.

"Jane Carter suffered a massive trauma, which in turn caused internal bleeding, and death soon after, from cardiovascular collapse – in other words, shock; other serious organ damage occurred, including a ruptured kidney."

Gardener rubbed his hands down his face. He wasn't quite sure what the pathologist was actually trying to tell him. "I want to come back to something you mentioned on Friday night. You thought that one of the two bruises was down to a footprint. Do you still think that?"

"I wondered if both bruises could be one injury, but they're not."

"Are you suggesting it was more than a shoe that caused all of this?" asked Reilly.

"It's possible. If her attacker had stamped on the stomach repeatedly, I feel sure we would have seen more bruises, and the pattern would almost certainly have been different. Although there were two bruises, only *one* was major – and very possibly the one that caused all the damage."

"Any idea what?" asked Gardener.

"I'm afraid that's up to you two. I believe the ruptured vein and kidney could have been caused by one blow, possibly the result of something like a knee into the abdomen, or maybe a fall against a padded object such as a sofa arm, or perhaps falling down the stairs."

"We found her in the bedroom, Fitz. Nothing in that room matches your theories."

"Not unless you count a knee to the abdomen. However, it must have been something pretty solid," persisted Fitz. "The blow ruptured her kidney, dissecting it

134

across its diameter, and fractured six of her ribs. It's not unusual for such injuries where someone affected by chronic alcoholism has a fall."

Gardener thought about that, but he wasn't convinced. A mental summary of the bathroom with the mess on the floor came to mind. There *was* a remote chance she could have fallen by the toilet bowl and managed to struggle back to the bedroom.

"Did you find any alcohol in her system?" asked Reilly.

"One unit of white wine was recorded in the toxicity report."

"That would tie in with what we've heard. She looked after herself, ate the right foods, and drank liberally."

"From what I've seen, I would agree with you. Jane Carter was fit and healthy."

Gardener's head was close to bursting. He needed a break but judging by what they were hearing, it would be a long time coming. Unlike DCI Briggs who would almost certainly be breathing down their necks before long.

"However, I discovered something that made me think it *could* have been the result of a natural process, because of a build-up of pressure in the vein as a result of a previous operation."

"Go on," said Gardener.

"Whatever it is, involved this little fellow here," replied Fitz.

"What is it?"

"It's a small tube. I found it placed between the aorta and the pulmonary artery, but I've no idea what it's doing there. It might be a pump of some description. After following the network around her system, I think it may have something to do with blood pressure. I suspect it might explain the tablets we found. I've done a little checking on those. *Pentoril Diazanem.* She had been taking them to purify her blood, which fits in with the tube being positioned where it was. We'd need her doctor to confirm.

135

I'm curious. I would like to know what's going on here. I've not seen anything like this set up."

"We dropped by her doctor this morning," said Reilly.

"He was busy so we had to leave a card," said Gardener. "There's obviously a lot more to tell us about your findings."

"She had some very old injuries. I don't think Jane Carter is a stranger to pain or accidents. Her doctor will almost certainly confirm something critical – possibly life-threatening – happened in her past."

"I'm sorry, Fitz, we should have mentioned this," said Gardener. "Her employer, Matthew Atkinson, did inform us of a serious accident years ago when she lived in Texas but he didn't know too much about it."

"Was he able to elaborate?"

"It involved horse riding," said Reilly. "I think she came off; maybe she ended up underneath the horse."

"That's certainly one explanation. She had some liver scarring. I think the valve may have been to bypass some blood around the liver, which normally has a huge blood flow. When the liver gets scarred from damage, usually cirrhosis, it restricts blood flow through it. The back pressure causes damage to other organs, especially the heart, leading to oedema – fluid collecting under the skin, around the legs, possibly in the lungs, which can be similar to drowning.

"A bypass valve would relieve this back pressure and prevent these symptoms. Before the operation, the patient might be taking diuretics, which cause the kidneys to produce more urine by reducing the amount of fluid in blood vessels slightly, hence reducing the back pressure of blood; or antihypertensives, which dilate blood vessels so that they can accommodate more volume of blood: that would also reduce back pressure.

"So, if you fit a bypass valve around the liver, it takes all this blood straight to the venous side and back to the heart, and therefore there is no blood backing up to cause high blood pressure or heart failure or any of those symptoms. Unfortunately, the liver's job is to manufacture proteins and other necessary biochemicals distributed through the bloodstream, and make safe any toxins from either metabolism or what is ingested already existing in the bloodstream. None of this can happen if the liver is bypassed completely. So it may only work for either a short time, or if the liver is only partly damaged."

"Hence the tablets," said Reilly.

"But what we've just discussed did not cause her death," offered Gardener. "Or the severe bruising we've seen."

"I don't think it would," said Fitz. "I was simply pointing out something I'd found that may or may not have a bearing on what happened."

"Could the blow have caused the valve to stop working?"

"It could have damaged the valve enough for it to partially work, or, as you say, stop it working altogether."

"But it wouldn't cause the damage Jane Carter had been subjected to," persisted Gardener. "We need to try and find out how she was killed, and who killed her. Was the mark on her abdomen clear enough to identify any tread pattern from the footwear?"

"No."

Chapter Twenty-seven

Gardener was the last person through the door. Despite the late hour the team were enthusiastic, huddled together in small groups, discussing what they'd learned during the day. He was hoping for positive results.

With the door closed, signalling the start of the meeting, he strolled down the left side of the room, noticing Maurice Cragg had once again pulled out all the stops. On top of one table they now had an old tea urn with a number of empty cups and saucers lined up. There were bottles of water and the usual leftovers from the bakery – most of which had been snaffled by the others. There was, however, one chicken salad wrap, which had his name on; he scooped it up as he passed, along with a bottle of water.

Cragg had updated the whiteboard with all the information discussed in the previous meeting, and more photos had been added.

Before starting, Gardener realised he wasn't last. One of his team was missing. "Anyone seen Colin?"

Most shook their heads.

"Not since this morning," said Rawson.

"Anyone heard from him?"

"Come to think of it, no."

Gardener found it very unusual that Sharp hadn't shown. He glanced at the clock on the wall. It said eight-thirteen.

"Okay, let's crack on. We have a lot to get through tonight, and if any of you have had the kind of day Sean and I have had, we'll be here forever. We spoke to Jane Carter's solicitor today, as well as Fitz. Both had some interesting things to say, but I'll fill you in later."

Gardener pointed to Dave Rawson first. "How did you get on with Carrie Fletcher?"

"Sorry, boss, couldn't find her."

"What do you mean?"

"She wasn't home."

"Why don't I like the sound of this?" Reilly asked.

"I went straight away after you called me," continued Rawson. "Knocked on the door a few times, went round the back – no answer. There was no car on the drive, and from what I could see, it wasn't inside the garage."

"Did you speak to her neighbours?" Gardener asked.

"Yes, one on each side. They hadn't seen her for a few days, 'since that nasty business' was how they put it."

Everyone knew what the neighbours had meant.

"How did the house look?"

"Not sure I follow you."

"Were the curtains open? Did you peek through the letterbox to see if any mail had built up? Did it have that abandoned look?"

"I wouldn't say so. Now you come to mention it, I didn't look through the letterbox, but the place looked clean and tidy. Curtains were open. I looked through the windows. Rooms were clean. Grass was trimmed."

Gardener leaned back against a table. "I don't like it either, Sean." He addressed the team. "We found out today from Jane Carter's solicitor that she changed her will about six months ago."

"Don't tell me," said Cragg. "She left everything to Robbie."

"Just the opposite," said Reilly. "He was in the first will, but not the new one."

"Who was?" asked Rawson.

"The stables, mostly. She left some for Atkinson to invest in training, some for an on-site vet, the rest to friends."

"Figures," said Benson. "She seemed pretty passionate about the horses."

"How does Carrie Fletcher fit in with all this?" asked Sarah Gates.

"She was a witness to the will."

"Which suggests she's a close friend," said Rawson.

"Her best, I should imagine," offered Cragg.

"What are you thinking, sir?" asked Patrick Edwards.

"You think she might know who the killer is?" asked Cragg.

"Maybe, which could suggest that the killer knows she knows. We're probably getting ahead of ourselves, and maybe there's a perfectly good explanation, but we have to consider every possibility. When was the last time the neighbours saw her?" Gardener asked Rawson.

"They're both pretty nosey from what I could tell. Both had seen her sometime on Sunday morning. She was pottering about in the garden. On Sunday afternoon, the car had gone from the drive."

"What car does she have?"

"Land Rover."

"No doubt supplied by Peter Strange," offered Reilly.

"Which reminds me," said Gardener, "anyone spoken to Strange about Jane Carter?"

Paul Benson signalled. "I have, sir. He hasn't seen her for about five or six months. They remained friends after the divorce and he's seen her about the town now and again. He said the last time they spoke she was fine."

Gardener didn't think the Land Rover dealer would be able to offer much. He addressed Dave Rawson again. "Did you manage to get the registration of Carrie Fletcher's vehicle?"

"Yes, it's a private reg: C1 FTR."

"Maurice, can you take the details from Dave and run it through the system? See if we can get a movement on it?"

Cragg nodded, strolled over to Dave Rawson, took the details and immediately added them to the charts, with a big question mark against Carrie Fletcher's name.

"Was she married?" Gardener asked Rawson.

"No. Carrie divorced her husband about fifteen years ago. Been single ever since. Had a couple of boyfriends but neither one has managed to tie her down. Neighbours reckoned she lives for her horses, just like Jane Carter."

"Okay, never mind, Dave. Sean and I will call back round in the morning, see what we can find."

Gardener cast his eye in the direction of Anderson and Gates. "Anything from the witness statements, or any more progress with Robbie Carter's neighbours?"

"Sorry," sighed Anderson. "It's a small cul-de-sac and it was too early in the morning for any of them. The people we've spoken to in the surrounding areas are pretty much the same: keep to themselves. Most were in bed at that time."

"Those that weren't in bed were working nights," added Gates.

"Anyway, realising it was a bit of a lame duck, we drove into Sowerby to check out this mill house place she used to rent."

"Anything?" asked Gardener, hopeful.

"Have you seen the place?"

"No."

"Miles from anywhere," said Anderson.

"Only reason we found it was because it had a mill; doubt we'd have found it otherwise," said Gates.

"What you're going to tell me is, no one was home and no one's seen who rents the place?"

"Pretty much," replied Anderson. "There isn't a neighbour for miles. And you're right, he wasn't home."

"But he might be back later," added Gates. "There were fresh tyre tracks."

"Yes," said Anderson. "Looked like someone had been recently."

"We also dropped in on a few of Jane Carter's contacts from the stables," Gates added.

"What did they have to say?"

"They all told pretty much the same story. She was well liked, always pleasant. She ran a tight ship where business was concerned, taught pupils properly."

"Basically, everyone liked her," said Anderson.

"What about him?" Gardener asked.

"Those that knew Robbie, or had seen him more than once found him a bit sullen, quiet. One even said they thought he was shy. He was confident when you got him on the subject of music, but other than that he had very little to say."

"Did anyone offer an opinion of them as a couple together?"

"No," said Gates. "If they went on nights out with her it was usually a girly thing. Most people assumed they got on all right because she never spoke ill of him."

"There was one who offered a bit more," said Anderson. "A woman called Cathy Smithson. She lives in Upsall, near Thirsk. There was a period about six months ago when Jane Carter wasn't her normal self. She was a bit quieter than usual. She noticed one time that Jane struggled getting on and off the horse."

"She say what that was?" asked Reilly.

"Cathy asked, but Jane Carter just shrugged it off as getting old. But she was quiet for about a week."

"Could have been a problem related to her medical condition," offered Gardener.

"What medical condition?" asked Cragg.

"We'll come back to that, Maurice," said Gardener. He continued to address Anderson and Gates. "I take it you have more contacts to speak to?"

"Yes."

The SIO turned and updated the board with the name and the incident before turning back to the team.

"Okay, we've made a note. If we get a few more saying the same thing we'll follow up. If we don't, we can go back to Cathy Smithson and see if she can elaborate on that point. Good work, guys, but I think we'll have to trundle up a few more paths and knock on a few more doors before we have a breakthrough."

Keen to press on, Gardener immediately turned his attention to Patrick Edwards. "Anything more from Seacroft?"

Edwards shook his head, dismayed, as if he'd failed in his mission. "No, sir. I covered a lot more ground today.

Robbie Carter did stop and talk to a couple in the car park: a Mr and Mrs Allen, live about ten minutes' drive in Alwoodley. But they only stayed a few minutes – too cold. They have a wedding anniversary coming up and they wanted to know if they could book Robbie privately. He said it was okay, gave them a card and left."

"And he didn't stop at any of the local fish shops before going home?"

"Not that they could remember. But as they said, you get a lot of people in at that time of night and all you're interested in is serving and getting 'em out of the door. I also tried all the fast-food places, showed his photo – no luck."

Gardener nodded. "Okay, Patrick, don't worry. You've tried your best. Tomorrow I want you to help Sarah and Bob to concentrate on as many of her contacts and customers as you can. Most of those will be friends but I suspect she will also have had friends outside the equine circle." He turned to Emma Longstaff. "Maybe you can help us there, Emma."

"I've really managed to delve into her Facebook pages." She reached into a folder, withdrawing sheets of paper. "I've made a comprehensive list of her friends here. Trouble with Facebook is, despite people being in your circle of friends, they might not necessarily be friends in real life."

Emma Longstaff passed out the photocopied sheets of the victim's friends. "There aren't as many here, which makes me think they really are her friends: there's only seventy-five."

"It's enough," said Gardener. "It's still another seventy-five possible people to interview."

"Who was in her top friends?" asked Patrick Edwards.

"I was just coming to that. The Atkinsons were there, as well as Robbie, and Carrie Fletcher. I was able to go back quite some time. In the very beginning there were quite a number of intimate messages from Robbie."

"Must have been when they first met," said Reilly.

"When was that?" Gardener asked.

"About three years ago."

"Did she say how they met?"

"Not in so many words, but I got the impression it was a dating website."

"Really?"

Cragg continued updating the charts so he immediately wrote that down and turned to speak to Emma Longstaff. "Did she say which one?"

"No. Not that I noticed."

"How do you know about dating websites, Mr Cragg?" asked Mike Atherton.

"Got to keep your finger on the pulse, son," he replied, with a wry smile that must have left everyone wondering what the hell he meant by it.

"Anything else from the social media angle?" Gardener asked.

"I haven't checked Twitter or Instagram yet, I've been a bit too busy with Facebook. But I thought you might like to know there was more interaction between her and Carrie Fletcher, than with Robbie."

"What kind of interaction?"

"Usual stuff: planning nights out, meeting up for meals during the day."

"Did you make notes?"

She consulted her sheets of papers. "Some."

"When was the last time they connected on Facebook?"

"Friday night, about eight o'clock. Carrie wondered if she wanted to meet for a drink but Jane said she was tired. She was going for a bath. After that, it was a glass of wine and a bit of TV."

"When was the last entry from Carrie Fletcher that didn't involve Jane Carter?"

Emma Longstaff dug out what she needed. "There was nothing from Friday night to Sunday morning. She was obviously devastated by the news, which she must have heard quite quickly. But then on Sunday there were three or four pictures and a beautiful verse as a kind of RIP. In fact, there were quite a few on there, nearly all of her friends. Something else which makes me think they're all genuine."

"More proof that her and Carrie were close," said Reilly.

"Nothing after Sunday morning?" Gardener inquired.

"No, sir."

Gardener grew more concerned. Where the hell *was* Carrie Fletcher? He returned to a point that Sarah Gates had mentioned.

"Sarah, you said Cathy Smithson suspected something might be wrong about six months ago." Gardener turned to Emma Longstaff. "Can you remember finding anything about any such incident on Facebook – privately or otherwise?"

"No, but I've only spent the day surfing through her friends and the messages they leave on her wall. I'll have to go through the private messages for that."

"Can you do that, please, Emma? It might give us something to go on."

The SIO was aware of the fact that Colin Sharp had still not made an appearance. As there were one or two more things to discuss he would see them out of the way before calling him on his mobile.

Gardener waited while Cragg added more notes to the boards, before addressing Mike Atherton.

"CHIS Handlers; Intel Cell?"

"Nothing concrete," replied Atherton. "But there was a mention of Manny Walters. They reckon he's mixed up in this somewhere. Word on the street says he's had a big pay day."

"Did they say why?"

"One of the guys I spoke to in Armley reckons Manny was spotted in a pub car park on Saturday night. The Black Bull in Rawston."

Gardener groaned and Reilly rolled his eyes. They were involved in something serious quite some time back in Rawston involving perverts, paedophiles and all sorts. It was a pretty rough area.

"Did your snout know what was going down?"

"No. It was all done in darkness. But later that same evening, Manny was also flogging a shed load of CDs and DVDs, biggest names in the collection all representing Glam Rock."

"Good work, Mike. Sounds to me like we've found our man."

Maurice Cragg shook his head. "But Manny isn't violent. It doesn't have his stamp on it."

"Maybe he panicked," said Rawson.

"If he'd have panicked," Cragg replied, "he'd have run, not fought."

"Pressure of being caught can make you do funny things," offered Reilly. "Under normal circumstances maybe he would have run. Let's say this wasn't normal. If he was in the bathroom when she came in, he'd be cornered. Only way past her was using force."

"I might go along with that, Sean," said Gardener, "but did he make it upstairs?"

"Maybe not, boss. I was just thinking outside the box."

"You'd have to," said Anderson. "It's a small fucking box inside your head."

Another roar of laughter ensued. Gardener loved the banter. He knew underneath all that his team had nothing but the greatest of respect for each other. "Did you pay Manny a visit, Mike?"

"Twice. Place was empty both times. I spoke to his neighbour, Mary Miller, but she didn't know where he was."

Gardener sighed. "Why is it that everyone connected to this case is disappearing?"

"Everyone *we* want to speak to anyway," said Benson. "Really does make you wonder what's going on."

Gardener added to the boards. "Okay, everyone on Manny's case. I want him found. I appreciate what Maurice says, that it doesn't seem to be Manny's style. If he wasn't there, he might know who was. If he was there, at the very least he could put himself in the clear for the murder by telling us what he does know."

"It's just possible that he was there and saw what's gone on and now he's in hiding," said Cragg. "Maybe he's been threatened."

"Even more reason to find him," said Gardener.

The SIO allowed the buzz to die down before updating them on what he and Reilly had found. The visit to Robbie had produced something of a result when he gave them names and addresses of Jane's doctor and solicitor. Gardener mentioned the lack of a laptop or any other computer, and that Robbie had insisted they could search the house again if they wanted.

"Doesn't mean to say he didn't have one tucked away somewhere," offered Patrick Edwards.

"I appreciate that, Patrick, but it would be like searching for a needle in a haystack."

"And he sure as hell isn't going to volunteer where it is," said Reilly.

"Emma, hack into his Facebook for me, see if there's any posts from him."

She nodded.

Gardener went on to inform them what Fitz had said, the most important point being what Fitz figured might be a blood pressure pump. Gardener described the small pump and held it aloft. He asked Cragg to take photos of it and then turned to Paul Benson. "I know it's a long shot but will you take that around the hospitals tomorrow and see if anyone recognises it?"

"Do you think it's imperative to the investigation, sir?"

"I don't know, Paul, but we can't afford to leave any stones unturned."

The clock informed Gardener it was nine-fifteen. As he pulled his mobile out of his pocket, the door burst open and in rushed Colin Sharp. His hair was unkempt, and Gardener could see he was concerned.

"What's up, Colin?"

"We've got a bit of a problem."

"We've had them all day, one more won't make any difference."

"This one will."

Gardener sighed. "It's about Robbie Carter, isn't it?"

Colin made for the left side of the room. "Give me a second, please, sir." He grabbed an empty cup and poured in some tea, picking up the final vanilla slice. "I haven't eaten all day."

No one spoke while he polished off the bun. Everyone knew Sharp to be one of the most dedicated professionals they had ever met and whatever he had to tell them would be important.

He took a quick slurp of the tea. "The man's a bloody enigma. I've spent all day trying to build up a picture on him."

"And?"

"I only know he's been in Bursley Bridge about four years."

"Where was he before that?"

"I don't know."

"What do you mean you don't know?"

"Just that. He seems to have blown into town on an ill wind. I can find no record of our Robbie Carter ever having existed before that."

Gardener was lost for words. "He must have done."

"That's what I thought. Trouble is it was late afternoon before I pieced all of this together, and I haven't had much of a crack at it since. I need more time."

"You can have more time, Colin. Find out everything you can."

Gardener turned to Cragg. "Has the tracker recorded any movement on his van, Maurice?"

"He's been home all day. Never moved."

"Has he signed in today?"

"Yes, this afternoon."

Gardener addressed Anderson and Rawson. "Will you two go and pick him up, bring him back here? I'd like to have another long chat with him about his mysterious past."

As both officers left the room, Gardener picked up his bottle of water and tackled the chicken wrap. He was starving, and it was going to be one hell of a night. He doubted he would make it home tonight. He suspected most of the officers were thinking the same; every one of them was on their mobiles already informing their loved ones.

* * *

Twenty minutes later, Anderson and Rawson returned.

Gardener noticed they were alone. "What's up?"

"He wasn't there," said Anderson.

Gardener glanced at Cragg. "Check the tracker, Maurice?"

"No need," said Anderson. "Van's still parked on the drive."

"Place isn't even locked up," said Rawson. "The back door is open."

"The whole scene looks just like it did on Friday night."

Chapter Twenty-eight

Ross Johnson stared into the sullen sky. The forecast wasn't good. Dry till dinnertime, then things would take a turn for the worse. Being late November, he couldn't expect much else.

He and his girlfriend Freya had spent the night at Bedlam Rocks. High up on the moors, it bordered North Yorkshire and the North East. It was rough, bleak, barren, and the last place anyone would want to be so late in the year. His mates had thought him crackers.

He and Freya spent most weekends together hunting for buried treasure, so why should the time of year make any difference?

Ross stared down at the ground. He had his pickaxe and shovel ready. The metal detector had lit up like a Catherine Wheel last night, but it had been too dark to do anything about it.

Being in the middle of Hangman's Bluff – Lord only knew who had called it that – the only choice they'd had was to bed down for the night. The bluff was one of those places that if you didn't stumble upon it by accident, you would never find it. Approximately six meters square, it resembled a small valley. On the right side, the rock face had an opening that led into a cave, which was where they had bedded down.

"Are you going to have some breakfast before you start digging?" shouted Freya.

Ross glanced at his watch. It was seven o'clock and approaching first light. "You start breakfast, I'll start this. I'll break off when it's ready." He bent down and hefted the pickaxe, speaking to himself, "Standing around daydreaming won't get me very far."

The last week had seen a fair bit of rain in these parts, so the ground wasn't so bad. It was pretty much wet peat, and slightly acidic anyway. After thirty minutes of digging using the axe and the shovel, the fruits of his labour were beginning to show. He'd dug maybe four feet down, and a couple of feet square.

He readied the axe once more as Freya shouted, "Ready when you are."

He ignored it, took the swing, and hit pay dirt as the tip of something white showed through the soil. "Nice one."

He took two more swings. More white appeared. He grabbed the shovel, carefully digging out some more. He peered closer in as Freya shouted again. He wasn't sure what it was, but he thought it was worth reaching down.

As Ross leaned forward, the wet ground underneath his feet gave way. He lunged in, grabbing at the object as the dirt collapsed around it. He dug in with both hands, removing soil much like a dog would with its paws around the now visibly round object. Eventually he was able to pull it free, before he landed on his arse with an audible thud.

Freya left the small cave with two cups of tea. "Guess I'll have to come to you, then."

Ross ignored what she'd said. He was too busy trying to work out what he had freed from the watery grave. Once he had, he let out a piercing scream and threw it back.

"What's up?" asked Freya.

Ross pulled out his inhaler, shoved it into his mouth, and breathed in deep.

"Police," he gasped. "Call the police."

Freya leaned further into the hole, dropping both cups. "Oh my God!"

Chapter Twenty-nine

At eight the following morning Gardener was staring at the whiteboard. He was still dressed in yesterday's clothes, having spent the night in a chair at the police station in Bramfield.

The news about Robbie Carter was disturbing. In view of everything that had happened – whether he was responsible for the death of his wife or not – the man was still of interest to them. They needed answers.

That was bad enough, but the fact that everyone else connected to the murder – Robbie Carter, Manny Walters, and more recently, Carrie Fletcher – was also missing caused further concern.

Once the shock had worn off, Gardener gave his team a number of actions. What they didn't know was how long Robbie had been missing. He'd signed on at four, but by ten o'clock he'd disappeared. He could be anywhere.

The team had left armed with photos and information, to try all local taxi offices, bus companies, train stations, and any other possible mode of public transport they could find. He'd run details out to all ports and airports to keep a watch for him but he'd considered that route unlikely, because they still had his passport.

Expenditure had to be a problem, so he had one of the officers inside the station checking Robbie's bank for cash withdrawals. His mobile phone had not been used for at least twenty-four hours. It was possible that he was now operating a cheap pay-as-you-go phone that was next to impossible to trace.

Finally, he had no choice but to issue the press office with as much detail as he could so that they could bomb all the media outlets. He would now have to rely on the general public.

One final thing he did was wheel clamp Robbie's van where it stood, on the drive, in the event that he returned.

It had been one hell of a night and the promise of anything better was slim.

The door to the incident room opened and Reilly brought in a tea and a coffee, sitting opposite Gardener.

"How are you feeling, boss?"

"Like we've failed, Sean."

"We haven't failed. He hasn't been gone that long. We'll find him."

Gardener took a sip of tea.

"Not just him, though, is it? Where the hell is Carrie Fletcher? If Robbie Carter *is* responsible, and knew about the will, then he must know about Carrie Fletcher's involvement. Maybe he's done something with her – like it's possible that he did something to his wife."

"Unless they were both involved in making his wife disappear."

Gardener thought about his partner's suggestion. "Doesn't make sense. Carrie Fletcher doesn't benefit from the will so there would still be nothing in it for them if they were together."

"True. And from what we've seen and heard, Carrie Fletcher probably has enough money."

"Which leads us to Manny's door. Is he controlling everything or is he in with Robbie?"

"The elusive thief?" replied Reilly. "I doubt it. Maurice Cragg reckons violence is not Manny's style. Robbie could have employed Manny to burgle the place, make it look like something it wasn't. But then, what does Manny have to gain?"

"Money, and whatever he sells on."

"There is another possibility."

"What?" asked Gardener, sipping his tea. His stomach rumbled. The last thing he'd eaten had been the chicken wrap the previous evening.

"Someone else is controlling the whole thing – someone we don't know about yet."

Gardener sighed. "That's a frightening thought."

"Even so, we might have to consider it. He might have all of them. Maybe something in the past connects them all and now it's payback time."

Before the conversation went any further the door opened and Cragg walked in with a sheet of paper in his hand. "Have you been sitting there all night?"

"Most of it," replied Gardener.

"You shouldn't have done that, sir, there's plenty of room upstairs and a couple of cells with beds in, we could have accommodated you."

"Cells with beds?" said Reilly. "You're all heart, Maurice. To be sure we'd have loved that."

"Have you been here as well, Mr Reilly?"

"Somebody has to look after him."

Cragg chuckled. "Well I've got some news for you."

"Go on," said Gardener.

"ANPR cameras have pinged Carrie Fletcher's car three times in the last hour. Seven o'clock in Skipton. Half an hour ago in Harrogate. And Ripon in the last few minutes."

Gardener jumped out of his seat and headed to the map of the area on the left-hand wall. He followed the route with his finger.

He turned to Reilly. "She must be alive and kicking and on her way home." Gardener grabbed his hat and jacket from a chair. "Come on, Sean, no time to waste."

"Do you want something to take to eat on the way?" Cragg asked. "You must be starving."

"No thanks, Maurice, there's no time."

Chapter Thirty

It took them thirty minutes to reach Carrie Fletcher's house in Sowerby. As they pulled onto the path, they saw the Land Rover parked in front of the garage. Gardener noticed the curtains twitch in neighbouring houses.

As he walked around the front of the car, he felt the bonnet. It was hot; the engine was still ticking as it cooled.

"Can I help you?" said a voice from the gate.

She was late forties, blonde hair tied back in a ponytail. Her slim figure filled out a pair of tight blue jeans rather nicely, and she was wearing a Barbour jacket.

Gardener held out his warrant card. "DI Gardener and DS Reilly, West Yorkshire Major Incident Team. Are you Carrie Fletcher?"

"Finally locked him up, have you?"

"Who?" Reilly asked.

"I think we both know the answer to that question. Yes, I am Carrie Fletcher, and you'd better come in. I'm not sure I want to talk on the doorstep with my neighbours listening."

Gardener followed her advice. The heat inside the kitchen was welcoming. Carrie Fletcher had an old-fashioned range, the type that had hot water running through it all the time. The walls and floor were tiled; the ceiling had dark oak beams. The appliances were silver and modern. Decorating the worktops were the usual kitchen crockery, with foodstuffs in canisters. Hanging from the beams were a number of pans and utensils. A radio on a windowsill provided background music.

Carrie Fletcher held a coffee pot aloft. "Drink?"

"I won't say no," said Reilly.

"I bet you never do."

Both officers took a seat at the table, and Gardener asked if he could have tea. She set place mats and joined them. In the middle of the table was a fruit bowl with apples, bananas, pears, and kiwi fruit.

Carrie Fletcher pointed. "Help yourselves, or if you'd like, I have biscuits."

"Now you're talking my language," said Reilly.

"We've been very concerned about you."

"It's Robbie Carter you need to worry about."

"You don't like him?"

"That's an understatement," she replied, peeling a banana.

"Before we get into anything, do you mind if I ask where you've been?"

"My sister's. She lives in Skipton. I had to get away, needed fresh scenery and to be left alone with my thoughts."

Gardener nodded. He knew that feeling all too well. "Okay. Let's start at the beginning. You were obviously a good friend of Jane's. When did you last see her alive?"

Carrie's eyes misted over immediately. "Friday, at the stables."

"What time would that be?" Reilly asked, having produced a small pad and pen.

"I was there most of the day." Carrie Fletcher finished the banana and deposited the skin in a bin close to the table. "I got there about ten o'clock. Matthew and Lizzie were around but they were leaving on a business trip. I spent most of the time in the stable. Jane was taking an early lesson. We had a bite to eat together in the tack room."

"When did you last see her alive?"

"It would have been four o'clock, when I left."

"What was she doing?"

"She was in the small arena with a pupil."

"How did she seem to you throughout the day?"

"Same as always. Very talkative. She really loved what she did. If she could have spent twenty-four hours a day, seven days a week at the stables, she would have done."

"That anything to do with Robbie?" asked Reilly.

"No. She loved horses – being around them."

"You say you left at four o'clock. Do you have any idea what time she went home?"

"No, but I think the lesson was due to finish at four-thirty, so any time after then and probably before six. I sent her a Facebook message about eight o'clock to see if she fancied going out for a drink."

Gardener knew that from Emma Longstaff but decided to not say anything.

In the background the radio rattled out a concession of sixties numbers.

"Did she reply?"

"Yes, pretty quickly. Said she was tired and fancied a night in."

Carrie Fletcher finished her coffee and poured some more, offering Reilly another. Gardener declined further tea.

"When you were with her on Friday, could you tell if anything was bothering her?"

Sitting back down, she said. "Nothing I could detect. And she certainly never mentioned anything."

"After the Facebook message, did you hear from her again that night?"

That was the straw that broke the camel's back. Carrie started to weep openly, shaking her head. "I'm sorry."

"Don't be," said Gardener. "You've just lost your friend."

Carrie Fletcher reached for a tissue, wiped her eyes and her nose and tried to compose herself.

"You were very close, weren't you?"

"Like sisters," she said eventually.

"We know about the will, Carrie," said Reilly.

"What do you mean?"

"We know you were a witness to the new will she made about six months ago."

"Yes, yes, but there was nothing in it for me. It was what she wanted."

"We realise that, Carrie," said Gardener. "We're just trying to build up a picture. Can you remember how she was on that day?"

"Pretty much the same as always. She wanted to make the new will and then go out for a spot of lunch afterwards."

"Did she tell you about her old will and the changes she was making?"

"A little, over lunch. Jane was a very private individual. She was always chatty but she very rarely told people about her business. I felt quite honoured to have had a friend like her. For the most, she kept to herself. That's two failed marriages for you. Learning who you can trust comes at a price. People often let you down, and they certainly did with her, so most of the time she relied only on herself."

"Let's come back to the will. Did she say why she was changing it? Why she was excluding her husband?"

"Marriage to Robbie was not good. It hadn't always been that way. At the start it was pretty much like any relationship in the honeymoon period."

"Do you know how they met?" Reilly asked.

Carrie Fletcher managed a smile. "That was down to me. She'd been on her own for about five years when I persuaded her to join a dating website – that was after one too many drinks over here one night."

"Which one?"

"*Findadate.com*. I'm on it, you see."

"And she met Robbie on the site?"

Carrie Fletcher took another drink of coffee and was deep in thought before she answered. "Not strictly speaking, no. She was there to meet someone else who had actually stood her up. Robbie was there for the same reason and somehow they connected."

"The person she was there to meet. Was that a date made through the website?"

"Yes. This guy had been messaging her, showed all the signs and the right signals. You know, winked at her, made her a favourite. Finally, they made a date. Maybe he got cold feet. Happens a lot."

"Did he offer any explanation?" asked Reilly. "For standing her up?"

"Not that I can remember."

"Did he contact her again on the site?"

"To be honest, I think his profile disappeared after that night."

"Can you remember his name?"

"No. Too long ago."

"Interesting," said Gardener. "So, what was Robbie Carter like?"

"At first, he was like any other bloke trying to impress a woman. Attentive, lots of text messages, emails, messages on the dating site. The magic wore off after a year or so and he became difficult."

"In what way?"

"Possessive. It was okay for him to go out, but he usually wanted to know everything about where she'd been. Sometimes he wouldn't let her go out."

"How so?"

"It's funny you should ask about this because the incident I'm referring to happened about nine months ago – so it wouldn't be that long before the will was changed.

"He was out all weekend doing gigs, up in the North West, so he didn't bother coming back, just stayed there all weekend. She came over here on the Friday after work. We had a night in, a meal, a bottle or two of wine.

"On the Saturday we did girly stuff, like shop all day. We arranged to meet up with friends on the night. We were getting ready. I slipped into the bathroom in something and she'd just stepped out of the shower. That's when I noticed the bruises."

"Bruises?" questioned Gardener. "Were they fresh?"

"Reasonably."

"How could you tell?" asked Reilly.

"I volunteered many years ago in a woman's refuge. I saw a lot of battered wives. I knew the signs. Women who were very quiet, and when pushed to talk would clam up, or they would blame themselves, never the husband. It was never his fault. He was under too much pressure. He didn't mean to hurt her. I've heard every excuse in the book in my time. And I'll tell you now, no woman deserves to be battered, no matter what the reason."

"We agree with you, Carrie," said Reilly.

"In your opinion, was Jane Carter a battered wife?" asked Gardener.

"Yes. I asked her about the bruises. They were hidden from view, you see, under clothing. That's something else wife beaters do, hit them in places where you're not likely to see it."

"How did she react?"

"Like all battered wives. She made an excuse. She'd fallen from a horse during a lesson."

"And you didn't believe her?"

"No. She was my best friend, the closest thing I had to a sister, and I desperately wanted her to tell me the truth. I did the best thing I could. I supported her and told her that if she ever wanted to talk, I would be there for her, twenty-four seven."

Carrie broke down into tears again. Gardener waited until she had regained her composure. "Did you know anything about the medication she was on?"

"She did tell me about the tablets. She had a terrible accident when she was younger, in the States. Apparently, there was an explosion and she came off a horse. It landed on top of her, causing her severe injuries, particularly to her liver.

"It was so badly damaged that it altered her blood pressure. Apparently, one side of her body had a reduced blood pressure flow. She had life-saving surgery, a pioneering operation that had never been done before. She had some kind of bypass valve fitted to circumvent her failed liver. The downside was the toxins. She reckoned they stayed in her bloodstream, creating real problems. She would have to remain on blood cleansing medication very possibly for the rest of her life. Which was why she was very careful with food and drink."

"Did you ever suspect the bruises were a side effect or a symptom of that?"

Carrie Fletcher snorted and chuckled. "No."

"Do you know if Robbie knew about her condition?"

"I'm not sure. He certainly knew something because one of the side effects was that Jane rarely felt like sex. That was a big problem for Robbie."

"So you think he hit her because their sex life wasn't up to much?"

"Who knows why he hit her."

Gardener waited for Reilly to finish writing. He had learned a lot from Carrie Fletcher. "Do you know if he had any friends or relatives?"

"None that come to mind. I was never introduced to any, and Jane never talked about them. If you're looking for friends of his I would start in the gutter."

"So you have no idea where he might be?"

Carrie Fletcher froze. "You mean *you* haven't got him?"

"No. We held on to him for three days. Questioned him relentlessly. But we had nothing to keep him on. He had a rock-solid alibi. We had to let him go."

"And you've no idea where he is now?"

"I'm afraid not. We went to pick him up last night but we couldn't find him. Have *you* any idea where he might be?"

Carrie Fletcher shook her head and clenched her fists. "No. None at all. I'll be honest with you, I'm not happy about that man being on the loose. I really do not trust him. He's a wife beater and an accomplished liar."

Reilly leaned forward. "He may be, but do you think he's a murderer?"

Carrie Fletcher returned the Irishman's stare, but never answered the question.

Chapter Thirty-one

Patrick Edwards entered the music shop to a grave-like atmosphere. It wasn't unusual for Terry not to have customers, but he always had the radio playing. Not today.

As he glanced around, Terry Jones appeared from the back of the shop and slipped in behind his counter. He was dressed as usual in a white shirt, brown tie, and a stained brown apron. "Thanks for coming, Patrick."

"Call sounded urgent."

"I think it is." To back up the statement, Terry's complexion was unusually pale. The shopkeeper was nervous. His body language spoke volumes. For some reason, Terry Jones was a man under pressure.

"Go on, then," prompted Patrick.

The two had known each other for about eighteen months, pretty much around the time that Patrick had started his own band. The bigger music shops in Leeds were okay, but the bass player in the band said his dad knew the man who ran the music shop in Bursley Bridge personally, and that he would treat them right when it came to buying equipment. "I've had that Robbie one in here."

"Robbie Carter? Today?"

Terry shook his head. "No, yesterday."

"What did he want?"

"His guitar."

"Surely he doesn't think anyone's stupid enough to bring it in here, does he?"

"I'd say he was covering all his bases. He told me his wife had bought it for him, and that it was stolen the night she died."

Patrick nodded. "What else did he say?"

Terry Jones dropped fifty pounds on the counter. "Said that was mine if I came across it and told him first, not the police."

"And you haven't seen him since yesterday?"

"No."

"He hasn't contacted you at all? Not even by phone?"

"No. Why?"

"Have you seen the guitar?" he asked, removing his pad and pen.

Terry Jones swivelled his head in the direction of the back room. "It's in there."

The shopkeeper shuffled out from behind the counter and locked the front door, turning the sign to "Closed". "Come with me," he said.

Patrick followed. Sitting in amongst the equipment was a young man with a terrified expression. He was late teens at a guess, wore a suit jacket, blue T-shirt, and a pair of blue jeans and leather shoes, all good quality. His hair was combed in short back and sides. He was clean-shaven. Patrick caught the aromatic fragrance of a *Lynx* deodorant.

"This is Stephen Whiteley," said Terry Jones. "Stephen, this is a friend of mine, PC Patrick Edwards. I'd like you to tell him everything."

"About what?" Stephen asked, glancing between the two.

"The guitar."

The young man didn't say anything at first. His body language was more worrying than Terry Jones'. Patrick glared back at the shopkeeper, who in turn stared at the youth.

"You have to tell him, Stephen."

The teenager quickly bit one of his nails and shuffled around. "I'm not sure."

"What are you not sure about, Stephen?" asked Patrick.

Stephen glanced at Terry and back at Patrick. "I don't want to get into trouble."

"Have you done something wrong?"

"Yes. No. Oh, Christ." He put his head in his hands. "I don't know."

Patrick Edwards motioned for him to sit down again. The young PC kneeled down in front of Stephen. "Look, why don't you tell me what you've done, and I'll be the best judge."

"Yes, but you can get into all sorts of trouble just for handling stolen goods, can't you? I'd be, like, an accessory."

"Did you know it was stolen?"

"No!" Stephen jumped out of his seat again. "But I'll get into trouble. I just know I will. And then I'll go to prison."

Patrick stood up. "Calm down, Stephen. No one's going to prison. I promise you. If you've bought a stolen guitar in good faith, and you didn't know it was stolen, then we will not prosecute you."

"You won't have to. He'll probably beat the living daylights out of me and there'll be nothing left of me to go to prison."

"Who will?"

"The man I bought it off. Oh, shit!" He threw his arms in the air. "I've said I've bought it now."

Patrick turned to the shopkeeper. "Which one is it?"

Terry Jones pulled a case into view and opened it, revealing a red Stratocaster.

"Is it Robbie Carter's?" Patrick asked.

Terry Jones nodded.

To Stephen, Patrick asked, "And you didn't know it was stolen when you bought it?"

"No."

"Where and when did you buy it?"

Stephen Whiteley had stood up now. He started pacing the small room, kept putting his hands in and out of his pockets. "Tuesday, at work."

"Where at work?"

"It was from one of the lads in the stores."

"It obviously wasn't his. Did he know it was stolen?"

"I don't know."

"What's his name?"

"Brian Parsons."

Patrick had never heard of him. "Where did he get it?"

"I don't think he did. He just said he knew a friend of a friend who was selling a guitar for another friend who had moved to Portugal."

That sentence nearly gave Patrick Edwards a headache. It was growing more complicated by the second. "This friend of a friend wouldn't happen to be called Manny Walters, would he?"

"No," said Stephen. "The bloke who was selling it came to work during my dinner hour. He had a big van with an amp inside so I could test it. I think his name was Baz Ronson."

Patrick had heard of him.

Chapter Thirty-two

Cragg returned the phone to its cradle. "I'm pleased you're back, we've got a problem."

"Another one?" Gardener asked.

"Go on, then," said Reilly. "It'll keep all the others company."

"We need to make a trip out to Bedlam Rocks."

"Where's that?" asked Gardener.

"About as far north as you can get without crossing the border into the North West."

"Love the answer, Maurice, but I'm still none the wiser," chipped in Reilly.

Cragg rose from the chair and shuffled into the incident room, drawing Gardener's attention to the map on the wall, and pointed.

Gardener rolled his eyes. "I'm guessing this has something to do with our investigation?"

"Not sure," Cragg replied. "A young couple hunting for buried treasure stayed the night because he'd detected something. Started work first thing this morning and discovered a body."

"When?"

"About seven o'clock. He did the right thing, called the police. A North Yorkshire team went out. They called Fitz, he's called us."

"Why?"

"He said to trust him."

That was the one sentence Gardener did not want to hear. His stomach rumbled again as if to remind him that he may not be able to go much longer without food. He checked his watch. "How long will it take to get there?"

"If I come with you, about an hour," said Cragg.

"If you don't?" asked Reilly.

"You might not be back this side of Christmas. Maybe you can fill me in on the way about how you got on with Carrie Fletcher, assuming you found her?"

Gardener nodded. "Phone Fitz back, tell him we're on our way."

* * *

Fifteen minutes later, following a drink and a sandwich, Gardener grabbed another PC from the Bramfield team and the four of them hit the road. The weather grew steadily worse. There had been some blue sky when they set off; upon reaching Bedlam Rocks, it was stark grey, a wind had reared, and the temperature had dropped at least three degrees.

Reilly parked the pool car in a clearing, and as they approached on foot, Gardener saw two more police cars, the vehicle Fitz used, and an ambulance.

The area was pretty bleak, with only two trees and a selection of different shaped rocks. Gardener could not tell what the trees were. Two rock faces closed in on either side to an opening of around eight feet, known locally as Hangman's Bluff according to Cragg. Standing guard in front of the crime scene tape was a uniformed PC. He held a log sheet in his hand.

Gardener displayed his warrant card, signed the sheet, and the three men advanced.

Through the opening, another rock face appeared with a cave entrance. A little way to the left, sitting on a boulder, wrapped in a blanket, a man sipped a drink from a flask cup. His expression was ashen. In his other hand he held an inhaler. A woman had her arm around his shoulder, talking softly to him.

"What's up with him?" Reilly asked.

"He made the discovery," replied Fitz.

In the middle, a marquee had been erected around what Gardener assumed was the burial place of whoever they'd found.

"Have you examined the body yet?" Reilly asked.

"As best I can," replied Fitz as he approached.

"What can you tell us about it, and how long has it been there?" asked Gardener.

"I think you should come and have a look. There's something I want to show you."

Gardener followed Fitz past another constable and into the tent, with Reilly and Cragg behind him. He nodded to the men in the paper suits carefully examining what was left of the body. Behind them was a police photographer.

"The man who found it is called Ross Johnson," continued Fitz. "He and his girlfriend were in the area treasure hunting. They stayed the night last night because his metal detector resembled the Northern Lights when he was searching the site. Thought he'd come across something valuable.

"He dug the hole, and eventually pulled out a bone. He dropped it and called us. He's a bit shook up. I've called a forensic archaeologist in."

Gardener stooped down and peered into the recess. What he could see of the flesh – which was really only the head – had mummified. The skin was tanned, like leather. A portion of the skull was showing, and the head still had some hair. The arms laid out by the side of the body were mostly bone with little flesh; some clothing remained.

"It's too neat for a walker to have fallen in and just died there for whatever reason," said Cragg.

"That's what I was thinking," said Gardener.

"It's been placed," said Reilly.

The whole middle section was skeleton, but the legs were partially clothed. The smell wasn't as bad as he would have expected.

"It's a fairly modern burial," said Reilly.

"And it's outside a graveyard," said Gardener. "Which suggests it's a crime."

"Is it male or female?" Reilly asked.

"Female," replied Fitz.

"How long would you say it's been here?"

"Best guess? Twenty, maybe twenty-five years. You asked me what was bothering me. I won't be able to tell you anything until I've examined it properly but there appears to be some serious damage to the pelvic area."

"What are you trying to say, Fitz?" asked Gardener, straightening up.

"It could be a coincidence..."

"We don't believe in those," quickly interrupted Reilly.

Fitz nodded in agreement. "I thought it might be worth mentioning that you already have another victim with very similar injuries."

The men in paper suits continued to brush the skeleton very carefully, stopping every so often to bag what they thought might be evidence.

Gardener spotted something. The left hand of the skeleton was closed up, the fingers gripping a silver object. Using gloves, Gardener reached into the grave and carefully teased out the item from the ossified digits; a solid silver, heart-shaped pendant on a chain. He turned it over. On the reverse, he read the inscription.

For my Mum, J
Love you forever, G

Gardener passed the pendant to his sergeant. "So who the hell is she?" asked Reilly.

"And how did she end up here?" asked Cragg.

"Finding out who she is will be a nightmare," said Gardener. "We'll need dental records, possible DNA samples from the bones. We'll need to check the missing persons file." He ran his hands over his face, wondering where to start.

He turned and asked the young constable who had come with them – and whose name he had not yet discovered – to take notes for the incident room back at the station. "We're going to need an entomologist to give us some idea of how long it's been in the ground."

"I doubt bugs are gonna help us much in this case," said Reilly. "Especially if it's been here as long as Fitz thinks."

"I agree, Sean, but we've got to start somewhere."

Gardener addressed Fitz. "We'll need a bone specialist, someone who can extract bone DNA."

"I think we should be able to get the bones dated," offered the Home Office Pathologist. "Might get a good idea then how old the skeleton is."

"And how old she was when she was stuck in there," said Reilly.

"And I'd like the soil sifted from ground level to two feet below the body," said Gardener. "There could be anything in there, fingernails, hair… anything."

"There's a bunch of weird little experts out there that can have a look at this site," said Reilly. "Tell us if the killer had special knowledge in locating and digging these things."

"Weird little experts," repeated Gardener.

"Come on, boss, you know what those people are like. You can't do what they do and be classed as normal."

Gardener glanced at the pendant as Reilly handed it back, studying the message. He could do with another weird little expert right now, to answer three more not so weird little questions: who's J; who's G? And what connection could it possibly have to his case?

Chapter Thirty-three

Manny was back in town. He'd had enough of living in someone else's gaff, especially when it belonged to Stitch. Manny wasn't known for his cleanliness. God knows Mary would attest to that. But Stitch was a fucking health hazard.

He was sitting on a bench, opposite the travel agent on the high street in Bursley Bridge, wearing a pair of working overalls and a fluorescent jacket. To his right he had his clipboard, to his left a discarded McDonald's bag that had held three Big Macs, two McFlurrys and two Red Bulls, all of which had now gone. He laughed at the thought that most nights he took a tin of baked beans, a spoon, and a tin opener to bed with him.

He glanced furtively up and down the high street before checking his watch. It was twelve-thirty. The main street was pretty quiet. The day had started off okay – blue sky, a few clouds. Now it had done what it always did: grown overcast and cold.

Right! Now or never. He picked up the clipboard and the false identity card, looping it around his neck. People were stupid. They didn't check things. No one would ask him if they could inspect the card more closely. He walked briskly and firmly toward the travel agent, leaving his shit on the bench.

He knew that the place was manned by two women; he'd seen one of them go for dinner, so it was easy pickings as far as he was concerned. In and out within five minutes, a wad full of cash if he was lucky; if not, at least he would have a credit card to play with for a while. All thanks to Stitch.

He opened the door, stepped inside. The place was spotless, smelled fresh. Two desks, wooden flooring. A number of potted plants decorated the room. On the window ledge a small radio quietly pumped out pop music. He thought the place was empty until one of the women came into view with a glass of water.

"Can I help you?" She stared at Manny as if he was something she'd stepped in. Snooty cow. He'd teach her a thing or two before the day was out.

He peered at her nameplate. "Miss Bunting?"

"Yes."

"I'm from Northern Fire." He held the identity card aloft, waved it around so she couldn't fix on it.

"And?"

And? What the fuck was that supposed to mean? Her attitude matched her appearance; black hair severely pinned back, piercing blue eyes, and a figure a rugby player would be proud of. Her dress sense was pretty butch as well: plain grey trouser suit and brown brogues. "I'm here to check your fire extinguishers."

"Says who?"

"It's the law," said Manny.

"What is?"

Fucking hell, she was making it hard. Still, when he was through the starting gate, he'd take the snooty bitch for everything. That would teach her.

"I've already told you."

"I beg to differ. You've said plenty, but none of it means anything. You're here to check the fire extinguishers and you say it's the law. So, what, have the police sent you?"

"No. My company has sent me. Every business has to have fire extinguishers, and they need checking every three years to comply with regulations."

Manny thought he'd handled that well. Word for word he'd said exactly what Stitch had told him. He should know. It worked every time for him.

"So your company have sent a letter to my head office to inform them that my fire extinguishers need checking?"

"I expect so," replied Manny. "But I don't get to see those. I just get my instructions, which tells me today that I have to come and inspect yours."

"And you're from Northern Fire?" asked Bunting.

Manny sighed. Was she completely thick or something? Perhaps if he was a bit tougher with her, she'd back down.

"Can I see your identity?"

He held it upwards but she was still standing behind her desk, somewhere in the region of six feet away. "What? You think I can see that from here?"

He could have a problem now. She wanted it on the end of her nose. Manny walked forward. As he did so, she reached into a desk drawer and drew out a pair of glasses, slipping them on.

As he stood there with the card in his hand, she surprised him.

"Take it off."

"Pardon?"

"I said, take it off. I need to look at it."

Manny wasn't keen. Stitch said it was simple, in and out. No one checked. Who the fuck did she work for, the KGB? He had to comply, so he held it out.

"Put it on the desk."

"The desk?"

"Yes, the desk. The big wooden thing. You know what a desk is, don't you?"

"Look, love–"

She stopped him in his tracks. "I'm not your love, now please put it on the desk so I can examine it properly."

She glanced behind her. "The fire extinguisher is through there."

Manny was surprised. "You want me to go through and inspect it?"

"No. I'd like you to go through and eat it. What do you think?"

"Pardon me for breathing." Manny lined up some more sarcasm. Instead, he held his tongue and slipped into the back. At last, the whole reason for being here.

The area was a small kitchen. Like the other room it was spotless, with tiled walls and floor. All electrical appliances had been PAT tested, and bore the labels. Half a dozen cups were suspended on hooks from a cupboard; tea, sugar and coffee in their own jars. The fire extinguisher was on the wall.

Ignoring that, Manny quickly checked all the small cupboards. He found nothing of interest. In the corner near the back door of the premises was another cupboard – a large one. He opened that and struck gold. On one shelf was a black leather handbag. Inside was a set of keys, perfume, a deodorant, items of personal hygiene and a purse – the very thing he was after.

He glanced behind him. Miss Snooty Tits hadn't come to find him, so he unzipped the purse. He found fifty quid and three credit cards, all major high street banks. Perfect. He pocketed the money and the cards, zipped up the purse, put it back in the handbag, threw that back on the shelf. Only, it fell on the floor and made a clattering sound because it hit the pedal bin on the way.

Manny jumped. "Shit, shit, shit."

"Lost something?"

Only the contents of my arse, thought Manny, staring in the direction of the voice. "Sorry?"

"I said have you lost something?"

Manny stared at the bag on the floor and then back at Miss Bunting.

"It fell on the floor."

"I can see that. I'm wondering why."

Manny tried to think his way out of the situation. The key was in the back door, but it was probably locked to keep out thieves.

"Correct me if I'm wrong, but that on the floor" – she pointed – "is my handbag. That there, on the wall" – she pointed again – "is the fire extinguisher. Am I wrong, or am I right?"

Manny had to leave. He'd been busted. The only way forward was through the door she was blocking.

"Cat got your tongue?" she asked.

She was only a woman. Be no problem decking her and pushing past, thought Manny, rushing forward.

It was the last thought he had before his world crumbled along with his vision, leaving him surrounded by total darkness.

Chapter Thirty-four

Twenty-four hours after skewering Wilson to a pub table, Robbie Carter was back in Carpenter's Yard. If the police were not going to do anything about the situation, he was.

He'd kept busy by putting together a list of the things he needed to sort out. He wanted his guitar back, not to mention the money he had earned that night.

He also wanted whatever had been taken from his music collection. All his vinyl, CDs and DVDs were missing. It had taken him years to collect some of the Glam Rock material, particularly the Slade stuff. Whoever had stolen his property was either very lucky or they knew precisely what they wanted – in particular, a piece of history tucked away at the back of the shelves in the cupboard.

Back in 1964, drummer Don Powell and guitarist Dave Hill were part of a Midland-based group called the Vendors. They appeared regularly on the club circuit, and at the time had recorded a privately pressed four-track EP. Noddy Holder wasn't with them. In today's money that pressing was worth a fortune. Robbie had a copy of that EP. Not anymore.

More importantly, it was imperative he retrieved the cameras. When he finally caught up with Manny Walters, the little bastard would never take anything that didn't belong to him ever again.

Robbie had kept an eye on Carpenter's Yard most of the previous evening and had arrived a little over an hour ago. There had been no sign whatsoever of the little toerag.

The entrance to the yard was set back between two shops, encompassing two flats – one of which belonged to the thief's so-called girlfriend. Though what Manny had done to deserve her, Robbie didn't know. There were two garages. A VW Beetle was parked outside of one of them.

That might come in handy. A number of potted plants decorated the area.

Robbie's watch showed two-thirty. The cretin would have to show at some point but there was every possibility that Robbie would need to provide an incentive for that.

He walked into the yard and up to Manny's front door. He knocked but figured it would be useless, so he tried the handle as well. Still locked, and as he'd thought, there was no answer.

Robbie sat on the wooden bench in front of the flat. Had it been yesterday when the weather was wonderful it would have been more than pleasant. Today was a total pile of shite. It was grey and cold and a fair old wind was battering the place.

Robbie checked his new burner. No missed calls, no text messages. To be fair, only a handful of people had the number. Most of those were contacts. They obviously hadn't seen the little parasite.

The door across the yard suddenly opened. Mary exited her place, waddling toward him.

What a sight, thought Robbie. She was definitely a few pounds heavier than was good for her. Mary's shoulder-length brown hair was tied back in a ponytail. She wore a beige dress with a light brown cardigan and a pair of shoes even her mother would have been embarrassed to die in.

"Can I help you?" she asked, standing about two feet away with her hands on her hips.

"I'm looking for Manny Walters," replied Robbie. "Is this the right place?"

"Manfred? Does he know you?"

"He will when I find him."

Mary folded her arms and stood with her legs slightly apart. "What does that mean?"

Robbie smiled. "Can you tell me where he is?"

"He's away at the moment."

"How convenient," muttered Robbie. "Any idea where?"

"I'm afraid I don't know?"

He'd grown tired of trying to find the little warthog. His absence was really beginning to irritate Robbie, to the point of distraction. He figured his best course of action was to take charge of the situation: it was the only way if you wanted results. "I think you do, Mary."

If her expression was anything to go by, she had soiled her pants with that sentence.

"How do you know my name?"

"I know quite a lot about you... Mary."

"I don't think I like your tone."

"You'll get used to it."

Her hands went back to her hips. "What did you say your name was again?"

"I didn't."

"Would you like to tell me what business you have with Manfred?"

"Manfred, is it?" Robbie stood up and approached Mary. To give her some credit, she didn't back away, which only served to make life easier for him. "I'm surprised at you, Mary."

She hesitated before answering. Her confidence was leaving her. "Surprised? What do you mean?"

"You look like a nice lady to me. You're clean, well dressed. You speak pleasantly. Why the hell are you mixed up with a scabby little shit like him?"

Another sentence that had knocked the wind out of her. She took a step back, glancing behind her. She turned back to Robbie, smiling. "I'm sorry, I'm afraid I have to be somewhere."

"Oh, yes, silly me. Your mother... in the care home."

Mary was so horrified, Robbie almost laughed. Instead, he leaned forward. "Don't you go worrying about your mother, Mary. She's in the best place."

Bravado had the better of her because she stepped forward. "Who are you?"

Robbie didn't answer the question.

Chapter Thirty-five

The waiting room was like most: large and clinical, with a receptionist fielding more calls than a call centre. Not to mention the fact that it was half full of ill people; two were coughing and sneezing, two were extremely pale. The remaining two were a mother and her daughter.

"What are you hoping for with Dr Travers?" Gardener glanced at his partner. They were sitting in the farthest corner of the room, nearest the doctor's door, well away from anyone with anything infectious.

"I'm not sure, Sean. I'll settle for whatever he can tell us. This has to be one of the strangest cases we've worked. Twenty-four hours ago everyone we wanted to speak to had disappeared."

"Well, at least we struck lucky with the thief, Walters."

Gardener and Reilly had been informed that a Paula Bunting from the travel agency in Bursley Bridge had called the police, and the two constables attending the scene had found Manny Walters out cold on the kitchen floor where she had left him. She explained what had happened, and that when confronted, Manny Walters had rushed forward in a threatening manner. Luckily, she had studied self-defence, and had reversed the positions in no time at all, causing Manny to have a nasty confrontation with a door frame. Manny was back at the station in a cell, nursing the mother of all hangovers without him having taken a drink.

"Didn't we! Wonder what made him surface?" As yet, neither Gardener nor Reilly had actually laid eyes on him.

"I doubt it was bravery," said Reilly. "He's a few peas short of a casserole, that lad."

"We're now in the position of having two out of three people and the elusive guitar, so where does that leave us?"

"Back at square one. Maybe Robbie Carter was telling the truth. The guitar *was* stolen."

"If that's the case, why disappear?"

"Because it's not the truth, the whole truth, and nothing but the truth," replied Reilly. "But he does have an alibi. And he may not have disappeared voluntarily."

The door opened, and Doctor Travers appeared. He was short and dumpy, dressed in an ill-fitting suit, wore glasses with thick lenses, and most of his patients were in better health if appearances were anything to go by.

"Mr Gardener, Mr Reilly?" Both men stood, producing their warrant cards. Travers nodded. "Please follow me."

Once in the office, each man took a seat and Travers said, "Okay, let's cut to the chase. You want me to tell you about a procedure called the Sano Shunt."

"That's the blood pressure pump?" asked Gardener.

"Yes, sir. Jane Carter did not have the Sano Shunt; she had the Sano procedure. The way this works is that the operation serves to make the right ventricle the main pumping chamber for blood flow to the body. The aorta is made larger to increase blood flow. A connection is made to enable the blood travelling through the aorta towards the body to 'shunt' through this connection, and flow into the pulmonary artery to receive oxygen.

"This may be accomplished with a modified Blalock-Taussig shunt, which is a small tube placed between the aorta and the pulmonary arteries, or by using the Sano modification procedure, in which a homograft conduit is placed between the right ventricle and the pulmonary arteries. The choice of which procedure is best is usually discussed with your cardiologist."

Gardener appreciated the information Travers was giving them but it did nothing to move his case along, leaving him frustrated.

"Thank you, Dr Travers."

Chapter Thirty-six

Gardener stood in front of the whiteboard with a pen in one hand and a bottle of water in the other. The tea urn and the snacks were on the side table, but he had no interest in food. He couldn't remember when he last had a case as tough as the current one.

"Thanks, guys," he said, turning to face them. "I appreciate the effort you're all putting in."

"Just wish we could get somewhere, chief," said Bob Anderson.

"Wait till you hear what we've got to say," added Reilly.

"Have we found Robbie Carter?" asked Rawson.

"No," replied Gardener. "But we have made a breakthrough today, starting with Carrie Fletcher."

"She's alive, then?" asked Sarah Gates.

"Yes, she's been staying with her sister in Skipton for a few days."

Gardener continued by outlining what they had learned from Carrie Fletcher, finishing with her discovery of the bruising on her friend's body.

"And she thinks it was him?" asked Emma Longstaff.

"She's convinced," replied Gardener. "She spent a lot of time at a women's refuge and she knew the signs when she saw them."

"Why didn't she do something about it?"

"What could she do?" asked Reilly.

"She could have reported it to the police," said Longstaff.

"That probably wouldn't have achieved anything, Emma," said Gardener. "It would have been Carrie Fletcher's word against Robbie Carter's, and it's very unlikely that a wife would have gone against her husband."

"Why not?"

"Had she been so minded, she would have reported it herself," said Reilly.

"Anyway," said Gardener. "We were really pleased to find Carrie Fletcher, and she's given us more to think about." He added his notes to the board before turning to address his men again. "So, before I continue, does anyone have anything to report on the man himself?"

"I'm no further on, sir," said Colin Sharp. "I've checked the electoral roll, which only goes to confirm when he moved into the area. He's been here four years, but I can't find anything previous to that. Well, not strictly true, I can find lots of Robbie Carters, but none of them are ours."

"Is it possible he changed his identity before coming here?" asked Rawson.

"That's a very good point, Dave," said Gardener. "And one we have to consider. All of this is assuming that Robbie Carter is the killer," said Gardener. "But he may not be. I thought you'd all like to know that Manny Walters is locked up in a cell as we speak."

A collective "nice one" was voiced from the team.

"How did we get him?" Rawson asked.

Cragg laughed. "He were up to no good, as usual." With Mike Atherton's help, he explained the incident with the fire extinguishers.

The team erupted with laughter.

"Have you interviewed him yet, sir?" asked Patrick Edwards.

"No," said Gardener. "We haven't stopped today, but letting him stew won't hurt. Maybe you want to tell them about your discovery, Patrick."

"There's more?" asked Anderson.

"Maybe things are looking up after all," said Gates.

"I got a call from the man at the music shop this morning, about a red Strat a young lad had just bought. To cut a long story short he bought it from Baz Ronson, didn't know it was stolen. We picked Ronson up this afternoon. He squealed the minute he realised it was part of a murder investigation. He bought it from Manny Walters, so that ties that bit up nicely."

"Are we sure it's Robbie Carter's?"

"Yes," said Edwards. "He'd been in the shop the day before, offering Terry Jones fifty quid if it turned up to tell him first, not us."

"Which means he isn't missing," added Reilly.

"But he must be desperate for that guitar," said Rawson.

"Why?" Benson asked. "Is it a decent bit of kit then, Patrick?"

"It looks old and well used, but according to Terry Jones, the neck is warped."

"Has he any idea why?" asked Reilly.

"Not really. He can only think that it's took a bit of a blow at some time."

"How does a guitar take a blow?" asked Rawson. "It's not the kind of thing you swing around or knock into walls, is it?"

"Depends who you are, son," said Reilly. "I remember years ago when The Who used to finish concerts by destroying their gear, smashing it up on stage. But it wasn't the real top stuff. They all used to come on for an encore with cheap instruments, and smash 'em up to get themselves noticed."

"Can you have another word with Terry Jones, Patrick?" asked Gardener. "Get him to check the guitar more closely, see if he can offer any explanation on the damage?"

"Will do, sir."

Gardener added further actions to the charts. Before he'd finished, the door opened and Fitz entered, waving a manila folder around. "I have those results you asked for on this morning's body."

"Body," asked Gates. "What body?"

"We were just coming to that," said Gardener. Nodding to Fitz, he asked the pathologist to continue.

"Once I had a line on a possible identification – and further information from Maurice here, I had them fast track the dental records to me. The lady in the ground is definitely Jane Browne."

"Thank you, Fitz. That gives us another line of enquiry."

Gardener knew his team was confused. He had not had time to discuss the body.

"I have found something else very interesting. She has three broken ribs and suffered severe trauma in the pelvic area, judging by what I can see."

Gardener noted the concerned expressions of most of his team. Tensions rose. They had to be thinking along similar lines to him: another body with similar injuries to the first – also called Jane. What exactly was going on here? "Any ideas on the cause?" he asked Fitz.

The pathologist raised his hands in defeat. "She was hit with, or by, something heavy."

"Thank you, Fitz," he said, waving the folder. "Much appreciated."

Fitz nodded. "Well, gentlemen, I've done what I came to do, so I'll leave you to your detecting. My wife assures me I have a home-made steak pie waiting for me, and a nice bottle of Merlot."

"Any more comments like that, old son, and you might not make it home."

"That's right, Fitz," said Anderson. "But don't you worry about your pie because we know where you live."

Everyone chuckled as Fitz left.

Gardener took them through the trip to Bedlam Rocks, and what they had found.

"What're the chances of that?" asked Colin Sharp. "Both women being called Jane?"

"That crossed my mind as well," said Gardener. "And I'm left wondering how many more coincidences we're going to find before two and two start to add up to four like they should. Anyway, I believe Maurice has some information about her for us. He's just spent the last two hours on the phone."

Gardener stepped aside to allow the desk sergeant to take over. He opened the manila envelope and placed the photographs of the buried body on the charts.

"So what happened to Jane Browne, Maurice?" asked Anderson. "How did she end up buried on the moors?"

"We're not sure. I've only had a couple of hours to make sense of any of this but I've spoken to the police in the North West and the North East. Seems Jane Browne went missing in the nineties. She was married to a man called Raymond Culver. They went away for the weekend, camping – presumably they ended up somewhere near Bedlam Rocks.

"Raymond eventually returned home alone. He acted withdrawn, said his wife had left him and he couldn't go on. Grace, the daughter, reported it to the police and they questioned Raymond but said they had nothing on him, nor did they suspect him of any foul play. He were blaming the daughter for making up stories. He'd said at the time he had no idea why because they'd always got on," Cragg said.

"So the wife just upped and left, and the daughter never heard from her again?" asked Anderson.

"According to the people I've spoken to, but like I said, I've only got the basics on this. We'll need someone checking it all out."

"Doesn't sound right, does it?" said Gates. "I can accept that the mother would want nothing more to do with the husband, but would she leave her own daughter?"

"Did you get a last known address, Maurice?" asked Gardener.

"Yes. Might not be much use."

"Maybe not, but at least it's a starting point. The daughter might still live there, or somewhere in the area."

"Aye," said Cragg. "And people have long memories. They'll remember this so we might strike lucky."

"Okay," said Gardener. "Colin, first thing in the morning I'd like you up in Billingham. Report to the local police station and find out everything you can. Dave, you go into the North West, to Brough. See what you can find about that incident. I know it's a while back but there's bound to be some records worth chasing."

"Like Maurice says, people have long memories," added Reilly. "There's bound to be an old lag on the team who was around at the time."

"Like me, you mean?" asked Cragg.

"I wasn't thinking that old," added Reilly.

"Do you honestly think there's a connection, sir?" Rawson asked Gardener.

"I don't know, Dave. It seems very coincidental. My gut feeling tells me something is amiss. I'm going to stick my neck out here and tell you that I don't think Manny Walters is responsible for the carnage. I still feel that Robbie Carter is the number one suspect, which is why I'm going all out on it. I'd also like you two to take a photograph of Robbie Carter with you. Show it around. With everything we've heard, it's just possible we're talking about the same man being responsible for both murders."

Gardener nodded to one of the HOLMES team. "From you, I want to know the deaths of every woman called Jane who has died in suspicious circumstances over the last thirty years."

"Pardon?"

Gardener held his hands up. "I know it's a long shot, and that HOLMES probably doesn't go that far back, but sometimes you have to think outside the box."

"I'll give it a go," said the HOLMES tech. "I don't hold out much hope."

Gardener nodded. He glanced at Emma Longstaff. "You get anywhere with the dating sites?"

"There's a lot of them, sir, be nice if we knew if he had a favourite."

"We can help you there," said Reilly.

"Christ," said Anderson. "You two are full of it today."

"*Findadate.com*," said Gardener. "Carrie Fletcher told us that's how they met. She herself uses the website. She persuaded Jane Carter to join. Eventually, Jane Carter received regular emails from someone wanting a date. It was set up but he never showed, and subsequently disappeared without trace – she never received another message."

"What happened?" asked Edwards.

"She turned up for the date. No one showed. She was about to leave when she bumped into Robbie Carter."

Reilly took up the story. "Ironically, the same thing had happened to him: his date had not shown, so they had a drink, a bite to eat, and the rest is history."

"So is *she* now."

"So, tomorrow, I'd like you digging around on that site if you can, Emma. We need to try and maximise the intelligence product. See if we can lift all known ID's and run open and closed source checks. If we do find anything, we should try to trace and interview all the girls he's made contact with."

"Do you think they're at risk, sir?"

"Who knows with this man, but we can't treat it lightly. Finding him has become the top priority. If we think he's going to kill one of them, we'll have to look at a safety plan for each."

"Can we force the company to provide personal information?" asked Edwards.

"Probably," said Gardener. "Best bet might be to email them an authorised data protection act form stating that we're investigating a serious offence and the info requested was for the prevention and/or detection of serious crime. Most companies in receipt of one of these will probably fold and give us everything."

Longstaff and Edwards made notes.

"The rest of you, I want you all to concentrate on the man himself. It's a manhunt: he's our number one priority. Is he innocent? Or is he guilty?

"If he's innocent, why has he disappeared? Maybe it's as Sean said. Someone else might be behind all of this. Robbie Carter may not have fled – he might actually be fighting for his life at this moment.

"If he's guilty and he hasn't fled, what the hell is keeping him here? The guitar? Why? What's so special about that guitar? Maybe we'll find out, because we have it. Is he still around because he didn't kill his wife but he knows who has, and wants revenge? We have the advantage over him there because we have Manny Walters, probably the number one suspect in Robbie's eyes. So he might consider it worth the risk waiting around to claim what's his.

"Which brings us back to a point made by more than one person earlier: the change of identity. Assume for one minute that the body buried on the moors is a victim of Robbie Carter's. Then he's been doing this one hell of a long time. That's a big problem for us. How is he doing it? How has he remained at large and undetected for so long?"

"Why is he doing it?"

"Find the answer to that and we may find out how," said Gardener. "Our number one priority is to find Robbie Carter. God forbid we should let this man slip the net.

"All of this ties in with something else that's been pointed out. If he is still here, why has no one seen him? Maybe it's because he's changed his identity. If he's innocent and not dangerous, then maybe he's in danger. If he's guilty and dangerous, he may just be the worst serial killer in history, and he's on our patch. We cannot let him walk again. I want another media blitz and I also want you guys to do what you do best. Concentrate your efforts on finding him."

Chapter Thirty-seven

Grace Browne, aka Jane Rogers, glanced around. Her ears were ringing. When did she grow old?

Ten-thirty on a Thursday evening, Silhouettes was bouncing. She couldn't remember the last nightclub she'd been in, but very little had changed. It was all leather seating, uncomfortable round stools, balconies. The walls were full of speakers and spotlights, with private booths. She'd been upstairs – all hush-hush with its tiled floor, black columns, secluded seating in front of arched windows, all of which she was convinced hid a number of offences. Sex, drugs and rock 'n' roll. People talked in corners under low-level lighting; the women wore short skirts; the men were drooling, hoping to pull them. She'd rather be elsewhere, but she hadn't spent more than half her life chasing a rainbow to back out now.

Earlier in the day she'd left work, showered, pampered herself before leaving the flat. She'd spotted the man she wanted, boarding a bus into Leeds, which she managed to catch before it set off. She'd followed him all around town. He'd eaten at The Orchid Lounge, before leaving and walking up The Calls, on to Crown Street. Grace followed, even though it was the last place in the world to be wandering around after dark. She didn't care.

Around the back of The Corn Exchange, he'd finally slipped into the nightclub.

Grace went to the toilet. When she returned, she couldn't believe her luck. Critchley was standing at the bar, next to her stool. She took a sip of her Baileys. He ordered a glass of red, before glancing in her direction while waiting for his drink.

Inwardly, she grinned. He had no idea who she was. Naturally, she did not resemble her photo on *Findadate*. Gone was the black hair in a bob, replaced by a blonde wig. She wore glasses and heavy make-up. Not his type in the slightest.

He'd also altered his appearance considerably; he was nothing like the photos he'd been using on the dating site. He'd cut his hair a little shorter, tinted it grey, and wore a pair of wire-rimmed spectacles.

"You don't look old enough to enjoy this stuff," he said, leaning in.

"I'm not. What is it?" she replied.

"Music for the soul, love, that's what it is."

She'd hooked him. He leaned further forward. She was close enough to inhale his favourite cologne, *Brut 33*. God, people still wore that stuff! Her skin crawled.

"A good decade for music, this," he shouted. "Forget the sixties, the Beatles and the Merseybeat sound. This is all you need."

"If you say so."

"What are you doing here if you don't know this stuff?"

She stood up quickly, knocking into Critchley, dropping her purse. They both went down to pick it up. She stopped, allowed him some chivalry. Her action was deliberate. She quickly managed to slip a pound coin into his back pocket. Not an ordinary one. She bought it recently on the Net. It had a tracking device.

He stood up and held out her purse.

"Thank you," she replied, reaching out, thoroughly disgusted that she had to take it from his hand. Wondering when he'd last washed it. "I'm meeting someone."

"Me, too," shouted Critchley, as his drink was placed on the bar. He paid and then took a sip. "Well, I hope she turns up."

Jane simply nodded as he made his way upstairs. It was obviously a good vantage point, but she doubted he would see much with all the flashing lights that had started. Mind, he wasn't going to see anything at all. She knew that. She also wondered how he would react later in the evening.

Furthermore, what would his reaction be when she finally confronted him? Grace couldn't wait for that day. Her thoughts wandered, once again, back to a point where she had really closed in on him, and discovered yet more victims.

The fourth had taken her completely across the country to Whitehaven, Lancashire. Her name was Jane Sullivan. She was his type – long black hair, blue eyes. They met at a caravan site on the coast near Cumbria. His name was Rupert Conway. Jane Sullivan was forty-one, single, no children, no family. She'd been left a tidy sum by her late husband Steven. She had ploughed that into a pub. Rupert had eventually moved in with her. He'd been living in Whitehaven in a small bedsit above a high street shop and working one night a week in the pub.

Things, as usual, must have gone wrong.

In the early hours one morning, an explosion in the cellar nearly blew the pub apart. He was injured severely enough to land up in hospital. Jane Sullivan died. Once out of hospital, he disappeared. The trail would have gone cold but for one elderly local who happened to make a comment that the fair was in town that week, and Rupert had been seen talking to the owner quite a lot. How ironic that when the fair left town, so did he.

So Grace had set to work again. She consulted the association of travelling fairs, which had kept scant records of all showground movement and travellers. It wasn't an easy job because they moved around so much and people joined and left so easily, there was no guarantee that the person she was searching for would be there.

In 2008, however, she discovered a man by the name of Roland Curtis who had drifted into the seaside town of Llandudno. When the fair left, he didn't. Roland started seeing a woman by the name of Jane Jenkins. She lived in the small village of Betws-y-Coed, North Wales. He was residing in the seaside resort of Llandudno, working as a deck chair attendant. The dating website was once again the link.

Jane Jenkins had never been married, never had children. Her only family was an aged mother and a sister; they took it in turns to care for their mother. She was a state registered nurse and travelled the area extensively caring for old people. She had a round in which she dropped in on most of them every day, and tended to organise a meals-on-wheels schedule for them. She was his type.

He eventually moved in with her and found work with a local carpenter. Once again, the relationship hit the rocks. Jane Jenkins was an asthmatic. No one had seen her for quite some time, but the news suddenly came out that she had died from a massive stroke. They'd heard that he'd called for an ambulance. There was nothing the doctors could do. Immediate family were informed. Everyone sympathised with Roland, reckoned it was the loss of her mother that brought it on. Within weeks he had left town.

Grace returned to the present as a drink was put in front of her. She stared at the barman. "I didn't order this."

"No, he did."

"Who?"

The barman glanced to his right. "Oh, sorry, he's gone."

A voice behind her said, "Me."

She turned. Standing before her was very obviously an out-of-town businessman. His dark hair had a hint of grey around the temples, with George Michael designer stubble. The open black shirt he wore was a size too small. The usual gold medallion and chain swung loosely in the black bush of chest hair. The trousers were definitely a waist size smaller than they should be.

"Nigel," he said, offering his hand.

She didn't take it, nor had she picked up the glass that had been put near her. When she'd arrived, she'd ordered a

Baileys, and would only accept it from the barman after she'd requested he wash the glass in front of her.

Nigel lowered his hand. "Do you come here often?" he shouted.

She stole a glance at Critchley. He was leaning over the balcony, staring into the crowd. "Never," she replied. "Which is probably more often than you."

He wasn't put off, and for the next half hour he tried his best to ply her with drinks, slobbering over her with his life story. It was the usual shit: boring job, working long hours, away from home, his wife didn't understand him.

"She has my sympathy."

"Pardon?" he shouted.

"I said I'm sorry."

"Her loss."

"I somehow doubt that," she replied. Another comment he never heard.

The volume of the music had notched up somewhat; they were now resorting to shouting, which Grace wouldn't tolerate much longer. She'd achieved what she came here to do. She glanced over at Critchley, who constantly checked his watch – his expression growing more miserable by the minute.

"What say we move on, sweetheart?" said Nigel. "Go and find somewhere more comfortable."

"Sorry?" replied Grace, still glancing in Critchley's direction, before staring at Nigel. "Are you still here?"

"I said–"

Grace held her hand up. "I know what you said, Nigel, but you're obviously not very good at reading body language, or taking the odd hint, so perhaps I should spell it out for you."

"Pardon?" he shouted, leaning in much closer than Grace would normally have allowed.

She backed away, as far as the bar would allow her, before slipping sideways and creating more room for herself. As she did so she noticed that Critchley had disappeared.

Nigel was about to speak but Grace cut him off. "If you continue to harass me, Nigel, there's only one place more comfortable that you'll be going."

His expression changed to one of mock disappointment before he smiled and asked, "Where might that be, sweetheart?"

"The morgue, Nigel."

Grace placed her glass on the bar, noticing the barman smirking.

She turned to Nigel. "Now if you'll excuse me I have a much more pressing engagement."

Grace pushed her way through the crowd and bolted down the stairs. At the bottom, she saw Critchley slip out of the front door toward a taxi rank. There were two in line. He caught the first.

She ran to the second, jumping in. "Oh my God," she shouted.

"What's up, love?" said the Asian cabbie.

"Quickly, please, follow that cab."

"What do you think this is, love, *The Italian Job*?"

"I'm serious. My husband is in that cab and he's really unwell. He's going home for his medication, only, he hasn't got the house keys. I have."

The cab driver's expression said he wasn't sure.

"For God's sake, hurry up. He might bloody well die if we hang around much longer."

Any doubts were quickly washed away when she stuffed one hundred pounds in his hands. They set off at the speed of light, and fifteen minutes later, the taxi in front pulled into a long drive that had a mill house at the end, in Sowerby. She had the driver stop so she could jump out.

"Is everything going to be okay, love?"

"Yes, thank you."

"What about your change? It's only cost twenty pounds."

"It's your lucky night, then."

Grace closed the door and strolled up the path, watching as Critchley's taxi passed her.

Outside the house, she stood, observing for ten minutes as lights went on and off in different rooms. He was pacing, obviously pissed off because he'd been stood up. Being in that house with him tonight would be no picnic.

Before Grace left she noticed a blue VW Beetle parked outside a garage.

She made a note of the registration.

Chapter Thirty-eight

Mary was brutally dragged into consciousness through a combination of three things; she had little time to decide which was worse.

The first was going from absolute darkness to an overwhelming amount of light, which not only dazzled but hurt her eyes.

"Wakey, wakey, rise and shine."

The second was the sheer amount of sound, from dead silence to someone screaming at the top of his voice at such a volume that it was enough to make her sick.

"Come on, Mary, for fuck's sake. It's six o'clock."

Mary was going dizzy.

"Please... please, whoever you are, please stop it."

The third was the bucket of freezing cold water.

Mary screamed from the shock. That was the point at which she realised she was naked.

An unseen hand slapped her right cheek, the sting equivalent to the cold water, forcing her head to bounce against the wall behind her.

"What have I done to you?" shouted Mary. "Please stop hurting me."

The hand grabbed and pulled her hair. "If you want me to stop hurting you, stop begging."

Dazed, cold, frightened, and shaking like a leaf, she finally focused her eyes. Glancing around the room, it was very stark. Four bare brick walls, with one door in and out. A couple of steel racks had been fastened to the concrete floor. A number of power tools were lined up, as was a big red toolbox in the corner.

Standing in front of her was the man who had been asking about Manfred yesterday – at least she thought it was yesterday. He had said it was six o'clock, but as there were no windows, she didn't know if it was morning or evening. He was wearing a dark blue boiler suit, which was also stained; from what, Mary had no idea. "Are you awake, Mary?"

She was on top of a dirty mattress. Her clothes were on one of the shelves. She was tied to a radiator. It was cold.

"I think so," she replied meekly.

He grabbed her ear and yelled into it. "Speak up, Mary, I can't hear you."

"Yes, yes. I'm awake. What do you want with me?"

"I trust you slept well. Don't bother answering, it wasn't a question. I don't care one way or the other. There are two things you need to know. One, I'm very intolerant. Two, I want information from you. If you annoy me and I don't get that information then we will play some games. You won't like those, Mary, because I make the rules up as I go along and I'm not inclined to tell you what they are."

She thought he'd finished but then he held up a finger. "Oh, and three, I'm in a bad mood."

"Where am I?"

"Why do you want to know that? Knowing where you are won't do you the faintest bit of good, will it, Mary?"

He had a point. She felt so helpless. She wasn't naturally one of life's fighters. She hated violence of any kind and was completely out of her depth. "No."

"Good."

Mary remembered something about yesterday when he was searching for Manny. He said something about Mother. "What have you done with Mother?"

"Whose mother?"

"Mine. Who else would I be talking about?"

"Nice one, Mary, that's what I like to see. A bit of guts. Though in your case, there's quite a lot."

Ignoring the insult, she continued. "If you've hurt my mother..."

"You'll what?" shouted the man, cutting her off.

She shuffled as close to the wall as was possible. God only knew what she had done to upset the man, but she was starting to think her situation would not end well.

"Never mind about your mother, Mary. If you want to worry about anyone you should start with yourself. Now I'm growing tired of all this claptrap so I'm going to move things along."

Mary pushed hard against the wall. "What are you going to do?"

He walked across the room, started rooting around in his big red toolbox. "Whatever it is you won't like it."

Mary's stomach lurched.

He came toward her with something in his pocket. "Your boyfriend turned my house over last week, and he took three things from me." He leaned in close, lifting her head. The whites of his eyes were so bloodshot they terrified her. The little red lines were like a map, small roads leading into his soul, one place Mary had no desire to see. "And I want them back."

Mary desperately needed a way out so the only thing she could think of was to cooperate.

"Are you sure it was Manfred? He wouldn't do a thing like that."

"I'm very sure, Mary, because I have the little weasel on film."

Mary hung her head and shuffled around on the mattress.

"What did he take?" she finally asked, still staring at the floor.

"My guitar and my collection of vintage cameras."

"That's only two. You said three."

He stood up. "My wife was killed, but I can't get *her* back, can I?"

"He killed your wife?"

"That's what I said."

"No," said Mary. "I'm sure you've made a mistake. Manfred would not do something like that."

He faced her, his expression hard and cold. "Are you calling me a liar?"

Recognition hit Mary like a sledgehammer. She remembered reading all about it in the newspaper. She even talked to her mother about it.

"Are you Robbie Carter?"

"Yes, love. Fame at last."

"But you don't look like him."

"Not fucking likely to, am I, the stress he's put me through. But at least they'll never find me."

"Who?"

"The police."

"What do they want with you?"

"They think *I* did it, can you believe that, Mary? They think I killed my wife, so they're not looking for anyone else. If I want the killer found, I'll have to do it myself. I abhor violence, Mary. I don't like doing this but I can't let him get away with what he's done. I need to find him, and the only way to do that is through you. Anyway, enough of this shit, Mary. I'm not here to answer *your* fucking questions."

"Don't be so coarse," said Mary, unable to help herself. "There's no need for such language."

"Really," said Robbie, leaning in again. "Well, I can promise you something, Mary. Before I'm finished with you, you'll be using it as well."

Mary was close to tears. She had no idea where she was, how long she'd been here, what he'd done with Mother; worse still, what he was going to do to her.

"Where is he?"

"Who?" Judging by his expression, Mary wished she hadn't asked that one.

"You know fucking well who," he shouted back. "Where is Manny bastard Walters?"

"I don't know."

Robbie Carter kicked her legs to one side. Mary screamed in pain. He must have had steel toecaps.

He yanked at the ropes holding her, loosening them from the radiator. When she was totally free, he punched her in the stomach, quickly dragging her upwards and tying the rope to a hook on the wall.

"Last chance," he said.

"For what?"

"You're trying my patience, Mary. Where is Manny?"

"Please, I don't know."

"Wrong answer."

"No!"

"Pardon?"

"I said, no. Don't you touch me!"

"Don't worry, Mary, I'm not in the mood and you're not my type. Anyway, where is this getting us?" He stepped back. "No fucking where, that's where. I'm not here to play games, Mary. I want the answers to my questions. And I want your boyfriend, and when I've finished with him, the police can have what's left. I don't like injustice, Mary."

He turned and shuffled over to his toolbox again. When he returned, he had a long length of electrical flex. Robbie dropped the cable and pulled out some rubber gloves from his pocket.

It was then that Mary noticed one end had a plug. The other end had bare wires.

He put his gloves on, plugged the flex in and picked up both wires.

Mary didn't hear or see anything else as her world darkened.

Chapter Thirty-nine

Gardener's first view of Manny Walters came coupled with a tirade of abuse. "It's a violation of my basic human rights, this is."

"Can you hear something?" Gardener asked Reilly.

The Irishman cupped his ear and feigned interest. "Nothing worth listening to."

Manny was on his feet. "Oh very funny, very funny. What do you do for an encore?"

"We arrest people," said Gardener. He closed the door and approached the table, placing a folder on top. Sitting down, he studied his suspect. Manny Walters was stick thin – undernourished at a guess, but when you had his lifestyle, you tended to run yourself on nervous energy. His hair was black and thinning, and he had a face like a road map. His teeth left a lot to be desired, as did his fingernails. His right eye was black and had puffed up nicely. He was also sporting a purple bruise on the left side of his face.

"Are you lot listening to me?"

"Do we have a choice?" Reilly asked, taking a seat.

"You can't keep me here all this time. I know my rights."

"You should do," said Reilly, "the amount of times you've been in and out of this place."

"You can't try me for past crimes."

"Oh my God," quipped Reilly. "He thinks he's in court now."

"He will be soon," said Gardener. "Sit down, Mr Walters, and make it quick. We have a lot of work to do and we don't want to waste our day on you."

Gardener leaned over and started the recording equipment, introducing everyone for the benefit of the tape. On the table, he also had a laptop.

"Am I under arrest?"

"No, you're helping us with our inquiries."

"Then why is that thing rolling?"

"So you can't claim that we said something when we didn't. And before you start, it's also there to protect you. We've been hoping to have a word with you for some time now, Mr Walters."

Manny took his seat. "What about?"

"All in good time."

"For someone who hasn't got all day, you seem to want to take the long way around things. Where's Maurice?"

"Mr Cragg to you."

"So where is he? Let's have him here and we'll sort this in no time."

"We'd like to talk to you about what happened at the shop."

"What shop?"

"Stop playing games, Manny, or you'll be here for a very long time," said Reilly.

"The travel agent," offered Gardener.

"Oh, that," replied Manny. "It was just a misunderstanding."

"Is that what you call it?"

"What would you call it?"

"We're not here to answer your questions, sunshine," Reilly said.

"Forgive me," said Gardener. "I'm a little old fashioned. I have it down as theft."

"No, no, officer, you've got me all wrong. Like I said, it was a misunderstanding."

"Take us through it."

Manny grew quiet. Gardener could almost hear the cogs whirring. "Well, I was there on business."

"What business?"

"I was checking her fire extinguishers."

"Are you qualified?"

"I was subcontracting."

"For who?"

"I forget now, but my mate knows."

"Name?"

"Whose name?"

"Your mate."

Manny put his hands on his head. "I think it was Graeme Sharp Electrical."

"Strange," said Gardener, "him being a mate of yours and you're not sure about his name."

"It'll be Stitch," said Reilly.

Manny's face dropped.

"So," said Gardener, writing in his pad, "we have our first charge, impersonating a fire officer. Go on."

"No, no, it was all kosher. I showed her my warrant card."

"Warrant card?" said Reilly. "So you were impersonating a police officer as well?"

"No," shouted Manny, "I didn't mean warrant card, you know what I meant."

"Not sure we do, old son, but we know why you were there."

"Stop wasting our time," said Gardener. "You went into the back and you did not check the fire extinguishers, you set about stealing anything you could find."

"I think you'll find you're wrong. As I said, it was a misunderstanding. I went through to check the extinguishers when I heard it."

"Heard what?"

"It was like a scampering sound."

"Coming from where?"

"The cupboard. I thought it was a rat."

"There was only one rat in the place."

"No, serious. I heard this sound and I know women don't like rats, so I opened the cupboard and the bastard thing jumped out, knocked her bag over and the money fell out. She came in when I was picking it up. Snooty cow accused me of all sorts."

"Let me get this straight. You were there to rob the place, she caught you stealing from her handbag, and now she's the snooty cow and she's in the wrong?"

"I was going to put the money back."

"If it was a misunderstanding, why did you attack her?"

"I didn't attack her."

"That's not what she says."

"Well she wouldn't, would she? Stuck-up bitch."

"Snooty cow, stuck-up bitch. Such language, Manny."

"You're right," said Gardener. "She does tell a different story. So do the cameras."

"Cameras?"

"Yes, the cameras. They'd been installed to watch the back door. Most shops have them. You know, for thefts? Would you like to see the film?"

Manny remained silent, so Gardener switched on the laptop. The black and white images confirmed the accusation of him being there to rob the place. Paula Bunting entered the room, a brief conversation ensued, and then Manny rushed forward. At the very last second, she fell backwards and brought up her right leg. She thrust it between Manny's legs and he stumbled. As he came down, she punched him on the left side of his face and the right side of his head hit the door frame. As it bounced off, she brought the right leg up again and slammed the left side of his face with her foot, causing his head to hit the framework again. Job done.

Gardener stopped the film. "Anything to say?"

Manny did as all good criminals had been brought up to do – he said nothing.

"That was a cracking piece of self-defence, so it was," laughed Reilly. "I wouldn't mind her on the team."

"Pity she's not available, Sean, she plays prop forward for the Bursley Bridge first team, hence the almost perfect rugby tackle," continued Gardener, smiling. He turned to Manny, "You've seen the film, you can't deny you were stealing her money, and she caught you red-handed."

No reply.

"You were banged to rights, so you attacked her in an effort to get out."

"Attacked her?" shouted Manny. "I didn't attack anyone."

"You ran at her. It's all there on the film."

"Not to attack her, to get out of the place."

"You wanted to get out? Is that because she saw you stealing?"

Manny said nothing.

"And when that didn't work, you attacked her."

"I did what?" Manny shouted. "I keep telling you, it was a misunderstanding and she got the wrong end of the stick. I was trying to leave."

"Fancy attacking a poor defenceless woman after you'd tried to steal from her."

"She can't have been that defenceless. I was the one who ended up on the floor knocked out. You want to get her in here, ask her what she did to me. I'll sue for assault, that's what I'll do."

Gardener picked up his pen. "Impersonating a fire officer."

"Theft," added Reilly.

"Assault," said Gardener. "The list just goes on, Manny, old son."

"This is out of order," Manny protested.

"You think so?" replied Reilly. "Tell you what I can't understand."

"I'm sure you'll tell me."

"If you've been wrongly accused here and we're fitting you up, why haven't you asked for a lawyer?"

"Maybe I will."

"It's your right," said Gardener. "I mean, we could fit you up with anything."

"Then again," said Reilly, "there is the problem of proof. You know – that little bit of film we've just seen."

"Of course," said Gardener. "You could just admit it and save us all some time."

Manny obviously thought about that one as well. "Why not?" he eventually said. "What are they going to do to me, slap me on the wrist?"

"Could be a touch more than that, old son."

"I don't think so," said Manny. "Okay, you've got me on checking the fire extinguishers and impersonating a fire officer, but you can't get me on stealing. After all, I never left the shop with the money. She took it back off me, so I haven't stolen it, have I? As for the attack, it's... well... it's her word against mine. I mean, your film doesn't actually show me doing anything, does it, apart from running?"

Gardener and Reilly remained silent.

"So yes, officers, I admit to a touch of fraud. So what you gonna do, charge me, lock me up, throw away the key? I don't think so. We'll set a date for a court hearing, I'm out of here, and with a bit of luck I'll get a slapped wrist and told not to do it again."

"Okay, Mr Walters." Gardener closed the folder. Both officers stood up.

Manny joined them. "We gonna go to the front desk, get this over with? So I can go?"

"Go?"

"Yes, leave. You've got what you wanted, an admission."

"To felony number one, yes."

"Number one?"

The officers left the room pretty much how they started, to another tirade of verbal abuse.

Chapter Forty

Grace Browne washed her hands and made herself a coffee. The Italian beans were medium roasted for a smooth flavour, with a hint of tiramisu. She absolutely loved it. Glancing out of the window, she noticed a weak sun. The early morning frost was all but gone. The leaves on the trees were stripped. There was always something sad about winter setting in.

Her apartment was comfortable as she padded through to the living room, placing her coffee next to the unread morning newspaper. Her thoughts wandered to last night in the club. Everything had gone pretty decently, with only the slightest of hiccups. She had enjoyed playing the game with Critchley, turning the tables, hoping it would leave him frustrated and angry. What was interesting however, was where the taxi had taken him: a mill house in Sowerby. How the hell had he ended up there? And what was he doing here? The man was a human eel, walking Teflon – nothing stuck. But she had an address now, so it wouldn't matter. His luck had finally run out.

In the bedroom, Grace fired up her computer, connected to the internet, and studied the electoral roll. The mill house actually belonged to Matthew and Lizzie Atkinson, who ran a stable in Thirsk. Some illegal software in her machine told her they were currently renting it to him. Bingo!

She made a note before starting up another illegal program she had developed for infiltrating the DVLA in Swansea. Within minutes she had the owner of the Beetle: one Mary Miller of Carpenter's Yard in Bramfield.

What was the car doing at the mill house in Sowerby so late at night? Grace didn't know Mary Miller; she had never heard of her. Had Critchley stolen her car? Was he involved with her? Was she working with him? Not likely. He almost always worked alone.

She wasn't happy. Something was wrong. The pattern was out of kilter. She was going to have to investigate. She could not lose control of the situation now, not having come so close.

She left the computer and went for a shower. Padding back to the living room for her coffee, she picked up the newspaper.

The headline and the following story completely stunned her. The body of a woman had been found buried up on the moors at a place called Bedlam Rocks, very close to where her life had completely disintegrated all those years ago.

Her head swam, her eyes went out of focus, and her legs simply wouldn't support her. Grace dropped the paper back on the table, sinking into a chair. The whole shocking episode came back and hit her like a tornado, making her feel sick. Her hands were clammy as she raised them to her mouth. She tried to suck in air, but her lungs failed her.

The floodgates opened, and Grace cried like she'd never done before. Her whole body shook with the pain and the sobbing. She suddenly felt like she'd been violently assaulted. She was shaking, regretting never having had the chance to say goodbye. There had never been any closure; no funeral. The years she had missed with her mother, who would still have been a relatively young woman, all because of that bastard.

And he was still at it.

Not for much longer.

Reaching for a tissue, she dried her eyes and forced herself to read the final paragraph: the police believed the body had been there for possibly twenty years, and were appealing for witnesses to come forward to help piece together the final movements of Jane Browne.

She clenched her fists, ground her teeth. "You fucking animal." Grace silently vowed to herself that witnesses would be of no use to the police, because Critchley would not live another full day on Planet Earth.

Then a thought struck her. Now that he was back in town, had Ronald Critchley been responsible for Jane Carter's death?

Chapter Forty-one

At precisely one o'clock Manny Walters was marched back into the interview room. Gardener had specifically arranged it so that Manny was sitting across from them at such an angle that he could not clearly see all of the room. In other words, he couldn't see what was behind them.

Manny was agitated as he took his chair, constantly rocking one of his legs like he had Parkinson's disease.

"Coffee, Manny?" asked Reilly.

"If it's not too much trouble."

Nothing further was said until Manny had his drink. During that brief period, Gardener assessed the file in front of him. Reilly simply stared at Manny Walters.

"Where were you on Friday, 24 November, Mr Walters?"

"Pardon?"

"It's a simple enough question."

"God knows," replied Manny. "How long ago was that? Over a week?"

"Old memory not so good now, Manny, old son?" questioned Reilly.

"It's ages, isn't it? Can you remember where you were over a week ago?"

Gardener nodded. "Investigating a murder."

No reply.

"So, I'll ask you again. Where were you?"

"Are you trying to fit me up?"

"You really haven't got the hang of this, have you, Manny?" said Reilly. "We ask the questions."

"Where were you?" Gardener repeated.

Manny leaned forward. "I'm not going down for something I haven't done."

"You might if you don't tell us where you were," said Reilly.

"Bit touchy, aren't we, Mr Walters?" said Gardener.

"I know what you lot are like. You're not pinning a murder on me I haven't committed."

"So you have committed some?"

"No," shouted Manny.

"Pleased to hear it. Last chance, where were you?"

Manny sighed and sat back. "At home."

"All night?"

"Yes."

"Can anyone corroborate your movements?" asked Gardener.

"What does that mean?"

"Can anyone confirm you were at home all evening? Your neighbour, perhaps?"

"Ask her."

"We will. Now, at the risk of repeating myself, were you at home all evening?"

"Yes."

"Alone?"

"Yes."

"Doing what?"

"Nothing."

Gardener found that hard to believe. Not the fact that he was at home all night – though he suspected that was a lie – but doing nothing; everyone did something.

"You're not making things easy for yourself, son. What were you doing? Watching TV, listening to music, reading a book? You must have been doing something."

"Look, I've told you, I don't know. Maybe I had something to eat with Mary."

"Who's Mary?"

"My next-door neighbour. She cooks things for me, casseroles and stuff, brings them over. Sometimes we eat together, other times we don't. She has to go and see her mother in the care home."

"What do you do, Mr Walters?"

"Do?"

"For a living?" Gardener figured he was wasting his time asking that question, judging by Manny's track record for arrests.

"Nothing."

"There's an awful lot of fucking nothing going on in your life," added Reilly. "How do you cope with all the boredom?"

"I can't work, see, because of my condition."

"What condition?"

"My nerves. Shot to pieces. Good days and bad days, mostly bad. I'm on tablets. Can't work, can't hold down a job."

"You seem to be able to hold on to everything else well enough," said Reilly.

"What's that supposed to mean?"

Gardener pushed a pen and paper forward. "Name and address of your doctor."

Manny wouldn't pick up the pen. Rather than sign it, Manny told Gardener, who wrote down the details.

"Were you in or around Swansea Court in Bursley Bridge on Friday, 24 November?"

"I just told you, I was at home."

Gardener leaned forward. "Are you sure?"

Manny also leaned forward, spreading his arms. "Are you?"

"Do you know where Swansea Court is?"

"Not really."

Gardener's pet hate for an answer. "You either do, or you don't. Which is it?"

"I'm not sure."

Gardener realised Manny's years in and out of police stations had taught him well. Always evade questions, never answer directly, try and change the subject. But he would slip up soon.

"It's on the outskirts of the town, heading towards Bramfield. Have you ever been to Swansea Court?"

"I don't think so."

Gardener changed subjects. "Does the name Robbie Carter mean anything to you?"

"Robbie who?"

"Carter."

"Who's he, then?"

"He's the man who lives at Swansea Court," offered Reilly.

Manny finished his coffee. "Sorry, why are you telling me all this?"

"Maybe you know his wife, Jane Carter?"

Manny placed his cup on the table, his eyes wide, his mouth open. "Here, is that the woman who was killed?"

"Might have been."

"Might have been?" repeated Manny. "She either was, or she wasn't. Which is it?"

Gardener opened the file, riffled through the paperwork. "Been a bit of a lad in your time, I see, Mr Walters. We've had you up before the judge on a number of theft-related charges. You have a record for selling stolen goods, dodgy Sky cards being one. Seems you also once had a problem with some fake Viagra tablets. You've been done for stealing cars and altering the number plates with black PVC tape."

Despite the coffee, Manny's leg was still shaking.

"Anything to say?"

"People take advantage of my good nature, lead me into all sorts of trouble."

Reilly leaned forward. "Let's cut the crap, shall we, Manny? You can stop evading questions and giving us neutral answers. The fact is, we don't believe what you've told us. We think you were in Swansea Court on the night of the murder. You see, Robbie Carter's house was turned over that night, and a number of items were stolen. A lot of little stuff that can easily be sold on."

"Rather fits your profile," added Gardener.

"There are more thieves in the area than me."

"So you admit to being a thief?"

"Not much point denying it, is there? You've got my records."

"But that wasn't all, Manny," said Reilly. "Something big was stolen, and Robbie Carter's wife was brutally murdered."

"Something big?"

Gardener didn't answer. He simply stood up, moved away from the table.

The red Fender Stratocaster came into view, resting in a music stand, with the open guitar case leaning on the wall behind.

Manny flinched. His reaction was slight, but enough for Gardener to sit back down and ramp up the tension.

"Do you recognise it, Mr Walters?"

"Should I?"

"It's the something big that was stolen," said Reilly. "Tell me, have you ever seen that machine before in your life?"

"No."

Not only was Manny's leg shaking, he continually rolled his hands around, clenching and unclenching them. He was worried, which told Gardener he knew a lot more about the situation than he was letting on.

"You see, Robbie Carter is one very unhappy man," said Reilly. "Wouldn't you be? There you are, out earning a crust, working late hours, your wife waiting at home for you. And when you get home, you find your house turned over, all your possessions stolen, including your guitar and your money. The guitar that his late wife bought him. It's all he has to remember her by. Now, according to rumour, our man Robbie has a bit of a temper, so he does. I wouldn't like to be in the burglar's shoes when he finds out who nicked the guitar and managed to kill his wife in the process."

"How could I have stolen his guitar if he was out working with it?"

"I didn't say he was out working with it," said Reilly. "In fact, I don't remember mentioning his profession." He turned to Gardener. "Did you?"

"Don't think so, Sean."

"So, how do you know what Robbie does for a living? You claim you don't know him, never heard of him?"

Silence.

"Does the name Baz Ronson mean anything to you?"

"No."

"So you didn't sell the guitar to Baz Ronson in the car park of The Black Bull public house in Rawston the day after it was stolen?"

"The day after the house of Robbie Carter was turned over and Jane Carter was murdered?" added Reilly.

"How can I?" said Manny. "I've already told you, I've never been to Swansea Court and I've never seen that guitar."

"We don't believe you," said Reilly, leaning forward, staring straight at the thief. "Are you working with someone, Manny, old son?"

Manny remained tight-lipped.

"Are you in partnership with Robbie Carter?" asked Reilly. "Does he have something on you? Maybe you did a job for him, cheated him out of the booty."

"Maybe Robbie forgave you but made you a proposition," said Gardener. "Let's assume he and Mrs Carter weren't seeing eye-to-eye. They were arguing all the time. He decides he wants rid of her."

"What does all this have to do with me?"

"Robbie Carter decides to give you another chance after cheating him. He figures if he can get rid of her legitimately, the insurance will cough up, and he will also collect from the will."

"And he gives you a nice little earner," said Reilly. "Not bad for cheating him in the first place."

"Only, things go wrong, don't they, Mr Walters?" said Gardener. "Maybe you were only there to burgle the place. Get everything of any value. You sell it on. He deals with her afterwards in the wake of it all. He collects the insurance, everyone's a winner."

"But even the best laid plans can go wrong," said Reilly. "So, what happened, Manny? Did she catch you? Maybe she was supposed to have gone out for the evening, meet up with a traffic accident on the way home – not sure what you two had planned."

"She comes home early and catches you red-handed. Or maybe she didn't go out at all. Either way, she caught you in the act and you panicked. Turned nasty."

Silence.

"We're not saying you meant to kill her, Mr Walters. Maybe it was an accident. Maybe she caught you upstairs in the bathroom. You two had a fight, stuff all over the floor, she falls, cracks her head. You run out, unaware that it's a little bit more serious than your average bang on the head."

"Is that what happened, Manny?"

Manny crushed his plastic cup. He was sweating, shaking. Gardener realised they were onto something but wasn't sure how much more it would take to crack him. "Are you being blackmailed?"

"No one is blackmailing me," he replied, through clenched teeth. "I have no idea what you're talking about."

Gardener figured he did. In his opinion, Manny Walters was a chancer. He was out for the night on the rob, came across a house with an open back door and took his chances. Only he had no idea what he was letting himself in for. Maybe he saw everything that happened, but if he did, why not admit to it? That way he would only face charges of theft. It really was puzzling the SIO.

"Is someone else pulling the strings, Manny? Is there a third party here who has a hold on all of you?"

"A minute ago I was working with Robbie Carter, now you think someone else is behind all of this shit."

"It would explain why Robbie has disappeared."

"Disappeared?" shouted Manny. "What the hell are you talking about now?"

"Didn't you know?" Gardener asked. "Interesting, isn't it? His house is burgled and his wife is killed. Then he disappears. No one has seen him; no one knows where he is. That leaves only you with a connection to the whole sorry incident. Does that mean you're going to disappear if we let you go?"

"What do you mean I'm the only one a connection to the incident? I'm telling you I was nowhere near that fucking house, I never pinched the stuff and I did not kill his wife."

"Oh, dear," said Reilly, standing up. "I think you were, Manny. I think you're in this shit, as you call it, up to your scrawny little neck. Now the way I see it, you could talk and tell us what you know and only go down for a charge of theft."

Manny's eyes narrowed. The pressure was mounting.

"Or you can keep your mouth shut and perhaps end up with a murder charge."

Manny's eyes widened again.

"I know which I'd prefer," said Reilly, putting his palms flat on the top of the table.

Manny ran his hands through his hair. "Oh fuck, fuck, fuck. This isn't happening."

Gardener stood up, stepped back to the guitar. "I'll tell you why we don't believe you," he said, pointing to the Stratocaster. "Because this guitar has your prints all over it."

Manny jumped up and pushed his chair back, which clattered loudly as it fell over. "No way has it got my prints! It can't have!"

"Why not?" Reilly shouted.

"'cause I was wearing gloves."

Chapter Forty-two

The pellet bounced off the radiator with a deafening metallic clang before burying itself in the plaster an inch or two above Mary's head. She jumped, screamed, and launched herself off the mattress onto the stone floor, panting for breath. She glared at the maniac who had fired it as he laughed himself stupid before firing another at the floor, inches from her face.

"What are you doing?" she shouted, bouncing back onto the mattress, trying to maintain some dignity as she used her hands to cover her private areas.

"Put your hands down, you stupid cow. I saw it all yesterday. Nothing impressed me then."

"You are a foul individual," shouted Mary.

"Compliments, compliments, Mary," shouted Robbie, reloading the rifle and letting off another couple of rounds: one into the mattress, the other into the radiator, which, sadly for Mary, bounced off and took a small piece out of her right arm.

She grabbed it with her left, slumping back against the wall, gritting her teeth, the pain shooting through her arm. "What are you doing, you stupid man? You could have killed me."

"I'm not aiming to kill you, for Christ's sake. Why would I want to kill you? I haven't got my information yet."

"I've told you, I don't know anything."

"Rubbish." Robbie slung the air rifle across his arm and slowly walked in. He knelt down at the edge of the mattress. "You're either very brave, or very stupid. Which is it, Mary?"

"I'm certainly not stupid."

"Then you must be brave, protecting your man like you are doing. So we're going to play the game again, and God help you if you don't give me something to go on."

Mary's insides rumbled at the thought of what that could mean.

"What do you know about his friends?" Robbie asked her.

"I'm cold."

"Pardon?"

"I said I'm cold, and I'm hungry. Perhaps if you looked after me a little better, I might be able to help."

"I don't think you've got the hang of this game, Mary. If the worst comes to the worst, I won't need you to find him. I'm just making things easier for myself and having a little fun along the way."

"Fun?" shouted Mary. "What's funny about kidnapping and torturing a defenceless woman?"

"It's amusing me." Robbie stood up.

"There'll be people looking for me, you know."

"Well, your mother won't be one of them, will she? She can hardly walk, and if she could, I doubt she'd remember the way."

"Don't you insult my mother."

Robbie grabbed her right arm where the pellet had removed a chunk of flesh, squeezing. Mary pinched her face so hard that all of her features ended up in the middle, as if she was in the hall of mirrors. She tried to screech, but her vocal cords failed her.

"Now what do you know about his friends?"

Mary was breathless, so Robbie let go. "Friends?" he persisted.

"I don't know any of his friends."

"What?" he shouted. "You're his girlfriend and you haven't met any of his friends? Mind you, type of company he keeps, you're probably better off."

"It's not that type of relationship."

"Oh yes, I forgot. He hasn't tupped you yet, has he, Mary? Given you a good servicing?"

Mary's face coloured quickly. "Stop being so vulgar."

"What about family? Or haven't you met those yet, either?"

"No."

Robbie turned to face the wall, obviously frustrated. "When did you last see him?"

Mary was staring at the floor; she mumbled something.

Robbie turned and grabbed a lock of hair and pulled so hard she had no choice but to stare straight at him, whilst trying to catch her breath. "Speak up, I can't hear you."

"I'm not sure."

"You're not sure. You live next door, not in the next fucking county. When did you last see him?"

"Tuesday... maybe Wednesday."

"Where?"

"At home."

"Why?"

"Pardon?"

"I asked why? Why did you go to see him? It won't have been to test the fucking bed springs, will it?" He pulled her hair tighter, and Mary stood up to avoid the pain.

"I took him something to eat."

"Eat?" said Robbie, relaxing his grip. "Who are you, Florence fucking Nightingale? You took him something to eat? Doesn't the lazy bastard feed himself now?"

"I like to make sure he's eating properly. I took him a casserole."

"Why? It's not like he does anything for you."

"He does plenty for me."

Robbie let go of the hair and leaned in closer. "Not as much as you'd want, though, eh, Mary? Never mind tasting the casserole, maybe you should offer him some beaver. What do you say?"

"You disgust me."

"I disgust you? It's not me parading myself naked in front of a stranger." Tiring, giving her no time to answer, Robbie pinched the bridge of her nose between his thumb and forefinger, cutting off her air supply. "You and your rat-infested, weasel-faced, thieving fucking scumbag of a boyfriend are beginning to try my patience to a whole new level."

Mary was reddening, finding the pressure uncomfortable.

Robbie dropped the gun. Mary jumped back. He didn't let go. "Are you going to tell me where he is?"

Mary lifted her hands and tried to break his hold on her nose. With his free hand, he grabbed her hair, pulling upwards again. Mary yelped.

"Are you going to tell me what you know, or are you going to continue protecting him?"

Breathless, with her voice barely above a whisper, Mary spoke back. "I don't know. I keep telling you, I don't know where he is."

"Wrong answer, Mary. I'm very tired now."

He strolled over to the other side of the room and rummaged around in his toolbox.

Chapter Forty-three

Gardener slipped into the incident room a little after seven-thirty in the evening, carrying a manila folder under his arm. He deposited the paperwork on the table, took a swig of water, and faced his men. There was a buzz of conversation like he'd never heard before. They were excited about something, especially Dave Rawson and Colin Sharp.

"Robbie Carter. I'm hoping you guys can bring something to the table. We really do need to find him soon."

Sharp and Rawson both raised their arms. Gardener nodded to Rawson first.

"I've got something positive at last."

Gardener breathed a sigh of relief. "Okay, Dave, what have you got?"

"I met the guys in Brough, as you asked. Only got back half an hour ago. Basically, it's as Maurice said last night.

Jane Browne and her husband Raymond Culver spent a weekend camping in the area, but not where the body was found at Bedlam Rocks. They were north of Brough in a place called Warcop Fell. They'd been there three days when he wandered into the police station at two o'clock in the morning, claiming his wife was missing. He hadn't seen her since he'd woken up at eight that morning."

"And it took him till two the next morning to report her?"

"His excuse was that, as far as he understood, people had to be missing twenty-four hours before anything would be done. As the Brough police explained, maybe under normal circumstances that would be the case. But they were in an area inundated with walkers, full of nature paths, therefore, the authorities took any disappearance seriously.

"They alerted the air rescue services straight away and a search was mounted. According to them, they looked everywhere but found nothing. We know now why – they were in the wrong place altogether. They questioned him for three days and he appeared devastated. Kept going on about how much he loved her, and he thought the love was mutual. The only explanation he could come up with was she must have upped and left him."

"Why? Did she take all her clothes with her?"

"Didn't take anything. The police searched the area and went back to their camping ground: she'd left everything."

"Doesn't sound right to me," said Reilly.

"So, what happened, Dave?" Gardener asked.

"They let him go after three days. They had nothing on him. They didn't believe he'd done anything to her. He apparently went home and told the daughter, Grace. She didn't take it very well. In fact, she reported the incident to the local police in Billingham. Even went to see the police in Brough."

"What was the outcome?" Gardener asked.

"She put her side of the story to them. She didn't like him. She figured the relationship between Raymond and her mother wasn't as he'd claimed, that they used to argue a lot, and there were times when her mother had bruises, personality changes, but she wouldn't talk about them. Grace reckoned it was all down to him."

"All starting to sound very familiar," said Reilly.

"Did they take her seriously?"

"Well, they had him back in the station at Brough," continued Rawson, "but he claimed that Grace didn't like him. They'd never got on from day one. Grace had it in for him. He told them all about her disruptive behaviour and how she often tried to wreck their plans, stop them from going away. He said her stories were not true. He and her mother had an excellent relationship."

"Despite the bruises and the moods and the fact that she'd supposedly left him?" persisted Reilly.

"So, it's possible something went wrong on the camping trip," continued Cragg. "Maybe they argued, it got out of hand, he struck her... maybe he went too far. She died as a result, and he got rid of the body, buried her on Bedlam Rocks."

Rawson held up the photo of Robbie Carter. "The police in Brough reckon this is Raymond Culver."

There was a gasp of interest amongst the team. Gardener felt the net was closing, and he noticed an agitated Colin Sharp who obviously had news along similar lines.

"What have you got, Colin?"

"Very similar story to Dave's. They also confirmed from the photo we have of Robbie Carter that was him."

"Did they back up Grace's story?"

"Yes and no. Although they weren't keen on Raymond, they said they never heard or saw anything that gave them cause for concern."

"Doesn't mean it wasn't going on," said Reilly.

"What about Grace? Have you found her?"

"No, sir. I did manage to find one of her best friends, a girl called Louise Warton, who said that after two years of putting her heart and soul into the matter, Grace eventually sold the house."

"Her heart and soul into what?" asked Cragg.

"Investigating what happened to her mother. Louise said that Grace would never rest until she knew what happened. She blamed Raymond from day one, and said she would continue to blame him for the rest of her life until she found out, one way or another.

"She sold her mother's house two years after the event. Grace had a heart to heart with Louise, and said that she was going to start a new life for herself, move away from all the bad memories. Louise was pretty pleased, I can tell you. She reckoned Grace's mother's disappearance and her refusal to accept the facts really had an effect on her health."

"Where did she go?"

"She moved to Hull. Worked as a secretary, took IT courses and, according to Louise, really moved on with her life."

"Is she still there?"

"No. About seven years ago she moved to Harrogate and took a job as a legal secretary."

"Looks like she has managed to put it behind her," said Gardener. "Do you have an address in Harrogate?"

"No. Her and Louise kept in constant contact until about three years ago."

"What happened three years ago?" Reilly asked, his tone intrepid.

"Grace disappeared off the radar."

"Just like that?" asked Rawson.

"According to Louise. One minute she was there, the next gone. She managed to get over to Harrogate herself, but all she hit was a dead end. The legal outfit said that Grace simply announced one day that she was leaving for

New Zealand. She worked a week's notice and disappeared."

"Just like that?" asked Rawson.

"Is your hard drive stuck or something?" Bob Anderson chuckled as he said it.

"It just seems a bit odd, that's all."

"I'm inclined to agree," said Gardener. "How long had Grace and Louise been friends?"

"Years."

"And Louise never heard from her again?"

"No."

"It doesn't sound right," said Reilly.

Anderson laughed. "Christ, his hard drive's stuck now."

"What if she continued to harbour the grudge in secret?" offered Gardener. "Maybe she found something out about Raymond, but she never told her friend. She continued to investigate him herself."

"Or maybe he got to her, made her disappear like her mother."

"But why go to her employer and say she was emigrating?"

"Maybe she had every intention," said Benson. "Perhaps Raymond Culver got to her before she could leave. Let's face it, everyone thought she was going, so no one would question the fact that she wasn't around. Maybe he'd found out where she was, followed her, spoke to people, got to know what she was planning. If he made her disappear for making his life a misery, no one would be any the wiser."

Gardener nodded his agreement. "Good point, Paul." He turned and added it to the chart as an action.

Emma Longstaff piped up. "Don't suppose Louise gave you a photo of Grace, did she?"

Sharp deflated. "Oh, God. I'm sorry, I never thought to ask."

"Have you got her mobile number?"

"Yes. I'll call her, see if she can email one over."

"Or point us to a Facebook account."

Sharp nodded and made a note. Gardener asked him if there was anything else. "Yes. The neighbours talked at length about Raymond Culver being a musician. They gave me a lead on an entertainment agent up in The Borders. McLeod Holden Enterprises."

"Hardly Simon Cowell, by the sound of it."

"No. The guys who ran it originally have both retired. The two people in charge now have been there for years. The secretary seemed to remember someone fitting that description. He was called Richard Clayton, but went out on the circuit as Rocker Richards, and he had a red Strat. Anyway, she's going to circulate the photo and come back to us. Hopefully, we should hear something in the morning."

Gardener shook his head. The initials RC were cropping up far too much and far too often for his liking. "Excellent work, you two. Seeing as you're both involved, I'd like the pair of you on those threads in the morning. See what else you can pick up on Raymond Culver, or Robbie Carter as we know him, and the daughter, Grace."

Gardener glanced at the clock. It was eight-thirty. They still had a lot of ground to cover.

"Okay. Who's next?"

Gates raised her hand. "We had something come in about an hour ago, sir. I think you'll like it."

"Go on," said Gardener.

Bob Anderson took up the reigns. "A man called Stephen Westgate came to see us. He lives on Carr Road. It's kind of a neighbouring street to Swansea Court, but there's a field between them."

"He works nights at one of the furniture factories about ten miles away," said Gates. "Starts his shift about two o'clock. Always takes his dog for a walk about twelve-thirty."

"I hope this is as good as it sounds," offered Reilly.

"It is," replied Anderson. "About twelve-forty-five, Westgate and the dog were walking around the perimeter of the field when they were approaching Robbie Carter's house. His van was parked in the lane at the back."

"What was he doing?" asked Gardener.

"Westgate doesn't know. He only saw the van, not Robbie Carter. He can't be sure, but he thinks he heard raised voices. Which means he was lying about where he was."

"Absolutely," said Gardener. "He claims he didn't get home until an hour later than that."

"He also said he'd parked at the front to unload the gear," said Reilly.

"Which he may well have done," said Gardener. "But we now have a witness that puts him at the house one hour earlier, and his van around the back."

"Puts a whole different slant on things," said Rawson. "Question still is, what did he find when he came home?"

"Well I can't imagine he found Jane Carter in a slinky negligee with Manny Walters," said Cragg.

"No," said Reilly. "Well out of his league."

"And Robbie's, come to mention it."

"But was she at home with someone else?"

"I'm not really convinced," said Gardener. "Carrie Fletcher mentioned nothing about an affair. In fact, she said the opposite, that because of her medication Jane Carter wasn't interested in sex."

"Doesn't make sense, does it?" said Paul Benson.

"Why didn't the witness come forward before now?"

"Basically, because he's frightened of Robbie Carter. He has a wife and children and he put their safety first."

"If Robbie Carter is as bad as we're finding out," said Patrick Edwards, "why hasn't he come to our attention before now?"

"If he keeps changing his identity like we suspect," said Cragg, "that's one very good reason."

"But surely he'd have to keep skipping town as well," said Rawson. "That's a whole lot of work to keep putting yourself through."

"Possibly a well-established pattern, Dave," said Gardener. "He sets up with a woman. All is well to start with. Something goes wrong. The result could be a serious accident for the woman, or worse. He changes his name, his identity, and his location. Maybe that's why he never gets caught."

"You interviewed him, sir," said Edwards. "Didn't anything strike you as odd?"

"I can't say we were pleased with all his answers, Patrick, but even so, we had absolutely nothing on which to hold him at that time," said Gardener. "He won't be the first criminal who was interviewed and let go. You only have to look at Peter Sutcliffe, the Yorkshire Ripper. He was interviewed four or five times and slipped the net."

"That were one of the main reasons HOLMES were introduced," said Cragg.

"We simply have to keep going," said Gardener. "Do what we are doing, find the cracks in his armour. All credit to the witness for coming forward, but he should have done so sooner."

Patrick Edwards put his hand up. Gardener nodded to him. "I've been thinking about something, sir."

"About what?" asked Gardener.

"The bodies of both Janes. Last night, Fitz said they shared the same injuries. It's a bit far-fetched, but what if he hit them both with his guitar?"

The room descended into silence, so he expanded his theory. "Maybe he lost his temper and cracked them with the Strat. Let's face it, that must be big enough and heavy enough, and Terry Jones reckons the neck is damaged."

"That's not a bad theory, Patrick," Gardener said. "We'll make a detective out of you yet." He turned to the desk sergeant. "Maurice, can you go and ask Fitz to come over? Whatever excuse he makes, tell him it's very urgent."

Cragg shuffled off immediately.

"What do we want the Pathosaurus for?" Reilly asked.

"We're going to put Patrick's theory to him, see if he'd like to speculate."

* * *

Following a short break, the team resumed. Gardener took another sip of water before continuing.

"Which brings me to HOLMES. I asked you guys to look into the deaths of every woman called Jane who has died in suspicious circumstances over the last thirty years. Has anything flagged up?"

The HOLMES tech – whose name was Edward Potter – had reams of paperwork with him and an expression that said he would rather work any other case but the one they were on.

"We started at eight o'clock this morning. The first lot of data was horrendous," said Potter, an anaemic man with patches of thinning grey hair all over his scalp, as if he had moles burrowing from inside out. "But the more we narrowed things down, the better it became. We could only go back to 1985 because HOLMES has nothing previous. Technically speaking, an early version of HOLMES was started in 1981, but we never kept much of the information. Anyway, something interesting finally developed."

Everyone waited for Potter to continue, but he didn't. No one could understand why, so Gardener asked him outright if there was a problem.

"Oh, sorry." Potter scattered paperwork all over the desk, most of which fell on the floor. "Ah, here it is. Something happened up in North Yorkshire in 1985. A big time drug dealer, originally from London, named Alfie Peterson and his wife, Jane, were found killed at their home in Whitby. Both had been tortured for quite some time before they were killed. Police found evidence of physical beatings with fists, possibly, and other instruments, stabbings, electrocution. Somebody had really done a number on them." Potter threw his paper down before searching for another piece.

Gardener finished his bottle of water, concerned about where it was leading.

Potter continued. "Police had it down as a drug related killing. But some of the notes taken suggested Alfie Peterson's wife was a bit of a loose woman. Apparently, she'd had a number of affairs. Used to lead blokes on, in particular, one called Robert Chilvers."

That remark caught Gardener's attention, the initials RC appearing again. "What happened with him?"

"Here's where it all gets interesting. The notes are scant and there are very few people around who can remember the account first-hand. Chilvers was a local musician. Bit of a Glam Rock fan by all accounts."

Gardener's hair nearly stood on end. Reilly stood and threw his hands in the air and a collective whoop rounded the room.

"From what I can gather," continued Potter, "he was seeing Jane Peterson sometime in 1981. Not sure what happened, but I suspect Alfie Peterson found out because some time afterwards, Robert Chilvers disappeared from the town altogether."

"Is this our man?" Reilly asked.

"A bit too much to be a coincidence," added Gates.

"And if it is him, was it the start of his killing spree?" asked Anderson.

Gardener glanced at Benson. "Paul, I'd like you in Whitby first thing in the morning. Call the station tonight, inform them of what you're up to, and see if someone can have the information you need as soon as possible?"

Benson nodded.

"Do you have anything more on that story?" Gardener asked Potter.

"No, but as I said, it's a long time ago."

"What about all the victims named Jane that have either died or disappeared in mysterious circumstances?"

"That's another big task," said Potter, consulting his paperwork. "In the last thirty-five years, we currently have a list of two thousand names."

"He can't possibly be responsible for all those," said Reilly.

Gardener spread his arms and leaned on the table in front of him. "Okay, here's something that might help. Go back to HOLMES and see if you can narrow it down further by adding this information in. I want you to look only at the names of the women who have disappeared or died, who had a partner or a husband, whose initials were RC. I also want you to include unsolved crimes, specifically deaths."

Potter nodded. "Want me to start now?"

"No time like the present." Gardener rubbed his hands down his face. The whole thing was a nightmare without end. It was beginning to feel like they had come up against the world's most prolific serial killer. His attention was diverted when the door opened and Fitz strolled in.

"Seems you have a habit of demanding my attention at odd times, gentlemen."

"Well, if *we* can't have our tea, we're gonna make damn sure you don't get yours," retorted Reilly, smiling.

"I wouldn't put money on it." The Home Office pathologist faced the SIO. "So, what's so urgent that you need me here immediately?"

"Did I say immediately?" Gardener asked Cragg.

"No, I did."

The rest of the team laughed, which was music to Gardener's ears. "Patrick?" Gardener asked. "It's your show, you can take the floor."

"Very strictly, Patrick."

Another roar broke the relative quiet.

"Oh, very funny." Patrick explained his theory regarding the guitar.

Fitz stood with his arms folded, and Gardener could hear the cogs turning. "I don't see why not," he replied at last. "It's big enough and heavy enough. It certainly could cause the damage we've seen. What made you think of that, young man?"

"Something Terry Jones said, sir. I wondered what could warp the neck of the guitar, and he said maybe it had taken a hard knock somewhere."

"If the neck was warped wouldn't it be out of tune?" Reilly asked.

"Well, Terry indicated that it was okay at the top end where the machine heads were, but the further up the neck you travelled, the more out of tune it became."

"Wouldn't Robbie Carter have noticed this?" Gardener asked.

"Probably," said Patrick Edwards. "But maybe he was clever enough to keep playing chords at the top end."

"Fitz, can you demonstrate action for us?"

"I can try."

The guitar was brought into the incident room, and after judging the weight and the size, Fitz asked Patrick Edwards to stand near the wall while he raised the instrument and swung it slowly, stopping short of the target. In order to satisfy himself, he repeated the exercise three or four times.

"It's very possible, Stewart. Do I detect you know who your killer is?"

"Let's just say we're getting there. Thank you, Fitz, you've been a great help."

Gardener continued as Fitz left. "There we have another nail in his coffin, gentlemen. Dave, I'd like you to get on to the station in Brough tomorrow morning. See if you can find anyone who was directly involved in the case, and see if they remember a red guitar. If not, ask someone to check the notes carefully to see if there's a mention."

"Will do, boss."

"You think he might have taken this thing on holiday with him?" Reilly asked.

"It looks that way, Sean."

"Terry Jones reckoned it was a present from his wife," said Patrick Edwards.

"Maybe it was," replied Gardener. "But he never said which one." Gardener thought for a moment. "I'd like to know why he does it. Whatever the reason, I want him caught. It looks like he's been doing this for years and he's obviously been getting away with it. The book stops with us. He's not getting away with it again, not on my watch."

A collective show of support went around the room.

Gardener turned to Emma Longstaff. "Anything from the dating sites, Emma?"

She sighed, her expression glum. "In view of what we've heard tonight, I haven't been using my time wisely."

"Why?"

"I've found a number of Robbie Carters but none of them look anything like him. I realise now that they wouldn't. He'll be using a fake photograph, maybe even a false name. There has to be something he's doing, or putting on the site that has a common thread. Trouble is, I'm not sure what it is. Bearing that in mind, I'm going to cross reference a few different sites. I'm going to google something called *The Way Back Machine*."

"What the hell's that?" Reilly asked.

"It's a site that scans and records the content of all indexed webpages online," said Longstaff. "It can be useful if you know one of the last IDs and roughly when it was used. It's almost impossible these days for someone not to leave a digital footprint."

She explained about usernames and nicknames being traceable, and the likelihood of people using them time and again for all social media sites. "It's a big job, sir."

"I appreciate that, Emma, and it's possible that we may have to pull an all-nighter. But you can use Patrick and one or two of the HOLMES team if they haven't already got their hands full. We're very close to this man. We cannot let him slip the net."

"I take it we're not still trying to pin it on Manny Walters?" Cragg asked.

Gardener sighed. "I'm not convinced he's a murderer."

"But he's involved in it somehow," offered Reilly, strolling back from the tea urn with a cup in one hand and a sausage roll in the other.

"Thing is," said Gardener, taking a swig of water from a fresh bottle, "he would not admit to the burglary, or having been anywhere near Robbie Carter's house."

"And you don't believe him?" said Colin Sharp.

"We didn't believe him before we trapped him," said Reilly.

"How did you trap him, sir?" asked Gates.

"Told him his prints were all over the guitar."

"He reckoned they couldn't be because he was wearing gloves."

Dave Rawson dropped his coffee and doubled over with laughter. "Oldest trick in the book."

"That's typical of him," said Cragg. "Hasn't got the sense he were born with."

When the laughter had died down, Bob Anderson asked, "Where does that leave us?"

"I've had his place searched."

The door to the incident room opened and a couple of the local Bramfield PCs entered.

"Talk of the devil," said Gardener.

One of them spoke directly with Cragg. "Telephone for you, sir. Female, said it was urgent."

"Me?"

"Yes, sir."

"What does she want?"

"Don't know but she said she would only speak to you."

Cragg shuffled off.

Gardener noticed one of the officers had a metal box under his arm.

"What's in there?"

"Some stuff we picked up from Manny's place. He'd definitely been in that house and on the night in question. We found a pair of Vans trainers."

"There's no way he can afford them," said Reilly.

"We cross referenced them to a list that Robbie Carter gave us, sir. There were a number of other items on the list, CDs, DVDs, that sort of stuff."

"You'd have thought he'd gotten rid of them by now," said Rawson.

"He has," replied the PC. "Most of them, anyway."

"And the rest of the stuff is in the box?" Gardener asked.

"No." He put the box on the table and opened it. "We had to pick the lock. This is full of cameras."

"Cameras?" said Reilly, approaching the table. "What the hell does he want with cameras? And look at the state of them."

Gardener poked one or two of them around with a pen. "How old are these?"

Benson came forward. "Older than me. My dad has a collection of old cameras, and they look like this lot."

"Is there anything on them?" Gardener asked.

"We haven't checked yet. Thought we'd come here first, they're just so out of place."

"To be honest," replied Gardener, "they don't really fit into place with anyone connected to this case, but let's have them opened and any film inside developed. You just never know."

The two constables nodded and retreated to the back of the room, taking a seat. Gardener added it to the whiteboard.

"Okay, gentlemen, I think that just about wraps our meeting up. You all have your actions so I'd like you all back in here tomorrow lunchtime: though some of us will probably be here all night."

"If you are, we are," said Rawson.

The team nodded in agreement, immediately reaching for their mobiles. It was a proud moment for Gardener.

* * *

Cragg entered the room, closing the door behind him. "That was Sandra Pearson, the matron in charge of the care home between here and Bursley Bridge. One of their patients is an old lady by the name of Elizabeth Miller. She has Alzheimer's. Not likely she'll ever come out, has good days and bad days. Anyway, seems her daughter, Mary, visits everyday come rain or shine. Never misses, not even on Christmas Day."

"Don't tell me," said Reilly, "she hasn't been today."

"That's right. But Mary not only visits her mother every day, she also works shifts."

"Maybe she's not well, Maurice. Everyone has an off day."

"Not Mary Miller."

"I have the feeling I'm not going to like this," said Gardener. "I'll bet you're going to tell us that she is somehow connected to the case."

"Looks like it. She's Manny's next-door neighbour, and possible girlfriend."

Chapter Forty-four

At nine the following morning, Gardener was in the incident room in front of the whiteboard. To his right he had a cup of tea, a bowl of cereal, and some fruit. Reilly was sitting opposite with two sausage, egg, and bacon sandwiches, and a large mug of coffee.

"That stuff will kill you," said Gardener.

"So will that stuff," said Reilly, pointing to Gardener's breakfast. "It'll just take longer."

The pair shared a moment of comfortable silence.

"Penny for them?" Reilly asked his boss, taking a large mouthful of the sandwich.

"I'm thinking about Mary Miller."

Her disappearance the previous evening sent shockwaves through the team, creating more questions.

Following a visit to the care home, Gardener and Reilly returned to the station around two o'clock in the morning, immediately setting a search in motion for Mary, which included all details of her and her car, alerting ANPR and CCTV. The pair of them then freshened up before grabbing a couple of hours sleep in an upstairs room, along with Cragg. The rest of the team continued to work through the night in shifts, allowing them a break as well.

"Employment in a care home must be very demanding," said Gardener. "It can't have been easy for Mary to complete her shift before spending time with her mother."

"Knowing that one day you can have a perfectly normal conversation, and the next, your mother wouldn't know you from Adam."

"Do you think everything got too much for Mary?"

"Maybe," offered Reilly. "Then again, maybe she just decided to have a day off after all?"

"Not according to Sandra Pearson," said Gardener.

The care home manager was a slim, mixed-race woman with the most piercing dark eyes. Sandra's calm nature and soft-spoken voice suited her vocation perfectly. The atmosphere within the building had been subdued as most of the residents were in bed. Sandra Pearson talked at length, had been a mine of information concerning Mary, even providing them with a photograph and car registration details.

The visit to Carpenter's Yard brought little in the way of compensation. She had not returned. The car was nowhere to be seen. The flat was extremely clean and tidy, and early indications were not good.

"I don't accept she just walked out of her life," said Reilly, "unless she went out searching for Manny?" Reilly washed down the last of his sandwich with a swig of coffee.

"I'm not so sure about that, Sean. Manny's been missing for days. She hasn't reported it."

"So, either she wasn't used to that kind of shit from him, or she wasn't his girlfriend."

"It's always possible he *is* running things. Perhaps he abducted her before we picked him up."

"Bit too far out there for my liking, boss. From what we've seen in the two interviews, he doesn't look capable of taking the skin from a rice pudding."

"Which brings us back to Robbie. Has he got Mary so he can find out where Manny is?"

"That's a far more likely prospect," said Reilly.

"Maybe Robbie has the car and her. After all, his own van is still parked on the drive at Swansea Court."

"So we could have a hostage situation."

Gardener ran his hands down his face. "It's the best and most fitting option. The only other possibility is once again a third party. Is someone wiping them all out one by one?"

"I don't hold with that theory, either. But it could link back to the incident in Whitby."

Gardener nodded. "Hopefully Benson might shed some light on that one."

The door opened and Cragg entered with the metal box that had been recovered from Manny's place.

Gardener glanced upwards. "You got something?"

Cragg nodded. "You're definitely going to want to see these."

Gardener and Reilly stood up as the box was placed on a table. Cragg opened the top. The cameras had gone. A mauve felt interior was all they could see and the box was bigger than they had first thought.

Cragg reached in, removing a false bottom. What he retrieved made Gardener's hair stand on end.

Gardener stared at dozens of photographs featuring naked and semi-naked women, all in some form of distress. They were chained to radiators, tied to heavy furniture, handcuffed, fastened to walls. Most had cuts and bruises, open sores, lots of which were fresh. Some had hair; others were bald. The one common thread running through every picture was the sheer expression of fear in their eyes.

On the reverse of the photos, someone had written names and dates. Jane Thornton – 1991. Jane Browne – 1999. Jane Sullivan – 2005. Jane Jenkins – 2009. And then came a few photos of Jane Carter.

There were however a number of photos, the oldest of them, that had no name written on the reverse. The woman was naked with dark brown hair – hanging limply around her shoulders – tied to a wooden kitchen chair and staring at the floor. She was bruised and battered.

"All these were in the bottom of the box?" asked Gardener.

Cragg nodded.

"What the hell's going on?" asked Reilly.

The photos were all different due to the type of film that had been used. Some were Polaroid, others had been developed. Some were large and grainy, others small and well defined. Some were black and white, others were colour.

"For what it's worth," said Cragg, "I don't think this box or these photos belong to Manny Walters."

"So what's he doing with them?" asked Reilly. "Whose are they?"

Gardener grabbed his hat and jacket. "No time like the present to find out. Maurice, can you have him brought to the cell immediately, and I'd like you to stay in on the interview."

Cragg nodded before heading out.

"I'm sick of this smarmy little thief, Sean," said Gardener. "Whatever he knows, I can guarantee that he's going to tell us today."

"There's only one way to do that, boss."

"I know. So, let's go and turn the pressure up."

Within five minutes, all four men were in the cell. Manny Walters feigned tiredness, complaining that they'd dragged him out before he'd woken properly. He'd had little time to dress – though Gardener thought that had made little difference – and he'd had no breakfast.

"Don't worry, Mr Walters," said Gardener. "When today is over, you'll get your daily quota of food."

"Especially where you're going."

"What's that supposed to mean?"

Gardener descended on Manny Walters like a car crash, throwing the photos on the table and spreading them around. "Explain these."

Manny's eyes flickered, and Gardener knew from his interested but puzzled expression they were new to him.

"Never seen 'em."

"They came from your house."

"My house?" shouted Manny, rising to his feet.

"Yes," said Gardener.

"All nicely hidden in a metal box," said Reilly. "With a lock on it. Mind you, if I was in possession of stuff like this, I'd want it under lock and key, so I would."

"You've been to my house without a warrant?"

"Don't need one," replied Gardener.

Manny was suddenly very pale but fought back well, slamming his hand on the table. "I'll sue the fucking lot of you. You have no right."

Gardener leaned on the table with his hands spread wide. He lowered his voice to a whisper, which should have been all the warning Manny needed. "I don't think you understand how much trouble you're in."

"Not as much as you lot, searching my house without a warrant."

"Change the record, son."

"We don't need a warrant," said Gardener. "You've seen the inside of enough police stations to know that, I would have thought. Once under arrest, section 32 of PACE says I can search where you are, or have been, for evidence of an offence. Once in the station, section 18 of PACE says I can search your home or place of work, no warrant needed."

"My solicitor will make mincemeat of you lot."

Gardener smirked. It was all bravado now.

"You have one, do you, Manny?" Reilly asked.

"Why don't you call him?" said Gardener.

Cragg intervened. "Manny, you're only making things worse for yourself."

Gardener could see the thief was torn to pieces over the latest evidence. He knew something about the whole sorry mess, but he simply wouldn't open up. Why?

Reilly pointed to the photos. "Who are these women, sunshine? How long have you been torturing them and taking photos?"

Manny was sweating.

"How many have you killed?" continued Reilly. "What have you done with the bodies?"

Manny's hands were deep red from the constant wringing.

Reilly added more pressure. "You do know what happens to men like you in prison, don't you, Manny? When the other cons get hold of this kind of information, you're going to know exactly how those women felt. Trouble is, in prison, no one can hear you scream."

"Actually, Sean, they can," said Gardener. "They just don't care."

"If I was you, Manny, I'd talk," said Cragg.

Manny opened his mouth but nothing came out.

Reilly leaned in again. "We know you burgled the house in Swansea Court, Manny. Which means *we* know *you* know something about Jane Carter. And if you add all this little lot into the mix, can you see where we're going with it? If someone else is responsible for all of this carnage, why are you protecting him?"

Manny had his head in his hands. Lord only knew what he was thinking. Gardener couldn't believe he would rather face what was coming to him from the police than what would happen in the outside world. It had to be serious.

Reilly was still leaning over the table when Gardener threw a picture of Mary on it.

"That's Mary," shouted Manny.

"You recognise her, then?"

Maybe they had finally pressed Manny's buttons. "Of course I do. Why are you showing me a photo of Mary?"

"Why do you think?" asked Reilly, before asking the question that knocked him sideways. "If you're not going to tell us anything about the night of the burglary, or Jane Carter, or the murders of all these other women, maybe you can tell us what you've done with Mary."

Manny stood up, his complexion ashen, emphasising the lines etched into his skin, which in Gardener's opinion had deepened since he'd been in the interview room.

"What do you mean, what have I done with Mary?"

"Oh come on, Manny," said Reilly. "Don't pull this shit on us. You know Mary is missing because you've taken her. What have you done with her?"

Manny flopped in his seat again. "I don't know what you're talking about."

"This is not helping you, son." Reilly had raised his voice. "Don't believe all the crap you see on TV about the right to remain silent. Right now you're up to your neck in shit, and you're sinking faster than the *Titanic*."

Manny was breathing like an asthmatic, his leg was shaking, his fists clenching and unclenching.

Gardener towered over him. "Mr Walters, we're going to leave the room for two minutes, and during that time I want you to think very carefully about your predicament. You either speak and tell us everything you know, or I'm going to charge you with theft from the travel agent in town and from Swansea Court. Also, threatening behaviour, and assault, with intent to harm. I will then charge you with the kidnapping of Mary Miller, and furthermore, I will also charge you with the murder of Jane Carter. And if I can add all these other women into the mix, I will. It's up to you. And at that point I would strongly recommend you call your solicitor."

As Gardener and Reilly were leaving, they heard Cragg tell Manny that he had better come clean for his sake. Outside the cell, Gardener addressed the other two. "What do you think?"

"I know what I'd do in his shoes," said Reilly.

"He'll crack," said Cragg.

Gardener allowed the full two minutes to pass before all three barged back in.

Manny was on his feet with his hands in the air. "Okay, okay. I'll tell you what you want to know." He fell to his knees all tears and snot. "Just please don't send me down for all that shit... please..."

Chapter Forty-five

The team was back in the incident room, with the exception of Paul Benson who had gone to Whitby. Gardener stood at the front with his back to the boards, his mood enhanced by the fact that Manny Walters had told them everything.

"Behind me you'll notice a number of photos," said Gardener. "These are what we discovered in the metal box that Manny Walters had been holding on to."

"Who are they?" asked Rawson.

"According to the names on the back of them, we think they are all victims of the same person who killed Jane Carter."

"And is that Manny Walters?" asked Anderson.

"No," said Gardener. "I don't think he's old enough. They have dates on them, the earliest being 1991. We do, however, have one photo with no name and no date."

"We reckon from the quality of the photo," said Reilly, "that it was before 1991. We just don't know who it is."

"To be fair," continued Gardener, "we don't know any of them, apart from Jane Carter."

"And neither does Manny Walters."

"So, what's he admitted to?" asked Sharp.

"He was there on the night Jane Carter was murdered, turning the place over," said Reilly.

"Yes," said Gardener. "Apparently, he heard two noises, both of which came from upstairs. The first time he heard a noise he was downstairs. He made the mess in the bathroom because when he was upstairs, checking to see if anyone was home, he heard another noise. Trying to get out in a rush, he lost his balance and crashed into the shelves."

"What was the noise?" asked Rawson.

"The first was a clicking sound, almost like a central heating timer clicking in," said Gardener.

"But we think now it was probably the alarm," said Reilly.

"So what was the second noise?" asked Sharp.

"Possibly a cry for help," said Gardener. "He wasn't sure."

"So Jane Carter was alive when he was in the house?" asked Sarah Gates.

"It would seem so," said Reilly.

"So why didn't he stay and call an ambulance?" asked Anderson. "He could have saved her life."

"He was frightened," said Cragg. "Didn't want to get caught red-handed for turning the place over."

"What kind of a weasel does that?" asked Gates.

"You've not seen Manny Walters, then?" Cragg asked. "A few minutes with him and you'd know."

Paul Benson finally made it through the door, apologising for his lateness.

"So if Manny didn't do it, who did?" Anderson asked.

"My money is still on Robbie Carter," said Gardener. "I still think that he came home and, for whatever reason, he was not happy. Maybe he'd had a bad night at the club, or an altercation with another motorist. Whatever it was, he was in a bad mood. Something then happened between him and his wife. He leaves, and in the meantime, Manny Walters stumbles across what he thinks is an empty house and decides to rob it."

Following a strained silence, Gardener glanced at Benson. "Anything from Whitby?"

"You could say that," he replied, taking a sip of coffee. "Turns out, Robbie Carter, or Robert Chilvers as he should be called, had a reputation for being a ladies' man. Rumour has it he'd been seeing Alfie Peterson's wife. Alfie didn't know that at the time, and could find no real evidence. From what I can gather, Alfie gave her a real beating when he found out.

"But when he finally caught up with Chilvers, he dragged him into The Ghost Train to torture him for a couple of hours, using all sorts of methods while he was tied up before letting him free. Alfie then warned him to leave town, never to return."

"He obviously did," said Reilly. "But maybe Chilvers came back and started his vendetta against everyone. It would explain why Alfie Peterson and his wife were killed."

Benson opened a folder and passed over a picture. "I have a copy of the cutting of the original news story from *The Whitby Gazette*, and a photo here of the Petersons."

Gardener took it. "Bingo." He placed it next to the photo from the box they had been unable to identify. "It's Jane Peterson."

"I can see why a lunatic like Robbie Carter came back for the gangster and his wife," said Rawson, "but I can't see what started him on a killing spree of all these other women."

"Are they all called Jane, every single one of them?" Benson asked.

"Yes," said Gardener. "Well done, Paul. We have a bit more information to connect the dots, and another nail in Carter's coffin." Gardener turned and asked Dave Rawson about Grace Browne.

"This is just as interesting. Believed to have disappeared three years ago, emigrating to New Zealand. I've been in touch with the major airlines that operate flights to New Zealand. There is no record of her on any flight at that time."

"So far," said Gates.

Rawson nodded. "Well, yes, there's still a couple to get back to me. I also contacted the passport office. It was around the time they started making them electronic, so all the details feed into a massive system that records when and where you go. If Grace Browne has emigrated, she must have done it covertly."

"Unless she changed *her* name," said Gardener.

"Oh Christ," said Reilly. "We'll never catch any fucker connected to this case. They're all invisible."

"It looks that way," said Sharp.

"I never thought of that," said Rawson. "If she has, it will be nigh on impossible to find her."

"And a minefield to trawl through even if we want to."

"Not necessarily," said Gardener. "Maybe she changed her name for a reason. Perhaps she wants to remain invisible so she can catch Robbie Carter herself. Maybe she feels that the police in the past have not done enough for her."

"In which case," said Reilly, "she might do our job for us."

"Or walk right into our hands," said Gardener. "Dave, did you get a photo?"

"Yes." He passed it over.

It was a glossy eight by ten. Gardener had no idea when it was taken, but he stuck it on the board. He was about to ask Sharp a question when Mike Atherton suddenly stood up. "She just has."

"Pardon?"

"You're right, Mike," said Emma Longstaff.

"What are you two talking about?" Gardener asked.

"That's not Grace Browne," said Atherton. "Unless I'm pretty much mistaken, her name is Jane Rogers, and she works at the estate agent in the town."

"Yes," said Longstaff. "I've been up most of the night tracking and tracing Robbie Carters on the dating site. But I've just seen where I'm going wrong." She searched through a number of photos before removing one, placing it on the table in front of Gardener. "That's J on the dating site, aka Jane Rogers aka Grace Browne."

Then she dropped the other one down.

"Who's that?" Gardener asked.

Longstaff pointed to the photo of a man. "He's been contacting J on a regular basis, even setting up meetings with her. They set up a date at a club in Leeds called Silhouettes a couple of nights back."

"So, what's his name, and why do we think it's Robbie Carter?"

"The initials, RC. This is Ronald Critchley."

The revelation hit Gardener like a sledgehammer. All the time he'd been searching for a link and it had been right under his nose. "Ronald Critchley," he said to Reilly.

"The Atkinsons," said Reilly. "They rented out the mill house in Sowerby to him."

Gardener glanced around the room, his eyes resting on Bob Anderson and Sarah Gates. "Can you two go round to the mill house and see if anyone is home? If there is, call back and keep the place under surveillance until we can join you." He then asked Maurice Cragg to send a couple of constables around to the estate agent to pick up Jane Rogers.

As they left, Gardener nodded to Sharp. "Colin?"

Sharp stood up and arranged his paperwork. "In view of what we've found out today, I don't think there's any reason for me to labour this point. I'll just give you the facts and save time. As you know we've been up pretty much all night, and HOLMES has narrowed it down to a small number of victims called Jane that have died or disappeared in mysterious circumstances over a thirty-year period."

He pointed to the photos on the chart. "That's Jane Thornton from Scarborough in 1990. When they were married he was called Richard Clayton, and they lived together in a flat near the post office in Flamborough. She disappeared in 1991. So did he."

"The next one we know about, Jane Browne. She married a Raymond Culver."

"How many names are we gonna end up with?" Reilly asked.

"There's one or two more. The next victim was Jane Sullivan in 2003. They met on a dating website. She had long black hair and blue eyes. He lived in Whitehaven in Lancashire. They met at a caravan site on the coast near Cumbria where, get this, Rupert Conway had been booked as part of a small selection of Glam Rock tribute acts."

"Jesus Christ," said Reilly. "Harold Shipman's got nothing on this bloke."

"At least we'll go down on record as nailing him," said Gardener.

"Jane Sullivan was a widower. She'd been left a tidy sum by her late husband, Steven, who had worked as an insurance salesman. She put that into a pub called The Golden Last in a little place on the Cumbrian Coast called St Bees.

"In the early hours of one morning in 2005, there was an explosion in the cellar. He was injured severely enough to land up in hospital. Jane died. He was questioned by the police. They were happy that he had nothing to do with it. Rupert was left alone, but the insurance refused to pay up. He disappeared."

Gardener continued to write everything down as Sharp was telling him. The rest of the team remained silent.

"In 2008, Jane Jenkins dated Roland Curtis in the small village of Betws-y-Coed, North Wales. Once again, the website played a big part. At the time, he lived in the seaside resort of Llandudno. He was working as a deck chair attendant and part-time musician."

"Doing what he's good at again," said Reilly. "What happened to her?"

"According to the neighbours, she went missing for about a week. The next thing anyone knew, he'd called an ambulance. The police appeared. She'd had a suspected stroke. The post-mortem report said her system contained a lethal dose of sherry mixed with nuts that had been ground into a fine powder, creating the drug Ephedrine, which brought on a massive stroke."

"So it must have all started back in Whitby in the eighties," said Gardener. "He felt let down by this woman called Jane Peterson, beat her up, took a beating in return, and was then forced to leave."

"So he starts up a relationship with a woman called Jane," said Longstaff. "His name is always different but he uses the letters RC. It still doesn't tell us why he's doing all of this."

"And where the hell does he keep disappearing to in between the times he pops back up?" asked Anderson.

"I might be able to help with that as well," said Sharp.

"Go on," said Gardener.

"Every time he skipped town, he did so when the travelling fair left. Seems to be a common link. A small fair was usually in the area for a week or so. When they left, so did he."

"That is worth knowing," said Rawson.

"And so is this," said Cragg. All eyes met his.

"You must have seen the posters. It happens every year, once a year. The fair comes to town and sets up on the car park of the railway station."

"Every year?" asked Reilly.

"Without fail."

"You wouldn't happen to know who runs it, would you, Maurice?" Gardener asked.

"I certainly do. An old lag called Sam Smith."

"Do you have his number?"

"I'll get on to it straight away."

As Cragg left, police constables Steve Smart and Dave Reynolds returned empty handed from the estate agent.

"She's gone, sir," said Reynolds.

"Who has?"

"Jane Rogers aka Grace Browne," said Steve Smart. "Her colleague said she hasn't heard from her for a couple of days and she wasn't at work yesterday. Jane Rogers lived in the flat above the estate agent."

"Lived?" said Gardener.

"Yes. Her colleague let us in. Place is pretty much cleaned out. All personal items have gone, and the only thing left was an envelope on the table. Inside, she found a month's rent and the bond in cash."

Gardener's phone chimed. When he answered, Bob Anderson reported that the mill house in Sowerby was all in darkness.

Chapter Forty-six

Mary was itching like mad. She had never been so uncomfortable in her life.

She had woken in the early hours of the morning, wrapped in a dirty blanket. When the itching started, the blanket had to go. She may have been shackled to a radiator, but it wasn't on. Although the tingling did not die down, she was too cold to stay naked. The whole blanket-on-blanket-off thing had continued throughout the day, and now the itching was driving her to distraction.

The door opened and Robbie strolled in casually. He was dressed in jeans and a T-shirt. In one hand he had an umbrella; in the other, a handgun. Mary's heart pounded in her chest.

"Okay, Mary," said Robbie. "If you don't tell me what I want to know today, it will be your last day."

"According to you yesterday, you didn't need me to find Manny." Mary could have bitten off her tongue as she said that. She'd spent her life correcting people when they had made mistakes. Her mother always said it would be the death of her. Maybe she'd been right. She couldn't help herself. Things had to be right.

He leaned in closer. "Today's the day I'm going to make the pain go away." Then he stepped back. "Or in your case, I'm going to make the whole fucking world disappear."

Mary didn't like the sound of that. Her stomach contracted, and she felt sick.

Robbie poked her with the umbrella. It was so quick she didn't even see the movement. All she felt was a piercing pain on her right breast. She gasped, held the breast, rubbed it vigorously. A red mark appeared immediately. Determined not to show her fear of the man, Mary confronted him again. "Hardly what I'd call making the pain go away, is it? Stabbing me."

Once again, her tongue had run free. Robbie poked the left breast equally as hard. "Pardon, Mary."

The pain was even more severe in that one. Mary slumped, gritting her teeth, holding her breath. Coloured lights swam in front of her eyes.

Robbie dropped the umbrella, grabbed her ear, and yanked Mary to her feet. "Did you say something?"

"No," she quickly replied.

Robbie let go, pushed her against the wall.

He strode over to the shelf, reached into his toolbox. She couldn't see what he'd removed, but it had to be bullets because he started loading the chamber of the gun.

The speakers on the wall came to life. Another Slade song: *Gudbye T' Jane*. She recognised it immediately. The level was acceptable but the implications heightened her tension, raised her blood pressure.

"I like this song, Mary. What about you?" Robbie asked as he returned to where she was shackled.

"Look, Mr Carter, whatever you're going to do, you should think very seriously about it."

"Why?"

"Pardon?"

"Why?"

"Because what you're doing is wrong. Don't you realise by now that I don't know anything?"

"You must know something, Mary. Everybody knows something. What you really mean is, you don't know the answer to the question I keep asking."

Mary nodded, all the time keeping her eyes on the gun. All thoughts of itching had gone from her mind; even the room didn't feel so cold.

"The problem with that, Mary," said Robbie, "is I don't believe you."

"Don't you think I'd have told you by now?"

"Depends how much you love the weasel. You're a tough old bus, I'll give you that."

"I've told you, I don't know where he is."

"So you keep saying."

The snapping of the chamber frightened Mary more than anything else since she'd been here. It was so final. "What are you going to do?"

"We' re going to play a little game, Mary. Do you like games?"

"Depends which ones they are."

"I believe they invented this one in Russia. Not sure when. But it's a very good one. Focuses the mind brilliantly."

"People will know I'm missing, you know."

"Of course they will."

"Doesn't that bother you?"

"Why should it?"

"Because they'll come looking for me."

Robbie stared at her. "Let's see, who have we got? Your mother? Very doubtful. She can't even remember what fucking room she's in, never mind where you are. I doubt she knows that you haven't even been."

"Don't you dare speak about my mother like that!"

"You're so naive," said Robbie, with a defeated expression. He levelled the gun, stared down the barrel. "And so fucking stupid," he shouted, at the top of his voice.

Mary flinched, backed away toward the wall.

Gudbye T' Jane finished and *Far, Far, Away* started.

"Of course, they know you're missing. What they don't know is where the fuck you are. How can they come looking for you when they don't know where you are?"

Mary didn't answer, so Robbie picked up the umbrella again and poked her right arm, where the pellet had taken out a chunk.

Mary nearly passed out such was the level of pain. He had managed to catch the wound full on, and the point had gone underneath her skin.

He pulled back. She grabbed the arm, screamed, "You stupid man!" She fell to her knees, rocking back and forth, holding her right arm tightly with her left hand.

He gave her no time to feel sorry for herself as he yanked her ear again, pulling Mary to her feet. She had no idea how much more she could take.

"Shut your whining, Mary, and listen to me."

She held her breath.

"See the gun?"

She nodded.

"Does that mean yes?"

She realised now was not a good time to correct him. He'd told her to shut up, but now he wanted an answer.

"Yes," she replied.

"Good. Take it."

She stared at it, trembling. She didn't want to take it, but how could she refuse?

"Mary." That one word was enough. She did as she was asked.

"Point it at your head."

She glanced at the gun and then at him.

"Having trouble with your hearing, Mary?"

She shook her head, the power of speech having gone. Rather embarrassingly, she broke wind.

Robbie doubled up with laughter. "Oh, Mary, that was a corker. How unbecoming of you. Does your mother know you fart like a docker?"

Mary screwed her face up. "You vulgar animal."

"Animal now, am I?" Robbie asked. His mood changed quickly. "Never mind all this shit, Mary. Point that fucking gun at your head now!"

She couldn't.

"If you don't, I will." She knew he would. He hadn't bluffed about anything so far. "Now!" he screamed into her face.

She urinated herself before raising the gun to her temple, very slowly.

"This game is called Russian roulette, Mary. Not sure why. Don't even know the origins of the game, but I find it funny. The chamber has only one bullet. Pull the trigger."

Mary was shaking like a leaf. She thought of her mother, on her own in the care home. She thought about the staff, who would wonder where she was. Even Manny might be wondering. How sad that they would probably never have an answer.

"Do it."

Tears ran down Mary's face. She had never felt so sad, so embarrassed, so humiliated in her entire life. Not to mention powerless.

Robbie moved so fast that all she felt was a stinging blow. She fell against the wall, dropped to her knees, and let go of the gun.

He was on her before she registered, weapon in hand. "It's quite simple, Mary, you just pull, like so."

Mary screamed as she heard the click of an empty chamber. "No, please, please don't do this."

"What's wrong, Mary? Nothing happened. No bullet in that one."

Mary sobbed heavily.

Robbie grabbed her by the throat. "Your turn. And so help me God if you don't pull the trigger this time, I'll pull it another five fucking times. Won't be so lucky then, will you?"

Mary had absolutely no idea what to do. Hadn't anyone noticed she had gone, set the alarm bells ringing? Hadn't someone seen her abducted?

Robbie spun the chamber and then put the gun in her hand. "Pull it."

She wouldn't. He kicked her hard. "I said, pull it."

She still didn't respond. Mary felt like she was shutting down.

Robbie grabbed the gun back. "Okay, you stupid cow, have it your way. Now I'm going to shorten the odds."

He put five bullets in the chamber and pressed the gun into her hand.

"If you didn't like the game before, you'll fucking hate it now."

Mary froze.

"Pull the trigger."

She couldn't.

"If you don't, I will. I'll count down from three."

Mary glanced around. Surely there had to be a means of escape.

"Three."

There were no windows and only one door, and she was shackled. What possible means of escape could there be?

"Two."

"Oh, Mother, I'm so sorry," she whispered.

"If you don't, I will, remember? Three bullets for you, and two for the old battleaxe in the home."

That phrase lit the blue touch paper.

"One."

Where she found the strength she had no idea, but Mary stood up. Her legs were weak, but enough was enough.

"Okay, Mr Carter, if that's the way you want it."

Robbie smiled.

Mary quickly turned the gun on Robbie, pointing straight between his eyes.

Then she pulled the trigger.

Chapter Forty-seven

The last time anyone had dared to cross Robbie was thirty-five years ago. They had paid the price. No one had crossed him since; not and lived to tell the tale. He wasn't about to change the habit of a lifetime.

Robbie shuddered as he re-lived the night in question.

He was twenty-one. As usual, it involved a woman. He'd seen a lot of her at the fairground where he worked. Seeing didn't mean going out with, or having an affair, it was simply the fact that he couldn't help noticing her. She had black, shoulder-length hair, and was about five nine – slim, attractive, nice white teeth. They started talking. Her name was Jane. She was unhappy. She hid her surname from him.

He tried to impress her. Let her on rides for free. Bought her a ticket to see Slade for a second appearance in the town. He was seen leaving The Pavilion with her on his arm. That was the night he finally found out how unhappy she really was. She claimed her husband treated her like garbage; he was tight with money despite having plenty of it, controlled her life to the point she didn't have one, and he beat her. Robbie pressed for more information. She finally gave in, told him her husband's name.

Robbie nearly fainted. She was married to a notorious gangster originally from London. An argument broke out. He accused her of all sorts: she had been using him. He wanted nothing more to do with her, despite his heart telling him otherwise.

Two days passed, and he figured he could no longer push his luck staying in the town. He packed his bags, took them to the fairground. Worked a shift, then decided to leave, but not before robbing the owner. From a safe he managed to steal three thousand pounds in cash and a box of cameras. Why he wanted cameras, he had no idea. After loading everything into his van, shutting the doors, he turned, only to be confronted by the gangster accompanied by two minders.

Robbie tried to flee. Alfie Peterson was not known for his patience. One thing he could not stand was a coward. He told Robbie he needed teaching a lesson he would never forget.

Robbie was dragged back into the fairground. Despite being a big lad himself, he was no match for Alfie's minders. They frog-marched him into The Ghost Train.

Once inside, Robbie found he wasn't alone. Jane Peterson was standing against one wall. She was crying, shaking, black mascara running down her cheeks; her face was covered with white powder, which made her more frightening than any of the things you were likely to meet on the ride.

Robbie lost his temper, shouted his mouth off, informing Alfie that if he had touched Jane, Robbie would kill him with his bare hands. He then experienced first-hand what Alfie's minders could do with *their* hands and a couple of knuckledusters. When they'd finished, his face had been rearranged so much that Lon Chaney would have been pleased with the result. While the gangsters brutalised him, the sound system continually played songs by his favourite group Slade, as if trying to demoralise him further.

When they finished, his eyes were swollen, his cheeks purple, and his face a variety of colours. He was shackled to a wall. Alfie asked his wife about what had been going on. Jane claimed it was all Robbie's doing, that he wouldn't leave her alone. She had tried to dissuade him, told him she wasn't interested, but he kept pestering her.

They turned their attention to Robbie. The music was lowered so Alfie could talk to him. Robbie tried to protest, told Alfie that Jane was lying. That didn't go down very well.

They spent a further two hours teaching Robbie the error of his ways, with a number of torturous methods: attaching electrodes to certain parts of his body, plugging the bare wires into wall sockets. They stabbed him with the sharpened points of a variety of instruments. Forced him to play Russian roulette. They even practised their spelling on every part of his body they could see, using scalpels.

Robbie begged and pleaded with the gangster to stop. He promised he would leave town. Alfie said that would definitely happen. He told Robbie he was going to forget Jane and that he was never going to come back, ever, because if he did, Alfie wouldn't be so patient with him.

But return he did.

Robbie shook his head, breathed in, and ran his hands down his face. The memory was still vivid.

He started the car and headed over to Manny's place. He had a guitar to find.

Chapter Forty-eight

The mill house in Sowerby was in darkness by the time Grace coasted her rented Isuzu to a standstill. Leaving the main road, she'd killed the headlights, driving the rest of the way using night vision goggles. She switched off the engine and sat back.

It had been a long journey – over twenty years if anyone was counting, and many identity changes along the way. Not as many as him, though. Jane Rogers no longer existed. The Isuzu had been rented with false documents, the fee paid in cash. In her mind, the trek had all been worth it.

The house was as dark inside as out. The Beetle she'd checked up on, belonging to one Mary Miller, was not in sight. Grace exited her own vehicle, leaving the door unlocked. She walked slowly toward the house, encircling the building twice. No one was home.

At the front door, Grace removed her lock pick set from the body armour suit she was wearing. She was taking no chances. She had not spent half her life tracking him to make a mistake now. She had no intention of ending up like her mother, or any of his other victims, for that matter. Tonight, he would be the victim.

Seconds later, she was inside the living room. It was larger than most, approximately fifteen feet square. A dining table stood to the right behind the door, in front of a window. A three-piece suite hogged the centre of the room. Along one wall she saw a pine bookcase. The usual entertainment systems were in place: a TV, hi-fi, and Sky. A number of doors led to different rooms.

Leaving the front door open, she crossed the room to a small lamp in one corner. She removed her goggles, felt for a switch. The light came on, which meant the electric was working fine. She switched it off. With the light out, she replaced the goggles and walked through all the downstairs rooms, removing every bulb she could find, depositing them all in a bin in the kitchen. She felt happier knowing that he could not take her by surprise.

Near the stairs to the upper floor, she saw two doors. She suspected one was a basement. She opened the other. It was an understairs cupboard, big enough to step into.

All she saw were a number of coats: two small jackets, and two full length ones hung on pegs.

She closed the door, opened the next one. What surprised her was the silence. It was so complete. Even the doors didn't squeak. She stared at the set of steps leading down. Grace saw the light switch, but decided to continue using the goggles.

She descended the stairs very slowly, stepping carefully on each. No creaks or groans gave her away, despite her tactical gear being fully loaded with all sorts of nasty little surprises should she need one quickly, including a 4.5-million-volt stun gun and a home-made Mace canister.

She reached the bottom. In one corner, huddled in a blanket, close to a radiator, she noticed a figure. It was hard to tell, but Grace suspected it was female. It didn't resemble Mary Miller, but she couldn't think who else it might be. The world was a small place these days.

"Who's there?" asked the frail voice in the corner.

Grace didn't answer immediately, but checked every corner of the room. Only when she was satisfied that it had one inhabitant did she remove her goggles and flick the switch. The figure in the corner shrunk back, suddenly surprised.

Grace was sickened by what she saw. As the lady blinked a few times, she could tell by the face it was Mary, but every inch of body hair had been removed, and she'd lost weight. Typical of that bastard.

When her eyes cleared, Mary's expression revealed the traumatic experience she had suffered. Her skin was ashen, her cheeks sunken. Grace noticed a flesh wound on her right arm. Mary had been shackled to the radiator. Next to her on the floor was a handgun.

"Please," said Mary. "Don't do this."

"I'm not who you think," said Grace.

Surprised, Mary was on her feet quickly. "Who are you?"

"It doesn't matter. We need to set you free."

"What are you doing here?"

"I've just told you. Why is there a gun on the floor?"

Mary glanced at the weapon, but didn't say anything. Neither did she raise her head to meet Grace's eyes.

"Don't tell me, you've been playing games."

Mary nodded.

"He made you play Russian roulette with a gun full of blanks, didn't he?"

"Yes," said Mary. "Only I didn't know they were blanks."

"Nobody ever did," said Grace.

Her expression darkened, the frown throwing up lines all over her forehead. "You mustn't let him catch you. I don't know who you are, but you need to go. He can be very nasty when he wants, and if he catches us both down here, we'll be in all sorts of trouble."

"I'm not leaving without you." Grace bent down and located her lock pick set once again.

"Where did you get all that gear? Are you with the SAS or something?" Mary asked.

Grace glanced up. "Let's just say I'm your guardian angel."

The lock was free and Mary was unshackled in seconds.

"Right, come on," said Grace.

Mary was reluctant to move. "Where are we going?" She pulled the blanket tighter around her body.

"Do you want him to come back and catch you?"

"God, no!"

"Then stop asking questions and follow me."

Grace left the light on and took the stairs two at a time. At the top she opened and reached into the cupboard with the coats, passing one to Mary.

"Get rid of that disgusting blanket."

Mary held steadfast. "How can I trust you? How do I know he hasn't put you up to this?"

"You don't, Mary. Once you put that coat on and walk out of here, you'll see an Isuzu pickup outside. You're going to get into that and drive to the police station in Bramfield and tell them who you are and what's happened to you." Grace showed Mary the car keys. "Trust me now?"

"But what are you going to do?"

"Don't worry about me. Just promise me that when you leave here you will not look back."

"But..."

"We haven't got time for this," said Grace. "Promise me, now."

Mary nodded. Grace noticed tears forming in her eyes. She threw the blanket down the stairs and put the coat on.

"Follow me," said Grace, replacing the night vision goggles. Although a small amount of light from the basement pierced the living room, the rest of the house was still mostly dark.

As they reached the front door, Grace heard a car engine screaming into the drive, the headlights on full beam.

"Oh, no," said Mary. "We're too late. He'll catch us. We need to hide. We need to get out of here." Her head was spinning in all directions. She was shaking. "I'm not going back down there. I can't."

Grace turned. "Do exactly as I tell you."

Without waiting for Mary to reply, she grabbed her left arm and pushed her to the front door, forcing her behind it. "Stand there and do not move until I let you know it's safe to do so."

"I can't. He'll find us, believe me."

"He won't."

There was no further time to talk. The headlights curved all the way round in front of the house, sweeping the whole façade. The engine died.

Grace crossed the room and stood against one wall, behind the bookcase.

The car door slammed. Footsteps urgently ran forward. As soon as he entered the living room, Robbie shouted out, "Who's in here?"

He tried the light switches. "What the fuck's going on?" He stepped into the room. Grace saw him peering into the darkness. His head came to rest in the direction of the basement, where a small amount of light filtered through.

"If that fucking bitch has gotten free..." Robbie left the sentence unfinished and ran clumsily forward, knocking into furniture.

Once he was out of sight, Grace moved to Mary. "Get in the truck and do what I said."

"What about you?"

"Do it now," said Grace. Mary was visibly shaken. Grace could guess what he'd done to her. "I will not tell you again, Mary. Now go." As she said it, she pushed Mary out of the door, but Mary turned.

Through clenched teeth, Grace said, "If you don't move, I'll put 4.5 million volts through you, and you'll have wasted your chance."

"I want to know one thing."

Down in the basement, Grace heard crashing sounds and Robbie cursing.

"I want to know the name of the person who has saved me."

More crashing and banging. Robbie was furious, and it wouldn't be long before he was back up to the living room.

Grace gazed at Mary. "My name is Grace Browne."

Grace gave her no time to say anything else. She turned and headed for the basement. As she reached the bottom of the stairs, he stepped in front of her and smiled.

So did she.

"Hello, Raymond."

Chapter Forty-nine

The incident room door opened. "We need you at the front desk, sir," said Cragg. "Quickly."

"What's wrong?"

"Mary Miller's turned up."

Gardener grabbed his jacket and his hat and followed Cragg. Reilly was close behind. Before he reached the front desk, he could hear the commotion. Emma Longstaff was trying to calm the woman down.

The sight that met Gardener's eyes shook him. He'd seen a lot of things during his years on the force, but he'd never seen a woman as tormented as Mary Miller. She was dressed in a long black trench coat and nothing else, from what he could see. He recognised her pale face from the photo, but she was completely bald. She'd lost weight.

"You have to go there now!" shouted Mary. "She's in grave danger."

"Emma," said Gardener, "take Mary through to the back. Get her a cup of tea."

Once in the back room, Gardener offered Mary a chair at the table. The woman was extremely agitated, and started on them immediately.

"He'll kill her. You have to stop him." She grabbed Gardener's hand. The strength of her grip surprised him.

"Please, Mary, just slow down for a minute. I'm Detective Inspector Stewart Gardener, and this is my partner, Detective Sergeant Sean Reilly."

Emma Longstaff returned with the tea. As she placed it on the table, Mary immediately grabbed the cup and took a sip. "We're wasting time, Mr Gardener. You need to get over there."

"Mary, where have you been?"

"Robbie Carter kidnapped me, held me captive at a mill house in Sowerby."

The rest of the team appeared from all corners of the station, crowding into the small back room.

Reilly addressed Mary. "Is he still there now?"

Mary nodded, her hands clasped around the cup of tea.

"When you said he'll kill her, who did you mean?"

"Grace," said Mary. "Grace Browne."

"She's at the mill house?" Reilly asked.

"Yes. She rescued me."

"Where were you?"

"In the cellar. Look, you need to get over there if you want to save her. Please, he'll kill her. You don't know what he's like."

"Is he armed?"

"There was a gun in the cellar. He made me play Russian roulette. But it was full of blanks."

Gardener turned to Maurice Cragg. "I want an armed response team to meet me there. Robbie Carter is dangerous, possibly armed, and we could have a hostage situation."

He glanced back at Mary. "I appreciate you must have been through an ordeal, but I would like you to stay here and tell Emma everything that happened to you."

"I just want to go home."

"I know you do, Mary, love," said Longstaff. "And you will, but you must tell me everything that happened to you."

Gardener addressed the team. "Every last one of you, in your cars. Follow us. This ends tonight."

Outside the station the night sky was clear, the atmosphere chilly and breezy. Gardener jumped in a pool car. Reilly drove. They reached the mill house in Sowerby within twenty minutes, racing up the drive, headlights and sirens blazing.

Gardener was not surprised to find a dozen armed officers waiting for him. Four vehicles were parked across the drive, blocking any entrance or exit. All the officers were standing behind their vehicles, rifles at the ready.

Once out of the car, he flashed his warrant card. Reilly stood behind him.

One of the men stepped forward. He was taller than Gardener, slim, black hair, blue eyes, and dressed in combat gear. "Simon Mason, sir. I'm the senior commander."

"How long have you been here?"

"Ten minutes."

The rest of his team pulled up, each parking their cars behind his. The drive was completely blocked.

"Have you been inside?" Gardener asked.

"No, sir. It's your show."

A wintry breeze skated the back of Gardener's neck, sending a chill through him. He had no idea what to expect. He glanced at the house. The building was in darkness. It was pretty total, out there in the middle of nowhere. He could barely make out the front door. "Were there any cars here when you arrived?"

"No, sir."

"And you haven't seen or heard anything?"

"No, sir."

"Have you checked the outside of the building?"

"Yes, sir, a complete full circuit. All quiet."

"I don't like this, Sean," said Gardener.

"You're not on your own."

"Do you guys have torches?"

Simon Mason nodded, quickly producing two from one of the vehicles. Gardener took them, passed one to Reilly, and spoke to his team. "If you have torches, bring them with you."

The senior officers set off in the direction of the house. Simon Mason followed with two of his men. He asked the rest to surround the building.

Gardener reached the front door, switched on the torch, peered into the darkened room. He was unhappy about what they were walking into. Not because he thought Robbie Carter was still there. Gardener had no doubt that he had somehow slipped the net. It was what he was good at. What he dreaded most was what the man had left behind in his wake.

Standing in the living room he saw no sign of life. He reached around the corner and tried a light switch. Nothing happened.

"Do you think he's cut the power, Sean?"

"Only if he's still here."

Gardener turned to his colleagues. "Split into teams of two and make a search of each room. For God's sake, be careful. If he's still here he could cause mayhem. If he isn't, he could have left a bunch of nasty little surprises."

Gardener turned and surveyed the rest of the room with his torch. It was spartan, with only the bare essentials in furniture. The beam of light came to rest on two doors near a set of stairs.

Paul Benson stepped over, opened the cupboard door, staring inside. "Only a few coats here, sir."

"What about the other door?"

Benson shone his torch down the stairs. "A cellar."

"That must be where he had Mary." Gardener addressed Simon Mason. "Would you mind?"

"Not at all, sir."

He raised his rifle and stepped forward. Two of his men followed, one lit up the way.

Gardener waited less than a minute for his answer, but it felt like a lifetime. "All clear, sir."

Gardener took the steps. Reilly followed. The tapping of their shoes sounded much louder than they probably were. He was about to speak when the room was illuminated. He glanced back up the stairs. Benson was at the top. "Didn't think it would do any harm to try it."

Gardener glanced at Reilly. "Why no lights upstairs?"

"No idea, boss. The element of surprise is pretty pointless if you're not here."

Gardener glanced around the room. It was bare. A few shelves, some tools. A chain was attached to the radiator.

In front of it was a gun. He knelt down. The chamber was open and empty.

"What the hell is going on, Sean?" he asked, standing up.

With nothing more to see, each man climbed the stairs into the living room.

Gardener was gutted. For over thirty years Carter had been abducting and abusing women. Perhaps killed most of them. He'd been right under their noses. They had interviewed him, had him banged up for two days. Then they let him go. And that was the last they had seen of him. Houdini had nothing on Robbie Carter.

"We've lost him, Sean."

"I don't know about that, boss. He wasn't by himself when Mary left."

"No. Grace Browne was with him."

"Exactly."

Gardener was puzzled. "Am I missing something?"

"Knowing what we know about Grace Browne, I find myself asking one important question."

"What?"

"Who's got who?"

Chapter Fifty

Elsie lifted herself out of the armchair. She banked up the fire to last them through the news. She then turned up the sound on the TV.

Eric closed the door into the kitchen with his left foot, balancing a tray with two cups of cocoa and a saucer of chocolate digestives. He stepped back and drew the curtain between the dining room and the living room to keep the heat in.

So commenced their nightly ritual. They never missed the news. Cocoa, biscuits, news, then bed. Been like that their whole lives. The chimes of Big Ben signified the start of the program.

"Wonder what's been happening today?" asked Eric.

The newscaster announced the headlines, shocking the pair of them. Each lowered their cup of cocoa back onto the table in front of them.

In the studio, the face of the newscaster was solemn. "Detectives in North Yorkshire have today reopened a thirty-five-year-old murder case. It started in the coastal town of Whitby when the bodies of Alfie and Jane Peterson were found at their detached home in Valley Road in 1985."

"Good God. What the hell's raked all this up again?" Eric asked.

The action switched from the studio to an outdoor shot of the resort. Unlike years ago, the street was quiet. No flashing blue lights or crime scene tape, or marquees. The reporter continued with the story, but Elsie couldn't hear anything because of Eric.

"Bloody place is doomed. Have they found someone else dead now?"

"Well we won't know if you don't keep quiet, will we, Eric?"

"I tell you, Elsie, love. You're not safe in your own home these days."

"I seem to remember you saying something similar when it happened. But we've done all right." But had they? Her son had disappeared at the time of the murder, and she had not laid eyes on him since.

The action switched back to the studio. Eric was still prattling on.

"Will you be quiet, Eric Chilvers? I'm trying to listen here. You're nowt but a damned nuisance. Drink your cocoa and shut your mouth."

"You should talk. Can't hear owt because of you now."

Elsie shot him a narrow-eyed scowl. When she finally returned her attention to the TV, she heard the jaw dropping line. "Detectives have stressed that Robert Chilvers is armed and extremely dangerous, and should not be approached."

Elsie's mouth remained wide open. Her eyes filled with tears as she focused on a picture of her son.

The newscaster finished the lead story and moved on to something else.

Chapter Fifty-one

Manny was back in Bramfield, approaching Carpenter's Yard. He was pissed, but happier than he had ever been. He'd cut a deal with the police. He wasn't going down for something he hadn't done. He didn't actually want to go down for something he *had* done, but burglary he could live with. Assault? That was a laugh. The mad bitch had attacked him, tripped him up, punched him, kicked him in the face. She's the one that should be done. Fucking would be, if he had his way.

But murder? No. He had not murdered anyone. Nor had he kidnapped his beloved Mary. When the police had dropped that one on him, he realised how deep his feelings actually went for her. All the stupid little things she had done for him, and still continued to do: cooking meals, shopping, watching out for him. She was besotted with him. Do anything he asked of her. Maybe she wasn't a supermodel. But who wanted one of them? Too up their own arses, they were. Stunners – and they knew it. Treat men like shit, saw them as buses. Miss one, and the next would be along in a minute. No. Give him Mary any day of the week.

From what he'd heard, she'd been found. He raised his head to the sky, cheering inside. Life was good.

Manny collided with a blue bin that someone had left out, which in turn caused him to smash into the post at the side of the gate, banging his knee into the frame. He pursed his lips as he fell backwards, hitting the ground with a thump. The chocolates went one way, the flowers the other.

"Clumsy bastard!" shouted Manny at no one in particular. "You wanna watch where you're putting things."

He struggled to his hands and knees, grasping at the box of chocolates. Then he fell forward, searching for the flowers. "Oh, Christ. Where the fuck have they gone?"

Eventually he had them both. Then he realised he couldn't stand up without using his hands, so he had to place everything back on the ground. The exercise lasted nearly five minutes but he finally drifted toward the two bungalows. Mary's was lit up like a Christmas tree.

"Good old, Mary." She'd been waiting up for him, probably cooked him another one of them casseroles she was famous for.

He fell the last few steps, crashing into the front door. Manny laughed out loud and farted. "Ooh, fuck me." He laughed again, realising he should have said, excuse me.

The door opened. Mary was standing there in a dressing gown, a towel wrapped around her head. She glanced down at him.

As he stared upwards, he wasn't so drunk that he didn't understand that expression. Manny fell backwards, laughing at the thought of her holding out a rolling pin behind her back, like every good wife.

"Mary, my darling. How lovely to see you. Isn't life fucking wonderful?"

"For some," she replied.

On his back staring up at her, Manny thrust forward the chocolates and the flowers. "For you, my precious."

Mary took them and retreated back through the front door.

Manny sat up. "The fuck's she gone?" As he tried to raise himself to his feet, he was given a helping hand. He left the ground so fast he literally fell through the door.

Mary pushed him the rest of the way into the living room, where he collapsed onto a chair. "What do you think you're playing at?"

"I've been for a drink."

"More than one, by the look of it."

"Maybe a couple, Mary, my love."

"Don't you 'my love' me."

Manny pointed at Mary. "Just you wait till I tell you what good news I have."

"Good news?" questioned Mary, leaning forward. "Have you any idea what I've been through?"

"Mary, just listen to me for a moment."

"No. I thought not."

"Mary, sit down. You need to listen to me."

"Are you the only person you ever think about, Manfred?"

Mary crossed the room and threw two more logs onto the fire.

Manny lost sight of her, she was moving too fast for his eyes. "Mary? Mary, where the hell have you gone?"

She was about to speak when Manny hushed her up. "Look. I got something to show you." He ran his hands through his pockets, ripping his coat in an effort to find what he wanted. "Here it is, Mary, love. You fucking wait till you see this."

"Language, Manfred."

He laughed again and fell forward, straight onto the floor. He banged his head on a small table to the right of the chair.

"Get up," shouted Mary. "You're drunk, and I've had more than enough of men who can't behave themselves to last me a lifetime."

Manny threw himself back on to the chair. "Mary, Mary, just read this and I promise I'll go. You read this bit of paper and all our troubles will be ending."

Mary took the newspaper clipping.

A gold-plated camera, thought to be exceptionally rare, is set to go up for auction. It's estimated to fetch more than £1.7million.

The Leica Luxus II has a 50mm Elmar lens and is housed in a crocodile skin case. It is one of just four original limited-edition models produced in 1932.

What makes the camera so unique is that the other three are untraceable. Its rarity suggests interest will be high when it goes under the hammer.

Although the camera commands a base price of £800,000, it is likely to sell for twice that amount after an earlier Leica 0 series sold for almost £2m last year.

She passed the paper back to him. "Why are you showing me this?"

"Why? Why am I showing you this?" Manny was so pleased he had kept the Leica out of sight of prying eyes – mainly the fuzz. "I'll tell you why, my precious little pearl. Because I am the proud owner of that camera, and when I sell it, we'll be rich beyond our wildest dreams. I can give you everything you ever wanted."

Mary sat down, opposite Manny. "So you did steal them?"

"Steal what?"

"Don't play the fool with me, Manfred. You were in that house on the night that woman was murdered and you stole a guitar, some money, and a box of cameras."

"Oh come on, Mary, it's all over and done with now, and you're back where you belong and we're gonna get some compensation for the shit we've been put through."

"As I said earlier, Manfred, you think only of yourself."

"Come on, Mary, that's not fair. I bought you flowers and chocolates."

Mary laughed. "Flowers and chocolates?"

"Yes, and there'll be plenty more where they came from."

"You're a millionaire and you bought me flowers and chocolates with your ill-gotten gains, your stolen money?"

"Mary..."

She held her hand up.

"Manfred, I've always known you were dodgy. I've never witnessed it for real until now. And because of that, I was willing to turn a blind eye. But I can't do that anymore. You left a woman to die and did nothing to help her."

"But..."

"Go home, Manfred." Mary stood up and helped him to the door. "There's nothing here for you anymore."

Epilogue

"My mother wasn't the first... was she?"

He made no reply.

"You killed her over twenty years ago, and you lied about what happened. You claimed she left you. You led me to believe there was some hope all these years. What kind of an animal are you?"

Grace and Robbie were sitting on wooden chairs opposite each other, only a table separating them. The room had four walls, with one light bulb dangling from a length of flex for illumination. A stone floor. No windows. In the corner behind Robbie was a portable CD player, currently playing the classic Slade track *Gudbye T' Jane*. The volume was low so the conversation could be heard.

He still gave no reply. The hatred in his eyes all but filled in the blanks, making up for his lack of words.

"I'm amazed that you managed to evade the police all those years."

Her sentence made him smile, as if he was proud of his achievement.

Grace pushed her chair back and stood up. "Didn't quite manage to escape me though, did you?"

He couldn't move from his chair because he was chained to it.

Grace lowered her eyes to the table. Nailed to the top was Robbie's tongue, which was why he couldn't answer back.

Acknowledgements

We've reached that stage of the book where we need to thank a few people, without whose help I'd never have made it happen. Writing a new book is always a challenge and I love having friends I can count on who happen to be experts and are able to dish out sound advice. I would like to thank Iain Ross for taking care of my website, which is no mean feat because he works more hours than anyone I know and still manages to keep it up to date. Andrew Gardener, the author of a number of crime novels, has a keen eye for detail and always keeps me on the right track. David Johnson, a brilliant editor and now, a really good friend, we get on really well, despite the fact that he is always taking me to task and making me kill my darlings. Arianna Bove, my in-house editor who has also done a great job in helping me to achieve the best from the story. Darrin Knight, a man who fought criminals for real in one of the toughest areas of the UK, the North East. He's recently retired but his help is still invaluable. To Bob Armitage, also a member of the retired club but served many years as a chemist at a hospital in Scunthorpe. He often acknowledges however that my books test his knowledge to its limit. One person I am indebted to is ex-policeman friend, Ian Harvey, without whose help, *Imposition* would not have been on the shelves in the first place. To Will and Harry of Edge Waes for producing superb trailers and continually pushing the world of Ray Clark forward. And to Peter James, fellow author and friend, who writes novels to such a high standard that it's almost impossible to keep the pace. But on a more personal level, Peter has offered so much help and support to me that I am eternally grateful. It's an honour to have such a close friend.

If you enjoyed this book, please let others know by leaving a quick review on Amazon. Also, if you spot anything untoward in the paperback, get in touch. We strive for the best quality and appreciate reader feedback.

editor@thebookfolks.com

www.thebookfolks.com

ALSO AVAILABLE

If you enjoyed IMPOSITION, the fifth book, check out the others in the series:

IMPURITY – *Book 1*

Someone is out for revenge. A grotto worker is murdered in the lead up to Christmas. He won't be the first. Can DI Gardener stop the killer, or is he saving his biggest gift till last?

IMPERFECTION – *Book 2*

When theatre-goers are treated to the gruesome spectacle of an actor's lifeless body hanging on the stage, DI Stewart Gardener is called in to investigate. Is the killer still in the audience? A lockdown is set in motion but it is soon apparent that the murderer is able to come and go unnoticed. Identifying and capturing the culprit will mean establishing the motive for their crimes, but perhaps not before more victims meet their fate.

IMPLANT – *Book 3*

A small Yorkshire town is beset by a series of cruel murders. The victims are tortured in bizarre ways. The killer leaves a message with each crime – a playing card from an obscure board game. DI Gardener launches a manhunt but it will only be by figuring out the murderer's motive that they can bring him to justice.

IMPRESSION – *Book 4*

Police are stumped by the case of a missing five-year-old girl until her photograph turns up under the body of a murdered woman. It is the first lead they have and is quickly followed by the discovery of another body connected to the case. Can DI Stewart Gardener find the connection between the individuals before the abducted child becomes another statistic?

IMPOSTURE – *Book 6*

When a hit and run claims the lives of two people, DI Gardener begins to realize it was not a random incident. But when he begins to track down the elusive suspects he discovers that a vigilante is getting to them first. Can the detective work out the mystery before more lives are lost?

IMPASSIVE – *Book 7*

A publisher racked with debts is found strung up in a ruined Yorkshire abbey. Has a disgruntled author taken their revenge? DI Stewart Gardener is on the case but maybe a hypnotist has the key to the puzzle. Can the cop muster his team to work some magic and catch a cunning killer?

IMPIOUS – *Book 8*

It could be detectives Gardener and Reilly's most disturbing case yet when a body with head, limbs and torso assembled from different victims is discovered. Alongside this grotesque being is a cryptic message and a chess piece. A killer wants to take the cops on a journey. And force their hand.

IMPLICATION – *Book 9*

When a body is found in a burned out car, DI Stewart Gardener quickly establishes that a murder has been concealed. But with a missing person case and a spate of robberies occupying the force, he will struggle to identify the victim. When the investigations overlap, he'll have to work out which of the suspects is implicated in which crime.

IMPUNITY – *Book 10*

After a young woman passes out and dies, the medical examiner makes a grim discovery. Someone had surgically removed her kidneys. Detective Stewart Gardener must find a killer evil enough to think of such a cruel act, let alone have the gall to carry it out. It looks like revenge is a motive, but what had the victim, by all accounts a kind and friendly girl, done to anyone?

IMPALED – *Book 11*

When Gardener is called to investigate a crime, he has no idea of the terrible scene that awaits him. The corpse of a man has been found with nails driven into his chest and no hands. There are no witnesses to the crime, just reports of a strangely dressed man seen nearby. Gardener feels a serial killer is at work, and the clock is ticking.

IMPROPER – *Book 12*

When a local actress is found dead in her luxury apartment, DI Stewart Gardener can't find any signs of foul play. Yet he is sure something is amiss. Investigating her last movements, he finds she associated with a known drug dealer, plus a mysterious man. Following his nose on what others see as a wild goose chase, has he lost the plot or will his hunch prove correct?

All FREE with Kindle Unlimited and available in paperback.

www.thebookfolks.com

Printed in Dunstable, United Kingdom